D1505563

# OTHERSPACE

ALSO BY

**DAVID STAHLER JR.**


The Truesight Trilogy

TRUESIGHT

THE SEER

OTHERSPACE


A GATHERING OF SHADES

DOPPELGANGER

# OTHERSPACE

## DAVID STAHLER JR.

*An Imprint of* HarperCollins*Publishers*

Eos is an imprint of HarperCollins Publishers.

Otherspace
Copyright © 2008 by David Stahler Jr.

Library of Congress Cataloging-in-Publication Data
Stahler, David.
Otherspace / by David Stahler Jr. — 1st ed.
    p.   cm.
ISBN 978-0-06-052291-9 (trade bdg.)
ISBN 978-0-06-052292-6 (lib. bdg.)
Summary: Now almost fifteen, Jacob leaves his good friends, Xander and
Delaney, and sets out for the distant planet of Teiresias, where he believes
he will find other Seers and learn about the visions he has had since gaining
his sight on his home planet, Harmony, where blindness is the rule.
    [1. Interplanetary voyages—Fiction. 2. Blind—Fiction. 3. People with dis-
abilities—Fiction. 4. Science fiction.] I. Title.
PZ7.S782460th  2008                                    2007029853
[Fic]—dc22                                                  CIP
                                                              AC

Typography by R. Hult
1 2 3 4 5 6 7 8 9 10

First Edition

*To my daughter,*
*Maida*

# PART ONE
## Watchers in the Dark

# CHAPTER ONE

Though the sun had only just passed its zenith, the ringed planet Duna—a vast gaseous orb that kept Nova Campi both temperate and tethered in space—was already breaking on the horizon as they approached the knoll.

"Go ahead. You take the lead," Xander murmured, shifting the rifle to his left arm and gesturing toward the rise.

"Me?" Jacob replied, his eyes widening.

"Why not? It's not like you don't know how to stalk gruskers after all this time," the soldier replied, his pale irises flashing against the darkness of tan skin and black hair. "Besides, maybe you'll have better luck than I seem to be having."

Jacob had been on nearly a dozen hunts with Xander, but none had proven this tough. They'd been having trouble locating the elusive herds all day and, when they did manage to spot several, were unable to move in close enough for a shot.

The pair had been on the plain since morning, taking the cruiser on a leisurely pace over the hills. From time to time, they would stop and get out. Sometimes they would take a brief walk, and Xander would scan the landscape for any sign of the large green-and-gold-striped herbivores that roamed in herds

1

across the planet, grazing with their massive, horned heads.

Jacob, meanwhile, would pause, look back, and—as he did now—follow the cruiser's tire tracks to where they disappeared in the distance, twin trails that would be gone by morning. It amazed him to think that nearly two years had passed since he'd first watched Xander's cruiser cut through the grass, barreling toward him over one of these very same ridges. He'd come so far since then. With a shiver, he imagined how different things might be now if Xander hadn't found him.

He'd been at his lowest: stricken with hunger and thirst, ready to flee back to Harmony, the only home he'd ever known, either to resubmit himself to the community of Blinders—a people engineered to be born without sight— and plunge back into the darkness, back into the world of Truesight, the set of principles and rules that guided them in their blindness, or remain unseen among them, hiding in their midst like some lonely ghost. He'd lived both ways already, first as a Blinder, born as one of them, then as a Seer when, at the age of thirteen, his sight had mysteriously appeared, showing him both beauty and pain, revealing the corruption in his midst before finally forcing him to escape when the terrible secret of his change was revealed.

He'd hated the thought of returning, but he hated more the idea of dying alone in the middle of nowhere, of ending up like the body of the lost Blinder he'd discovered on the plain, its bleached bones and tattered smock tangled in the grass with only its sounder—a metallic badge all Blinders wore, a device that both identified them and helped them navigate the blind world—providing any clue to its identity.

But he hadn't returned, and it was that cruiser—and more

importantly Xander, the man driving it—that had marked his first contact with the outside world, the world of the Seers. It hadn't been the warm welcome Jacob had hoped for; the grumpy loner had dismissed him with a scant offering of food and little encouragement. Never would Jacob have guessed that day how important Xander would become in the weeks that followed, when first he gave him a place to stay, then helped him find his friend Delaney.

Delaney had fled Harmony too, depressed and disillusioned and blind, though when they'd finally found her in the port city of Melville, Jacob was stunned to discover her unseeing eyes replaced by a gold-rimmed pair of synthetic, jeweled orbs, a gift from Mixel, the corporation that had taken her in. The excitement she'd felt—both for seeing and for life with Mixel—quickly faded. Soon, even the vision itself faded as the synthetic eyes failed, returning her to darkness.

Mixel wouldn't let her go, refused to relinquish its claim on her in spite of her misery. It was with Xander's help that Jacob managed to rescue her from the corporation's grasp. The weeks afterward had proved difficult as they fended off Mixel only to have Delaney suddenly seek a return to Harmony in the hope that her father, the colony's high councilor, would take her back. The return was brutal and short: Afraid to have his own corruption revealed, Delaney's father had tried to kill her, would have killed her if Jacob hadn't stayed behind to save her.

They'd left Harmony together, this time for good, and settled into Xander's home far from Harmony, far from Melville and Mixel, settled into a life together, three battered souls finding solace in one another's company. Comfortable, familiar, safe.

3

"Hey!" Xander called.

Jacob blinked and looked away from the nearby cruiser. "Sorry," he said, turning back toward the hilltop.

"You okay?" Xander asked, stooping as they neared the crest.

"Sure," Jacob said. "I was just thinking."

"About what?"

"Things," Jacob replied, shrugging.

They'd reached the top of the hill now. While Jacob stayed low and hidden, Xander rose, lifting the hanging goggles up to his eyes to probe the valley below with its magnified lenses.

"You weren't having another vision, were you?" Xander asked.

"No. I pretty much stopped having those, anyway."

"Yeah, until this week," Xander murmured.

It was true. Though the visions—strange moments of prescience where the future, or its possibilities at least, seemed to open before his eyes—had begun to fade over the last few months, Jacob suddenly found himself troubled by disturbing dreams these last few nights—images of eyes, dozens of them, watching him. Glowing eyes that moved in ever closer, burning in the dark. The vision had even come upon him last night as he stood on the deck listening to Delaney play the piano, a beautiful antique Xander had bought for her. The image had come from nowhere—so fast and intense that he'd cried out. Xander rushed out onto the deck, scanned the darkness, but the only eyes he'd uncovered were those of a stray cat lounging in a nearby tree. Still, Jacob couldn't shake the feeling that he was being watched, a feeling that had all of them on edge.

"Well, they're down there, all right," Xander said, dropping beside Jacob. "Same herd, probably." He gestured once more. "After you, Blinder."

"Thanks," Jacob replied, crawling forward down the far side.

They'd only gone about fifty yards when Jacob heard a string of bellows. Even with the thick grass beneath his hands, he could feel the vibrations as the ground shook. He didn't need to look to know the herd was on the move. Behind him, Xander swore.

"Not again," the man growled.

Xander always insisted on making the kill at close range. Parking behind a ridge, they would proceed to slither through the grass at what seemed to Jacob to be an agonizingly slow pace. Still, in spite of the long, quiet approach, there was a certain thrill in sneaking up on a herd of creatures so much larger than themselves. Then, when they'd crept so close they could hear the gruskers' snuffling breaths, Xander would rise beside him in the grass, pause in a moment of perfect silence, and fire. Jacob would watch the red streak of light—a deadly bolt of plasma—as it zipped across the surface and found its target, sending the remaining animals thundering off toward the next pocketed valley.

Then came the hard part as the animal was skinned and dressed. The first time, Jacob had been nervous, expecting to be repulsed at the sight of blood in grass, the viscera glistening in the sun. His people back in Harmony raised their own meat, butchered animals regularly, but he had never seen, or even heard, the process. To his surprise, it was a quiet affair—even peaceful in its own strange way, quick and precise as Xander went to work with his knife.

But for the second time in the last hour, the herd had

bolted without warning, moving out of range before the pair had crossed even half the normal distance, leaving Xander without a shot.

Jacob liked hunting, enjoyed the time he got to spend with Xander on the plain, the two of them working together toward a goal. But today seemed different. And it wasn't just the lack of success that left him troubled. The sense of calm Jacob normally felt was absent. He felt ill at ease, as if the remnants of last night's vision still lingered, transforming the landscape into a barren, unfriendly place. Maybe the gruskers could sense his uneasiness.

"Downright discouraging is what that is," Xander said, rising from the grass, watching through the lenses of his goggles as the herd disappeared.

"Don't blame me," Jacob quipped, trying to shake his agitation. "I didn't say anything to them."

Xander smiled, lifting the goggles onto his forehead as they headed toward where the herd had been grazing. "I was beginning to worry you didn't like hunting after all," he replied. He sniffed his jacket. "Maybe we stink."

"Well, I didn't want to say anything earlier, but . . ." Jacob looked up at Xander and the two laughed. "I do like hunting. It's a lot of work, though."

Xander nodded. "It is. But knowing you're feeding yourself, taking care of your own needs, makes it worth it. It's easy to let someone else take care of you, but there's a price attached."

"I guess," Jacob said. "It depends on who you are, though, doesn't it? I mean, we take care of Delaney, right? She needs us to."

"True. But she also takes care of us." The man looked

away. "Of you, at least. She's like a mother to you half the time."

"She reminds me of my mother, sometimes," Jacob said, nodding. "Probably because they were so close."

"Probably," Xander said, glancing back down at him.

They had reached the spot where the herd had last lingered. Xander examined the ground, poking the trampled stalks with one foot before slipping his goggles back down over his eyes.

Watching him, Jacob felt a sudden prickle along his spine, felt the hairs on the back of his neck rise. He glanced around the valley. The breeze died. Even the birds seemed to have stopped their singing. He took a step toward Xander, suddenly eager to be closer to the man, and peered over his shoulder.

*Splop.*

His foot slid. Jacob didn't have to look down to know what he'd just stepped into—the smell of fresh dung, its thin sun-baked crust now broken, was enough. A wave of frustration rose, the pricking surge from a moment ago forgotten.

"What are we doing here, anyway?" he muttered, trying to scrape the purplish goo from his boot. "This feels like a waste of time."

"No such thing when you're hunting," Xander replied, still scanning the horizon. "That's the whole point. Besides, I told you before, I like to see what the critters are up to. Sometimes you just have to open your eyes and look at the signs. For instance—"

There was a pause.

"Yeah?" Jacob said, glancing over to see Xander staring up the far ridge.

7

The man finished his sweep, then pulled his goggles down so that they hung around his neck. Then he turned and, without a word, began walking back toward the cruiser on the far side of the opposite ridge.

Jacob watched him for a moment.

"Where are you going?" he called out, but Xander didn't reply. He just jabbed the air with one hand in the direction of the cruiser and hoisted the rifle up onto his shoulder.

Jacob watched Xander march away. It reminded him of the old days when he'd first met Xander. Back then, it wasn't unusual for Jacob to be left bewildered by his host's erratic behavior, his sudden mood shifts. But it had been a while since Jacob had witnessed anything like this.

His body stiffened, and he gasped as the prickling sensation returned, almost burning him with its intensity. Watching Xander's determined gait, he realized this was no mood shift. Something was wrong.

"Slow down!" Jacob called, bounding through the grass in an effort to keep up with Xander's giant strides, suddenly afraid to look around.

Making a line for the closest rise, the former soldier made no attempt to moderate his pace. In fact, he sped up, breaking into a trot a few dozen yards below the summit of the ridge, his large rifle bouncing where it rested on his shoulder.

Scrambling up after him, Jacob gasped for breath, watching in exasperation as Xander slipped over the top of the hill and disappeared from sight. A moment later Jacob was at the top and then over, his momentum just starting to carry him down the other side when a pair of hands grabbed him and pulled him down into the grass.

He looked up at Xander's pale gaze. Jacob didn't need to be

told to be silent. He nodded. Xander released him and began crawling back toward the top of the ridge. Jacob followed.

They had crept forward only a yard or so when Xander stopped and reached into his jacket, producing a brass rod a few inches long. He pulled his goggles off, fitted the cylinder into the top of them with a click, and flipped a switch on its side. A green light above the switch lit up.

"What is that thing?" Jacob whispered.

"Periscope. Nice one too. Cutting-edge—or at least it was when I left the service. A nice little retirement gift from Mixel. One of many I gave myself on their behalf."

"What does it do?" Jacob asked. He had never heard of a periscope.

"Watch this," the soldier said with a quick smile.

Xander lifted the pair of lenses to his eyes. Jacob started as a thin metallic hose crept out of the cylinder, weaving like a serpent as it rose up out of the grass and into the air, its tip just cresting the ridge.

"Humph," the man muttered. He handed the goggles over to Jacob.

Jacob gazed through the lenses. There was a moment of disorientation as the view came into focus. Instead of the ground in front of him, Jacob was startled to be looking over the hilltop directly across to the far western ridge.

But far more startling was the sight of the two men on top of the ridge, silhouetted against the afternoon sky. One was gesturing, pointing toward their position, while the other appeared to be scanning with a pair of goggles of his own.

"Seen enough?" Xander asked. Jacob nodded.

Xander reached over and pressed the button on the brass cylinder. The periscope retracted, slinking back into its case.

Jacob lowered the lenses and dropped down as far as he could, hugging the ground even though he and Xander were surely not visible.

"Do you think they see us?" Jacob said, trying not to let his voice crack in fear. It helped that Xander didn't seem particularly bothered.

The man shook his head. "We're far enough over the ridge," he said. "But it doesn't really matter. They've probably been watching us all day."

"The gruskers," Jacob said.

Xander nodded. "The critters must have sensed them. Though I don't know how. Maybe they're using some sort of scanning frequency the gruskers are sensitive to. They couldn't have seen them—I didn't spot them until just now. They've been doing a pretty good job staying out of sight."

"So who are they?" Jacob asked.

Xander shrugged. "More importantly," he said, "why are they spying on us?"

"Maybe they're just like us," Jacob offered. "Maybe they're just out hunting gruskers."

"You don't really believe that, do you?" Xander said.

Jacob looked away, shivering at the thought of the electric waves along his spine, the prickly feeling of eyes on him.

"So what do we do?" he asked.

"Let's go talk to them," Xander said. He crept back down the bank, then rose and headed for the cruiser.

"What?" Jacob cried, scrambling after him.

Xander stopped and turned. Jacob could see his mouth moving in answer but heard nothing as the light around him muted and grayed, the colors fading. Jacob had long since learned to let himself be taken through the doors of perception to the other place without resistance. Sure enough, a second later Xander faded out of sight.

He was home, slowly heading up the steps that led onto the deck. But his feet felt heavy and slow, and as he stared down at the railing in the silver-blue light he realized the hand gripping it wasn't his own. It was older, with blond hairs along its back, a gold ring with an unfamiliar insignia on the pinky finger. Looking up, he saw a man in front of him. No— there were two. Large men dressed in nice suits.

Jacob fought off a wave of dizziness. Though he had had many visions since leaving Harmony, this sensation—looking through the eyes of another—had happened only once before, with Delaney's father. In his nightmares he had seen the man's hands close many times around his daughter's neck. It had been a strange mixture of relief and horror to discover the hands were not his own. Jacob wondered whose hands these belonged to now.

Reaching the deck, he walked behind the pair as they slid open the glass door and headed inside. Jacob started to follow, then suddenly paused to examine his reflection in the window. Another wave of dizziness struck as Jacob saw the face staring back at him with a thin smile.

*LaPerle.*

It had been over a year and a half since he'd last seen Jack LaPerle, Delaney's snide Mixel handler, but he could never forget that face with its narrow eyes, slicked-back hair, and bronzed complexion. Most of all, he could never forget the executive's smile—a grin that managed to be self-satisfied, conniving, and greedy all at once.

The face faded from the glass, its smile disappearing last of all. Jacob stirred as color rushed back into the world and

11

Xander reappeared before him, now gripping his shoulders. He could hear himself gasping.

"What did you see?" Xander demanded.

"I saw men at our house," Jacob replied between gasps. "I was . . . I saw LaPerle."

Xander's face darkened. "Delaney," was all he said.

He turned and ran to the cruiser. Still panting, Jacob struggled after him. By the time he reached the cruiser, Xander was already revving the engine anxiously.

"Let's go, kid," he said, reaching down and grabbing Jacob's arm. Though Jacob was now nearly as tall as Xander, he felt himself being practically lifted off the ground, and before he knew it he was pressed back against his seat as the cruiser leaped toward the hilltop.

"Strap yourself in!" Xander shouted over the roar of the engine, but Jacob was already fumbling with the harness, just managing to click the belt before the cruiser left the ground as it cleared the ridge.

For a moment time seemed to stop as the cruiser floated through the air. But the stillness ended. The cruiser came down with a thud, bouncing on its tires several times, drawing a yelp from Jacob. Normally, Xander would have laughed at the response, but when Jacob looked over, Xander's face was set, his eyes fixed solely on the horizon.

Jacob couldn't remember having ever gone this fast in the cruiser before. Already they had crossed the valley and were heading up the opposite slope toward where they'd seen the watchers.

Clearing the second rise, Jacob started to point at the floater rapidly disappearing into the west.

"I see it," Xander barked. "Forget 'em."

Jacob wanted so badly to ask Xander why—if the vision he'd just seen was true—LaPerle was coming for Delaney now, after all this time. Even more, he wanted to ask if Xander thought she was okay.

But he didn't. He didn't say anything. The way the man was driving made him too afraid of what the answer might be.

It took them only twenty minutes to get back.

"I never should have left her," Xander said at one point. It was the only time he spoke the entire trip.

They were nearly home, just outside the little valley where Xander had built his house, when they spotted the floater waiting in the shadow of the zephyr trees. As Xander slowed to a stop, the sleek craft crept out into sunlight and maneuvered up beside them. Jacob wondered if the two men in suits occupying the floater were the same pair from his vision.

Xander killed the engine. "You fellows lost?" he asked, his voice steady but sharp.

"No, Mr. Payne," one of the suits replied, "we know exactly where we are."

"Well, good. Good for you," Xander snorted. He stretched his neck out the cruiser's window. "So where's LaPerle?" he asked. "Not hiding in the backseat, is he?"

The two men glanced at each other. Then the second suit spoke.

"No, but Mr. LaPerle would like to invite you to join him in Melville. We've reserved a beautiful suite at Mixel Tower. Enough room for all of you."

"Sounds special," Xander retorted. "But we'll pass."

"Perhaps just Jacob then," the man said. "We'd like to talk to him."

Jacob's heart began to race. What did they want him for? He looked over at Xander in alarm. Xander raised a hand slightly to calm him.

"What about?" Xander said, trying to hide his surprise.

"We'd prefer to discuss it back in Melville," the first suit said.

"I'm sure you would," Xander murmured. He looked over at Jacob. "Jacob, do you want to go with these men to talk about whatever it is they're so eager to talk about?" he asked.

"No, thank you," Jacob said, trying to muster what courage he could.

"Well, that settles it then," Xander said, turning back to the men with a smile.

"Please, Jacob. This isn't anything bad," the second suit said. "We're not here to hurt you. Or Delaney, for that matter," he added. From beside him, Jacob could feel Xander stiffen.

"Sorry, boys, but you heard the kid," Xander said. The cruiser's engine growled back to life. "Give LaPerle a big kiss for me."

"Another time then, Jacob," the first man said, leaning over to catch Jacob's gaze. He turned back to Xander. "By the way," he said, "you should be more careful about your friend. A girl like that—pretty, blind—she could wander off. Get lost."

The floater slipped quietly away, rising over the trees before disappearing. Xander watched it leave, then hit the accelerator.

"Bastards," Xander muttered as they took off.

"Why do they want me?" Jacob asked.

"I don't know," the man replied, "but I don't like it."

The cruiser raced down the short road between the trees

and into the clearing, skidding to a halt before the house. They had barely stopped when Xander was leaping out of the cockpit, hitting the ground running. Following as quickly as he could up the steps, Jacob noticed the stunner in the man's hand. Once again, the old sickness rose in his throat at the sight of the weapon.

Reaching the top, they both suddenly froze. Their reflections stared back at them from the glass face of the house, the horizon unbroken behind them except for a two-foot gap where the door had been left open.

Xander gave Jacob a dark look. Raising his stunner before him, he stepped silently through the open door. Jacob followed over the threshold, his heart pounding harder than ever. Stepping into the open room that comprised most of the main floor, he felt a numbness come over him.

The place was a mess. Books lay scattered across the floor. Tables and chairs were overturned. Drawers were left open, their contents emptied onto the floor.

"Delaney!" Xander called out.

No response. Jacob blinked and glanced around. There was no sign of her.

Xander dashed up the side staircase to the second floor and hurried down the balcony, glancing into her room, before coming back to the railing and shaking his head.

Without a word, Jacob rushed out onto the deck.

"Delaney!" he shouted. He could hear his voice echo through the clearing. He shouted again, as loud as he could.

"Up here!" she called out.

Jacob raced down off the deck, around the side of the house, and up the steep bank behind it, the adrenaline coursing so hard through his body he could barely register his relief at the sight of her standing at the top of the hill.

"What are you doing up here?" he gasped, reaching her side.

Delaney smiled, pulling her black hair back into a ponytail. The gold lines and twin jewels of her eyes glittered against the sun as she turned to face him.

"I came up for some sun and fresh air and ended up falling asleep," she replied with a shrug. "The cruiser woke me up. You know how loud that engine is."

"You okay?" Xander called out, rushing up the slope to join them, his stunner still in hand.

"Yeah," she said with a laugh. "What's the big deal?"

Neither Jacob nor Xander spoke. As the silence grew, her smile faded. "What's wrong?" she said at last.

"We've got a problem," Xander murmured.

# CHAPTER TWO

"Doesn't look like anything's broken," Xander said, surveying the damage.

Jacob watched from the doorway as Xander stooped and began collecting books, gently gathering them in piles and returning them to the empty bookcase. He helped Delaney inside and over to the couch, the one piece of furniture left untouched, then set to work helping Xander.

"I can't believe they did this," he muttered.

"Forget about it," Xander said, standing with an armful of books.

"What do you mean forget about it?" Jacob cried. "Look what they did to your house!"

Xander shrugged. "Just a trick. The work of some cheap muscle."

"So what were they looking for?" Delaney asked.

"They probably weren't looking for anything. They just wanted us to know they were here. They did this on purpose. Like that little stunt on the other side of the clearing, and those watchers out on the plains."

"But why?" Jacob demanded.

"To let us know they can get to us," the man replied. "All part of the game."

"I'm not afraid of them," Delaney said. "I just wonder what they want with Jacob."

"Do you think Mixel knows?" Jacob asked, turning to Xander.

"That you're from Harmony?" the man replied. "They've probably figured it out."

"No," Jacob said, reaching down to pick up a lamp. "I mean about . . . you know, the visions." He was nearly whispering now.

Xander shrugged.

"Maybe they haven't been just watching," Delaney broke in. "Maybe they've been listening."

Jacob knew that Delaney remembered as well as he did the listeners back in Harmony. The listeners kept track of what people said, enforced the colony's rules. Everyone knew that when the listeners came to your house, dark days were ahead.

But now the idea that there were others out there taking in their words, monitoring their conversations—it almost seemed worse than the watching. He started thinking back to everything they'd been talking about over the last week. His stomach sank.

"Let's just get this place cleaned up," Xander said.

Xander had been right—nothing was broken or appeared to be missing. Before long, the place was put back together and swept for bugs, for any kind of eavesdropping device. The house was clean. It was as if nothing had ever happened. Except for one thing.

The basement had been left untouched, or at least left intact, as had the upstairs. But as Jacob walked down the balcony toward Delaney's room, the hairs on the back of his neck rose. It was as if he could feel the presence of Mixel's men passing through him along the walkway, could feel their footsteps beneath his own as he turned into the bedroom·where he kept the few possessions he had in a drawer.

But they weren't in the drawer anymore. There, neatly arranged on Delaney's pillow lay the two sounders—both Delaney's and the one he'd recovered from the body on his exodus over the plains. Between them lay the finder, the device he'd used to track down Delaney.

Staring at them Jacob couldn't help but feel that the very objects that had once helped him so much had now betrayed him.

Jacob sat on the hilltop above the house. Beyond the clearing dotted with trees the land spread out, stretching west toward the city of Melville, which twinkled meekly on the horizon in the early evening light. There were dark clouds across the western sky, blocking the sunset, illuminated ever so slightly by Duna hovering above, varying wisps of purple that signaled an approaching storm.

Aside from the fire pit in the woods, this was Jacob's favorite spot, particularly in the late afternoon when the sun would light up the hillside and the rippling crests of nearby ridges. It was also the time when the hawks took to the sky, wheeling and dancing in circles above him as they hunted or played games with one another.

But there were no hawks this evening as the air thickened and the grasses turned their pale backs to the breeze. Jacob lay down and for a long time stared up, watching Duna slip into view as it raced across the sky, its rings piercing the upper corner of his sight.

They'd finished picking up a couple of hours ago. Afterward, Delaney had settled into the piano, pounding out whatever fears or frustrations had built up through a series of ornate songs before slipping into something peaceful.

Listening from where he stood out on the deck, Jacob couldn't help but feel envious, not just of her skill, but of her form of catharsis. He wished he had some kind of outlet, somewhere to direct the anxiety still lingering from the day's events.

*I should be playing too,* he'd thought.

Like Delaney, like his mother, he had always wanted to be a musician, had hoped to be assigned the specialization in Harmony, the one that would allow him to spend his life performing and composing for the people of his community and for its parent Foundation back on Earth. But as much as he loved it, no matter how much he practiced, it had never seemed to come easy to him, not the way it had to his mother, or to Delaney. Their obvious talent made him constantly doubt his own. And though he'd never know for sure if he would have been chosen for a music specialization, deep down he believed it wasn't going to happen. He could still remember his mother hinting at the fact not long before his sight emerged, probably trying to prepare him for the disappointment.

"You are a good player, Jacob, but it may not be your greatest talent," she'd said. "I know that no matter what happens, you'll do something special. You *are* special."

Little did either of them know what was right around the corner, the changes that would ultimately drive them apart. He often wondered if his mother still believed what she had said about him. Most of all, he wondered if she was right.

Would he ever do anything special?

Delaney was still playing when Xander came out onto the deck. He came over to the railing and leaned beside Jacob.

"Scared, Blinder?" he asked.

Jacob shook his head.

"Good. 'Cause you don't need to be. I won't let them get to you. You know that, right?"

"I know that," Jacob said.

"They probably won't even come back," Xander continued, then paused. "But in case they do, I want you to take this."

Xander pulled the stunner out from his jacket pocket and pushed it into Jacob's hands. Jacob stared down at the weapon. It felt heavy, its metal cold. He'd been offered it once before, on his way back into Harmony to confront the ghost-box but had turned it down. He wouldn't need it, he'd said at the time. But this wasn't Harmony, and Mixel's men weren't blind listeners he could easily evade. His fingers closed around the handle. He looked over at Xander.

"You'll have to show me how to use it," he said.

Xander nodded. He proceeded to show Jacob how to aim and fire, how to recharge the weapon, and how to adjust the settings on it.

"Just be careful how high you set it."

"What about this far back?" Jacob asked, pointing to the highest setting, hardly daring to touch the dial.

"It won't kill them. Probably," Xander murmured. "Here, let me show you one other thing." He took the pistol. "This isn't just any old stunner. It's been modified—an old merce-nary thing. If you hold the trigger halfway down, like this, and turn the setting all the way back, it'll overload, set off a nasty little explosion. Just be careful—once it starts, you've only got ten seconds to get rid of it.

"That's all there is to it," he said, handing the weapon back. "Think you can handle it?"

It was the question Jacob had been asking himself for the last hour, thinking over everything that had happened as he sat on the hilltop. Reaching down from time to time, he would feel the stunner at his side in the holster Xander had given him, a weight against his leg, reassuring, terrifying.

By now Duna was straight overhead, its mass nearly filling his entire range of view as he lay back in the grass. A single black speck—most likely a cargo liner in the upper atmosphere—stood out against the swirling gases of the planet. He watched it carefully as it crept along, like a tiny insect floating in the air, before it finally disappeared with a blue flare of its engines, just another one of the myriad ships he saw nearly every evening cruising into space, breaking free of Nova Campi's orbit to climb into the stars. As always, he wondered where it was going. And in the back of his mind, like so many times before, came the whisper of that one word.

*Teiresias.*

It was almost two years now since the strange figure of the boy had come to him in a dream as fever ravaged his body. Before disappearing, the visitor had told Jacob that he wasn't alone, that there were others like him, others with strange powers waiting for him to join them so that they might help him understand what he had become. The vision had stayed with Jacob, pushing him back to Harmony, back to the ghostbox, the colony's central computer, looking for any clue to the mystery of the other former Blinders. The ghostbox hadn't told him much, but it confirmed their existence and—most important of all—gave him a name, the name of a suspected hiding place, the name of another world.

*Teiresias.*

For months afterward, Jacob had kept the name hidden in the back of his mind as he, Xander, and Delaney settled into a life together. They had all been broken in one way or another, and while they healed one another, the knowledge slept. When he'd finally asked Xander about the planet, there was little the man could tell him. Teiresias was a distant world on the far side of the Outer Rim, a strange planet that never turned as it circled around its sun, keeping one face toward the light, the other to the dark, a jealously guarded mining planet owned by one of Mixel's rival corporations.

Though it wasn't much, it was enough to rekindle Jacob's hope of finding the strange visitor and his friends. But only for a while.

A year had passed since then, and though he still thought about the distant planet from time to time, the memory of that dream seemed to be growing fainter every day, the visitor's words slipping away no matter how hard Jacob struggled to keep hold of them, just as the visions had begun to fade too, appearing more infrequently and in shorter bursts these last few months. Jacob had wondered if the powers were slipping away. And worse—if they went, would his sight go as well? Would he be like Delaney, blind again? It didn't seem to be the case. Everything had remained as sharp as ever, the colors still rich. It was all still real. This valley, this house and the people he shared it with—sometimes they seemed to be the only things that were real, this place the only place he wanted to be. And lately he'd begun to wonder if some dreams were meant to fade, to slip away and disappear and not disturb the world.

Not anymore.

He closed his eyes and took a deep breath, tried to quiet the pulse that throbbed louder in his ears as the old hope roused itself. Leaving behind everything he knew, everyone he cared about—he'd been down that road before. And like before, the same question rose up before him, a gnawing fear: How could he make it on his own?

Then again, he wasn't the same person he'd been two years ago. He was older now, stronger. Why shouldn't he try? Besides, he'd already started the journey the moment he'd fled Harmony, alone. Wasn't it time to continue it now? To finish it?

"Mind some company?"

Jacob sat up. He hadn't heard Delaney approach. But there she stood, dark against the western clouds, blocking Melville from sight.

"Sure," he said, moving aside to make room for her in the pocket of grass.

"Listen," she said, "you don't need to worry."

He laughed. He couldn't help it, though he tried not to make it sound bitter.

"That seems to be the refrain. Xander said the same thing to me earlier. Then he said it again. Then he gave me one of his stunners to hold on to."

"I know. It's kind of silly," Delaney said, nodding. "Okay, I'm worried too. But we're all in this together."

"You're right," Jacob replied. "That's the problem."

"What do you mean?"

He sighed. "You know what happened today, what's been happening all week. This isn't like before, Delaney, when LaPerle came to get you back. There's something else going on here. I feel it. It's me they're after now."

He paused.

"As long as I'm here, you're both at risk."

She was silent for a long time.

"You're leaving, aren't you," she said at last. "You're going to that place, that world from your dream."

"Teiresias," he whispered. "I don't know. Maybe. I think I need to."

She sighed. "I thought that you'd forgotten," she said, "that you were going to stay here with us."

"Part of me wanted to forget. After everything that happened, all I wanted was to be someplace safe."

"But you don't feel you have that anymore," she said, reaching over and taking his hand.

"It's not even that, Delaney. Not entirely. Whether Mixel ever came back or not, the other part of me has always known I can't stay here forever."

"Xander won't like it if you decide to leave. He'll try to stop you."

"I'm pretty much counting on it." He hesitated. "What about you?"

She leaned over, put an arm around his shoulder, and drew him in close. "I don't want you to go, Jacob. But I would never try to stop you. I remember how you supported me when I decided to go home. You didn't want me to, but you helped me, and I'll never forget it."

"Yeah, and look how great that turned out," he murmured.

"Don't say that, Jacob. It was good that it happened that way. I needed to experience that, to truly understand what my father had become. I had to learn that I could never have a place in Harmony. Besides, I only went back because I was scared. I was scared of Mixel, I was scared of the future, and I didn't know what else to do."

"So how am I any better?"

"It's not the same at all. Forget Mixel. Like you said, you need to do this. You've been called. I never was. I just ran into the darkness."

"I'm afraid I'm doing that too. I know Teiresias is a real place. I know where it is, a few things about it, but I don't know for sure the others like me are really there."

"Deep down, you do. You sense it. That's your gift. I'm sure of it."

"I'm glad *you* are," he joked.

She squeezed his hand. "My place is here. This is where I belong. It's the first time in my life I've ever had that feeling. That's why I understand."

She released his hand and stood up. "Supper's almost ready."

"I'll be down soon," he said.

She nodded and turned. He watched her walk back to the house, moving serenely down the slope as if she could see the beaten path beneath her feet.

After she had disappeared around the corner of the house, he lay back and stared at the sky one last time. Duna was still overhead. Another ship had appeared, emerging from the planet's dark rings as it moved toward the orb's outer edge, soon to be swallowed up by space.

He could still feel the eyes out there watching, could sense the weight of Mixel hovering at the edges as well as he could feel the metal weight of the stunner strapped to his waist. But for the first time in a week, he felt a little less frightened.

# CHAPTER THREE

"I knew it," Xander said, shaking his head as he threw a thick chunk of zephyr into the flames. A cascade of sparks rose up into the night, dying as they turned and fell.

"As soon as you came in for supper, I could tell you'd settled on something," he continued. "Didn't take much to figure out what it was."

Jacob swallowed, holding back from speaking. Sometimes it was best to just stand out of the way and let Xander talk.

"A bunch of muscled suits toss a few books around, spill a few drawers, and suddenly you're heading to the other side of space. Why? Because a computer told you there might be a few Blinders hiding out on some backwater planet on the edge of nowhere."

"It wasn't just the ghostbox," Jacob said. "There was the boy too."

"Oh, right. Some garbled hallucination during a tangle with the Aurelian Flu. Give me a 104-degree fever for three days and I guarantee I'd be hearing voices too."

"You don't believe it was real, then?"

Xander growled. "I already told you, don't worry about Mixel. I handled them before, didn't I?"

"You did. And it worked. But I don't think it will this time.

And I don't want you to get hurt trying to stop them." Jacob paused. "I don't want her to get hurt."

Xander's eyes narrowed.

"You can't go out there by yourself. You're just a kid," the soldier said at last. Hearing the man's voice start to shake, Jacob looked away, remembering the box of toys in the basement, remembering the story of Xander's own lost children.

"I'm almost fifteen," Jacob said, "and I'm only two inches shorter than you now."

Xander snorted. "Big deal. You don't know what it's like out there."

"I know. That's the point."

"Yeah, that *is* the point," Xander snapped. He hesitated. "I'll go with you. We'll all go together."

"Delaney can't make that kind of a trip. Besides, the whole point is to get away from the two of you. She needs you, Xander. Here."

"And how are you going to get to Teiresias? Space travel's expensive, Jacob. And all the passenger liners are owned by Mixel."

"There are other ships," Jacob said. "Smugglers have ships, right? I can work for one of them. I can earn my keep. Just like in those old stories you read me, about the water ships on Earth. Remember those cabin boys?"

"Now you're really talking crazy. You don't want to go to space with a bunch of smugglers."

"I need to get to Teiresias somehow. They're waiting for me."

Xander laughed bitterly and shook his head. "Do you know how crazy it sounds when you say that?"

"I don't worry about how it sounds. I just think about

what I've seen. What I feel."

Xander leaned back and looked up toward the sky, where a few stars twinkled between the dark leaves. For a long time he stared upward, not moving. Jacob remained still as well, listening to the fire crackle, watching the embers break apart and fall beneath the weight of logs. This moment was like many nights when they sat at the fire, sometimes exchanging only a handful of words the whole evening. Jacob could feel the quiet passing, could feel the moment's end as Xander finally spoke.

"You and Delaney. Both alike. Both too damn stubborn."

"You're one to talk," Jacob said, and grinned.

Xander raised his eyebrows, a brief smile crossing his face. But it quickly faded. Jacob could see his pale eyes grow sad.

"I can't really stop you," the man said at last. "If I were your father, I would. But you're not my son."

"No, I'm not," Jacob whispered. "But you still have to let me go."

Their eyes locked for a moment.

"When?" Xander asked.

"Soon. Before Mixel suspects it. I think tomorrow we should try."

"No point putting it off, I guess, now that you've made up your mind," Xander said, nodding. He sighed. "So this is our last night together, huh?"

"I suppose it is," Jacob said, trying to keep his voice from breaking. Hearing Xander acknowledge the fact somehow made it real for the first time. A sudden pang welled up, a bitter mix of relief and regret.

The man rose, brushing a few fallen ashes from his pants.

"Guess I better get more wood then," he said. He turned to go.

"Xander," Jacob said, holding out the stunner. "Here."

Pausing, Xander looked back, then shook his head. "Better keep it," he said. "You're going to need it."

He turned and disappeared into the darkness.

It was sunny that night in Jacob's dreams.

*I'm back*, he thought.

It had been quite a while since he'd last had the recurring dream of flying over the plains, soaring like a hawk above the swirling grasses as Duna's rings broke the horizon's edge, alternating bands of darkness and light that seemed to pull the orb up into the afternoon sky.

It was his favorite dream. He'd forgotten how much he'd missed it. Until now.

*There they are*, he said, tilting right and dropping down against the warm cushion of air toward the pair walking below. As always, Delaney and Xander came cutting through the grass, determined, smiling as they held hands. Jacob looked around for some sign of himself. He'd begun seeing his figure in the dream shortly before it went away—but not always, and not always completely himself, often appearing older, more grown-up, though the differences between himself and this other version had begun to diminish with Jacob's growth spurt.

But he was nowhere to be found below, and now the dream had taken on a new permutation. Jacob always loved the little changes, the subtle variations that made the dream fresh, but tonight was different as Xander and Delaney halted and began pointing to the sky, waving to where he hovered above them. Their faces had taken on a look of fear, and now they were gesturing for him to join them, pleading with him to come down out of the sky, but he wasn't coming. He tried looking over his shoulder, but his head refused to move. He tried willing his body to the ground, but it too seemed frozen in the air. Whether a force from above was pulling him back or one from below was pushing him away he couldn't be sure. All he knew was that his body was no longer his own, and that he'd never felt more helpless, not even when the listeners were taking him to the council house to stand in judgment before the colony's leaders, or when he'd fled Harmony and stood lost on the open plain, half-starved and withering from dehydration.

And now he could feel himself being pulled away just as Delaney's eyes came to life, glowing like he'd never seen them before, twin points of radiance that flared then faded as he drew farther and farther away. He watched them shrink as he rose through the atmosphere until all that could be seen below was the tiniest glimmer of her eyes, just a single flicker like some distant star weakly pushing its light through space. The light was extinguished, taking with it the surface around it, the clouds above it, leaving only darkness.

Just when Jacob felt he couldn't stand another moment of the black, felt as if he were being smothered by impenetrable night, the light came back as one star after another flickered to life. Soon stars surrounded him. Hundred, thousands, tens of thousands of them, bathing him in their glow. He looked around for Nova Campi, for anything familiar or solid, but all was space.

Slowly, bit by bit, like the stars a moment ago, music filled the space. A chorus of notes sounded, not made by human

31

voices or any instrument he could identify, just music, a single chord ringing, throbbing in overtones so intense, so beautiful he could feel the tears on his face, for he knew he was hearing the music of the stars, knew that they were singing to him the song they had always sung and always would sing, only no one had ever listened before now.

His hands were gripping hair now, he was speeding through space on the back of a grusker. He could feel its muscles flowing between his legs, could hear its snorting breaths heaving in time to its galloping hooves. The tears on his face burned cool as the stars blurred into streaks of light stretching behind him to infinity. He tightened his grip and leaned forward until his body and the grusker's seemed one.

A planet appeared before him, hurtled past, and disappeared. Then another, and another, until one rose before him and the streaks of light became stars again. They were slowing. The planet grew and grew, pushing out the stars, and still Jacob rode the grusker. All he could do was hold on, helpless as it continued its drive straight into the atmosphere.

And then he was falling, falling, burning, flames curling off the grusker's cage of horns and licking at his skin, the two of them a ball of fire, streaking toward the ground, the grusker bellowing in pain, him crying out in terror.

*We're going to crash,* he thought, breaking through the clouds only to discover the curved earth beneath was nothing more than an eye, a whirlpool pupil floating black amid an iris ocean, shrinking against the light of his falling, drawing him in.

"You're coming, aren't you."

Jacob opened his eyes to white. He hadn't felt the impact. At some point the fiery roar, the grusker's cries and his own, all had given way to silence. But he hadn't noticed when.

He turned to see the boy. It had been a while, but he could never forget the strange unearthly face, shifting and dancing in the white light, the voice rippled in static.

"It's you again, isn't it?" Jacob cried. "I wasn't imagining it before. I wasn't just sick."

"We lost you for a while," the boy said, "but we've found you again. You're coming, aren't you," he repeated, his face breaking into a smile.

"I am. I'll be leaving for Teiresias soon."

The figure nodded through a crackle of static, his frame shifting and fracturing, then joining back together. "You heard me then. I wasn't sure you knew where to find us."

"No," Jacob said. "The computer told me, the ghostbox, at Harmony. I went back there. I asked it and it told me about Teiresias."

The boy frowned, a look of worry crossing his face.

"Then they know," he said. "We were hoping they hadn't followed us."

"It's just a suspicion. They don't know for sure," Jacob offered. "I didn't get a chance to ask it what else the Foundation knew. I just know they're looking."

"They don't look themselves," the boy said, his voice slipping into momentary distortion. "They can't. But they have others looking for them. We are hidden, though. Protected. For how long, I can't say."

"Long enough for me to find you, I hope," Jacob said. The boy was beginning to fade now, his figure breaking up. Jacob knew he had only a few more seconds.

"Come, Jacob. Hurry. Even from here, we can sense danger all around you. Someone is—"

The voice became garbled to the point where Jacob couldn't make out the words. Then it cut out altogether, leaving nothing but the boy, a figure shifting in and out of shadow.

"How will I know where to go when I get to Teiresias?" Jacob shouted, hoping for one last moment of clarity. But the boy kept on talking. He hadn't heard Jacob.

And then he was gone, dissolving into a shower of dark specks, and Jacob was alone once more.

Pushing aside the glass door, Jacob stepped out onto the deck in the early light of dawn, his breath clouding in the cold. Wrapping his cloak around him, he slipped off the deck and stole up the hill one last time, his boots darkening with the thick layer of dew. Reaching the hilltop where only hours ago he'd sat and decided, he turned in a circle, taking in the land. The smaller moon Drake, a pink crescent, hung in the western sky. Prairie birds called to one another, singing the morning cries he rarely heard. The world seemed a different place.

He stamped his feet in the grass and shivered against the cold. But the shaking was deep inside him as he stood in the half-light and thought about the days ahead. He'd felt strong on waking, clear, having heard the boy again, having made contact with the visitor. The path was set, the destination known.

The clarity now made everything real, made the future real, just as it made this place, this world he was about to leave, seem suddenly unreal, as if it were slipping away all around him.

He wrapped his cloak even tighter around himself, closed his eyes, and tried to take it all in—the sounds of the birds and of the breezes rustling the grasses, the smells of the flowers and the last remnants of smoke from last night's fire being carried up and over the hill. And in his mind's eye, he tried to focus on the little house below him, on the two people inside now stirring with the morning, soon to rise and join him, soon to help him on his way, soon to say good-bye for who knew how long. Not forever.

# CHAPTER FOUR

Melville's skyscrapers, which seemed to sprout higher from the plain with every minute they drew closer, now stood before them, though none loomed higher than MixelCorp's single black tower at the center of the round city—the hub of a gleaming wheel situated on the plain. Though Nova Campi was home to several settlements—including Harmony, one of five outposts the Truesight Foundation had established on various worlds—none even came close in size to Melville, home to Mixel's regional headquarters, as well as to the planet's lone starport.

But they passed by the starport and headed downtown instead. Though the port was their ultimate destination, Xander thought it best to avoid the attention they'd likely draw openly going from one hangar to another in search of passage. They needed information first—the names of captains, the names of ships—and they all knew the one place to get it.

It had been a gloomy ride in, spent mostly in silence, each lost in his or her own thoughts. Thoughts of sadness mixed with worry, at least in Jacob's case. He'd always imagined his leave-taking would be a moment of excitement, of eager anticipation, not this dark cloud hanging over all of them. It made him angry—angry toward Mixel, toward LaPerle as he remembered the man's face from yesterday's vision. He'd tried so hard to forget that face, had convinced himself that it was gone for good. But in the silence of the drive in, he'd realized it had never really disappeared. And now it was looking for him.

Of one thing he was sure—there were eyes upon them. The same feeling as yesterday, the same nagging twinge he'd felt all week only grew stronger as they cruised down the main boulevard between the glass structures flashing an endless array of video ads and corporate logos. Looking up at one particularly tall tower, Jacob remembered seeing Delaney's own visage adorning its side on one of his very first visits to the city.

They pulled over to the side of the street and parked. There were plenty of spaces. Wheeled transports like Xander's weren't exactly rare, but most people used floaters. Jacob had asked Xander once why he didn't use a floater.

"I like to stay connected to the ground," was all the man said.

They got out of the vehicle and started down the street, ignoring the looks Xander's worn cruiser always drew from passing crowds.

*At least they're not staring at her anymore,* Jacob thought. A few paused at the sight of Delaney's eyes, but it was nothing compared to the intense stares and whispers she'd drawn from passersby the first few times they'd returned to Melville. Then, she'd still been a familiar face, a burgeoning star mysteriously fallen from grace. But as the wheel of celebrity ground on, as new singers and starlets had risen, some to fall as quickly as she had, she seemed to have been quickly forgotten.

He'd told her of the change during a recent trip.

"Too bad," was all she'd said, though a wry grin said otherwise.

They turned off the main street and headed down a narrow lane. By now, it was a familiar turn to Jacob, one he'd made many times since he'd come to live with Xander. As always, the lamp glowed over the doorway of the little shop, inviting those willing to leave the familiar path of the main thoroughfare.

They opened the door and passed in one at a time, Jacob last, savoring the sound of the bell. Of all the sights Melville had to offer, this shop, with its warm lights, antique books, and dry, earthy odors, was just about the only place he felt at ease in the city.

"Well, look at you," Xander said.

Jacob turned as the woman came around the corner, flashing her familiar grin. He gasped at the sight of her brilliant red skin and emerald hair.

"You've changed, Kala," he said. The last time he'd seen her, her flesh was still dyed deep purple, her hair the color of deep space, her eyes a pair of stars. But the gold lenses were gone now, replaced by jeweled greens to match her hair.

She laughed and gave him a quick hug.

"Kala doesn't change, kid," she said. "Just time for a new look, that's all. Need to shake things up a bit now and then."

She turned and gave Delaney a quick embrace.

"And how are you doing?" she asked. "Still not missing the spotlight?"

"Still not missing it," Delaney replied with a laugh.

"Those eyes are something," Kala said, reaching up to

trace a finger along the golden rims. "I still get shivers whenever I see them. If they didn't cost three fortunes, I think I could go for implants like that. A few of the divas have made the switch to synthetics. You must have started something."

Delaney's smile faded. "Trust me—they look better from the outside."

"We need your help with something, Kala," Xander said. "And I'm sorry to say it isn't books this time. Or pianos for that matter."

"I know," Kala said.

"You do?" Xander said, exchanging a quick glance with Jacob.

"I was hoping you'd come by soon," she said. "Let's talk back here."

They followed her between the stacks toward the rear of the shop and into a small office. Kala shut the door and sat down across from them at her desk. Jacob watched as she opened a thick book. Its center had been hollowed out. Inside lay a network of circuits encased in a glass cube. He watched as she touched two sides of the device. A faint hum filled the room like a distant insect on a warm night. Xander gave her a quizzical look.

"A blocker, huh?"

"Don't think they've got the place wired, but just in case," she said.

"You mean Mixel?" Xander said. Kala nodded. "But why would they be interested? You're not in the business anymore. Are you?"

Jacob knew what the business was. According to Xander, the smugglers who kept the underground economy rolling did well along the frontier, an economy to which Mixel and the other corporations—when they weren't taking part themselves—turned a blind eye.

She shook her head. "No, but I still like to mingle with the boys," she said. "They need a shot of style now and then, something to get their blood pumping. And every once in a while, they give me gifts." She gestured to the cube.

"Besides," she added, "a girl needs her privacy, no?"

Xander laughed. "She does if she's you."

"So why were you hoping to see us again so soon?" Delaney asked.

Kala nodded, her face growing serious. "They came in here last week," she said. "A pair of Mixel suits, asking lots of questions."

"Let me guess," Xander broke in, "they wanted to know about Jacob."

A brief flicker of surprise crossed Kala's face. "That's right," she said. "Guess they caught up with you, huh?"

"You could say that," Xander replied. "What did they want to know?"

"All kinds of things. How long had he been with you? Where did he come from? Was there anything different about him?"

"Different how?" Jacob demanded.

"They didn't specify."

"You didn't tell them anything, did you?" Delaney said. Jacob could hear the worry in her voice.

"'Course not," Kala said. She turned to Jacob. "Told them as far as I knew, you were Xander's nephew. That your parents were doing research out in the Spiral. Probably wouldn't be back for another two years."

Jacob breathed a sigh of relief. Kala knew just where

Jacob had come from and why he'd left Harmony. But they had never told her about his visions. And even though he trusted her, he was just as glad they hadn't.

Xander nodded. "Did they buy it?" he asked.

"No," Kala said. "But for whatever reason, they didn't hassle me. All smiles. They know I used to be one of them, just like you. One big happy family, right?"

"Yeah, right," Xander snorted. "Listen, like I said before, we need your help. We're looking to book passage offworld. Not on a liner, something low-key. Figured you might know somebody with a ship."

Kala frowned. "That's a tough one. Not many captains take on passengers these days." She paused, looked over at Jacob. "Still, I know someone who might help. Just caught up with him a few nights ago. A smuggler. Decent enough guy, though. But you'd better hurry," she added. "He's leaving today."

"Thanks, Kala," Jacob said.

Kala wrote something down on a slip of paper and passed it across the desk to Jacob with a wink. "Anything for you, kid," she said.

The blocker's hum intensified for a second then faded before dying completely. Kala put her finger to her lips and closed the book.

"Some gift," she murmured.

*220.* That was the number inscribed over the hangar entrance. The same number written on the slip of paper Kala had given them, accompanied by a single word: *Bennet.*

The three of them paused in the street and watched for several minutes, standing aside as men came in and out of the hangar, pushing the hovering stacks of crates loaded on floatpads. Like Kala, many of them had skin changes of all different colors—blues, reds, greens, some a swirled mix of different hues—while others had normal tan skin decorated with colored designs of every image imaginable, the sights and creatures of more than two dozen worlds. Interestingly, their hair reminded him of Harmony. Aside from the fantastic array of colors, most of the men—like those in the colony he'd grown up in—had long, flowing hair that ran down past their shoulders or hair that was shorn off altogether, right down to the scalp.

In spite of their wild appearance, most of the men Jacob observed coming in and out of the hangar seemed relaxed and easygoing, flashing smiles and trading jokes as they worked at a steady clip. He could feel the knot that had formed in his stomach as they approached the starport begin to ease. Just a little.

Seeing them stare, one of the men broke off and approached them.

"Need something?" he asked.

He was short but not little. Squat, solid, like the hills that dotted the plains. His reddish hair was shaved close, and he had a face thick with whiskers to match, so that his whole head seemed to bristle. Besides that, Jacob couldn't tell what was more startling—the web of scars crisscrossing the man's face, or his left forearm, an intertwining mix of plastic and gold ending in a hand whose fingers rippled like five miniature serpents, reminding Jacob of Xander's slithering periscope. His eyes remained stolid, waiting.

"Bennet," Xander said. "We're looking for Bennet."

The man's eyes narrowed. "Captain's not available. I can take a message."

"I don't care to leave one," Xander said. "We'll wait."

"I'm the first mate," the man said, his fingers rippling faster, becoming a blur. "Don't worry, I'll see he gets it."

Expecting tension, Jacob was surprised to feel none as both men regarded each other impassively.

"It's okay, Silas," a man called out.

The man ambled toward them through the hangar gate. He wore cargo pants and boots similar to Xander's, but over a white shirt he sported a black jacket with gold stripes along the sleeves. His long auburn hair—the same color as the first mate's—was tied back in a ponytail and matched both the color of his beard as well as his amber-tinted eyes. But what made him stand out was how ordinary he looked otherwise. Aside from a diamond glittering against the lobe of his left ear, he lacked any adornment. Amid the assortment of multi-colored, tattooed, wild-haired men scuttling about him, he seemed so tame, so mild mannered. But the blandness of his appearance was offset by the way he carried himself. He moved with a rhythm that was both languid and controlled, unassuming yet totally confident. No matter how pedestrian he seemed at first glance, Jacob could tell right away that he was the captain of a starship.

"Lucian Bennet," the man said, reaching out to shake Xander's hand. "I'm captain of the *Odessa*."

"Xander Payne," the other responded.

The captain looked down at his first mate and nodded. Silas glanced at them one last time, then disappeared back into the hangar.

"We're looking for passage on your ship," Xander said. "Just one." He put his hand on Jacob's shoulder.

Bennet looked Jacob over for a moment.

"We're not a passenger ship," he said at last.

"I know," Xander replied. "Kala sent us here. Said she thought you might be able to help us."

"Kala, huh?" Bennet said, flashing a grin. Looking back at Jacob, his grin faded. He shook his head. "Why don't you just take a liner?"

Xander didn't respond. Bennet shook his head.

"Okay," the captain said. "Where's the kid going, anyway?"

Xander looked over at Jacob and nodded. "Teiresias," Jacob said.

"Teiresias? That's a long ways. Lot farther than I'm going."

"So where *are* you going?" Xander asked.

"New Jupiter. With a few stops along the way."

"That's in the same sector," Xander offered.

Bennet shrugged. "How much you got?"

"Eighty thousand."

The captain snorted. "That doesn't even come close. You're looking at least two hundred to even make it worth considering."

Jacob's heart sank. Listening to the exchange, he'd felt for sure that this was the person, and the ship, that would get him to where he needed to go. It was strange—as soon as Bennet joined them, Jacob had felt the pressure along his spine ease, the watching eyes dim. It was as if there was some kind of energy field radiating from the man, shielding Jacob from whatever was out there threatening. He'd never felt anything like it before. Not even around Xander.

"I could work for you," Jacob said, trying not to sound desperate. "I could help out. Whatever you need me to do. Like a cabin boy?"

"Cabin boy?" Bennet said. He broke into a laugh. "The *Odessa*'s no sailboat, kid, and we're not pirates—despite our appearance. We're businessmen. Have you ever worked in the business?"

"I've never been on a ship before," Jacob murmured, looking down.

"Never been to space?" the captain exclaimed. He shook his head. "I've got all the help I need, thanks." He began to walk away.

"Wait!" Delaney cried. At her call, Bennet stopped, then turned back.

"How can it cost so much?" she asked.

As if seeing her for the first time, Bennet returned and peered in closely at her eyes.

"Air, water, food. Only so much to go around. The kid takes up weight and space. And space is what it's all about in our business."

"Come on," Xander retorted, "Jacob doesn't take up that much room. And he can bring his own rations."

Bennet frowned. "I don't like kids, don't like them on my ship. They have a way of getting into trouble."

"Jacob isn't like that," Delaney said.

Bennet glanced once more at Jacob. Jacob could see him hesitate. He turned back to Delaney.

"Who made your eyes?" he asked.

"Mixel."

"That's what I thought. Those are worth a lot of money. You know that, don't you?"

"Yeah, I've been told," Delaney replied. "But they don't work."

"Doesn't matter. The circuitry in them is top-shelf. Just

45

hitting the market now. Those would cover it."

"Cover what?" she asked. "You mean Jacob's passage?"

"Forget it," Xander snapped. "I know where you're going with this. It isn't going to happen."

Bennet shrugged. "Suit yourself." He turned once more to leave.

"So where would I go to sell them?" Delaney asked.

"There's a clinic on the other side of Melville. Mortimer's. He'll buy them. And he can take 'em out. When it comes to synthetics, nobody does a better job."

"How do you know?" Xander demanded.

"He did my brother's arm," Bennet replied, and gestured toward Silas, who was walking by.

"No way," Xander said, shaking his head. "I'm not taking you to any chop shop."

"Just listen, Xander . . ." Delaney pleaded.

"Forget it," Xander repeated.

Bennet broke in. "If you'll excuse me, I need to get back to work. We take off in a few hours. If you change your mind, come back. Otherwise, good luck."

He turned and strode away, back into the hangar. Jacob shivered as the captain left. The watching eyes had brightened once more.

# CHAPTER FIVE

Even in the middle of day, the neon sign seemed to light up the street in front of them—the cool blue letters of *Mortimer's* out-glowing the distant sun. They'd taken a quiet floater ride across the city to the shop, and now there they stood, side by side in the shining blue. Jacob wondered if the others felt as nervous as he did.

"This is all happening too fast," Xander said. Jacob could hear him trying to control his voice, keep his anger in check. Both of them knew it was pointless. Anger didn't work on her.

*So I'm not the only one struggling,* Jacob thought. It was all so overwhelming to begin with—the life-changing decisions hanging over him, driving him. Or rather, driving by him, ready to pass away to a place beyond reach, forcing him to jump on before it was too late. And now this.

"You don't have to go through with it, Delaney," Jacob said, squeezing her hand.

Delaney sighed. "That's enough. Both of you." She let go of their hands and turned to face them. "Look, even I can see that Jacob needs to be on that ship. This is the only way."

"Who says?" Xander snapped. "Besides, when those fancy Mixel synthetics of yours are gone, that's it. You'll never get them back." He hesitated. "I guess I always thought that sooner or later you'd decide to . . ."

Jacob could see her face soften. "I'd decide to get them fixed," she murmured, finishing his thought. "Did it ever occur to either of you that I might want to get rid of these metal sockets grafted into my skull? The wires running into my brain, the weight of these cold stones—I have to live with them every day. Trust me, they're worse than the darkness. And if I can help Jacob by selling them, then all to the good."

She reached out and took Xander's hand. "I don't need them to be happy," she said.

Xander looked over at Jacob and shook his head. Still holding Delaney's hand, he headed into the shop. Jacob watched them disappear together inside before following.

"State of the art, no doubt about it," the man said, leaning back in his chair.

Mortimer was younger than Jacob had imagined he would be, younger than Xander, with bushy black hair and skin almost as dark as the soil the growers worked in Harmony. He leaned in close to Delaney's face once more and studied each eye through a small glowing monocle before giving a second low whistle.

"Very impressive."

"They're broken," Delaney murmured.

Mortimer shook his head. "Not broken. They may not be functioning at the moment, but nothing appears damaged."

"So you could fix them?" Xander broke in.

The doctor shrugged. "Probably." He turned back to Delaney. "When did you go blind?" he asked.

Delaney hesitated. "I was born blind. I never saw until these were put in a year and a half ago," she said at last.

"Impossible," Mortimer said. "First of all, this generation has only been out for a month. Second, they've had implants for people like you for well over a century now, even organics—though they can't do the job of these. Besides, no one's born blind these days except for . . ."

He paused, then his eyes went wide.

"You're her, aren't you? That singer. The Blinder."

Delaney nodded. "They worked for a while," she said. "Then they started to break down. It was horrible."

"Makes sense," the doctor said. "Usually, people who get implants have already seen. Something just happens to their eyes—an accident, disease, whatever. Point is, the images are already stored in the brain—a whole lifetime of them. When the circuits go in, they're tapping into a whole established network."

He reached out and gingerly touched the gold rims.

"But you were starting from scratch with nothing to tie into. Probably just overloaded the circuits. A reboot, a few recalibrations with some time to adjust, and you'd probably be fine."

"How much can we get for them?" Delaney asked.

Mortimer hesitated. "New, they're worth over five hundred thousand. But these are likely prototypes, unique but potentially problematic." Delaney's sudden bitter smile made him pause. "More to the point, there's a good chance Mixel might have issues with their sale. I'm surprised they let you keep them at all."

"So in other words, they're hot," Xander broke in.

The man shrugged. "I'd have to turn them around fast." He cast a quick glance at Xander and Jacob. "You're sure you don't want me to just fix them?"

49

Delaney hesitated. "How much will you give us?" she said at last.

"Three hundred."

"Fine. How long will it take?"

"An hour. Maybe less." He turned to Jacob and Xander. "You'll have to wait in the other room."

"Hold on," Xander said as the doctor started to rise. "Have you done this before?"

"Don't worry," Mortimer said with a grin. "I'm the best. Ask anyone."

Xander nodded, then rose. "Fine. See you in an hour."

He glanced over at Delaney for a moment, then turned and headed to the waiting room. Jacob rose and came over to where she sat in the examination chair.

"We'll be close by," he said, giving her hand a squeeze.

She smiled. "I'll be fine."

He took one last look at the almond-shaped jewels sparkling amid the gold, then closed his eyes and turned away.

"She's resting now," Mortimer said, appearing an hour later. "I'll get her in a moment."

He opened a small case and turned it toward them. Jacob leaned in for a better look. Against the black fabric, the eyes seemed to sparkle brighter than ever. The rims curved back and into the velvet. Away from Delaney's face, the set looked like nothing more than jewelry.

Jacob lifted one of the eyes from the bed. Tucked underneath lay a small network of coiled wires. He shivered at the thought of the tiny cables grafted into her brain.

Mortimer handed a thin gold card to Xander.

"Three hundred thousand. Just like we said."

"What about Delaney?" Xander asked.

"She'll have a headache for a day or two. The bone sockets were undisturbed, so it's just a matter of tissue regeneration. I inserted some seed cells of my own design—she should heal quickly. Come back in a week. We'll need to find suitable replacements. Even if they're not functional, something for aesthetic purposes." He gave Xander a quick look. "You know what I mean?"

"I got it," Xander said. "Can we see her now or what?"

The doctor nodded, then disappeared out back. A moment later, Delaney emerged, Mortimer leading her by the arm. Jacob started at the sight of the bandage—a light blue piece of cloth—wrapped around her eyes. Though she was no blinder than before, the folded cloth made her suddenly seem so vulnerable. Jacob met her at the desk and gave her an embrace, fighting back the tightening in his throat.

"I'm sorry," was all he said.

"Don't be silly," she assured him. "I'm just glad I could do this for you."

While Mortimer gave Xander a package of fresh bandages and went over instructions, Jacob escorted Delaney to the doorway.

"Thank you," she called back. "And good luck finding a buyer."

"Won't be a problem. Before long, someone else will be seeing with your eyes."

"They were never mine," she said, then headed out the door.

They stepped out of the floater taxi to find Bennet in the shadow of the hangar bay doors talking to a man in a suit. The man's pale skin and cropped hair—a shock of blond so fair it looked white—stood out against the darkness of his suit so that his head appeared to float in the shadows. Even stranger were his eyes, which seemed to have no whites to them at all, though Jacob figured it was probably a trick of the light. Seeing them, Bennet broke off his conversation and strolled over. The other man turned inside the hangar and disappeared.

"I had a feeling you'd be back," the captain said. "Got the money?"

"Yeah, we got it," Xander said. He nodded toward the hangar. "Who was that guy?"

"New passenger. Just showed up about twenty minutes ago."

"Yeah, but who *is* he?" Xander pressed.

Bennet shrugged. "Some suit. Isn't one of Mixel's, I know that much. Had some business here and needs to get back. He's going your direction, you'll be happy to know. I'm guessing he works for BiCo. Those guys own Teiresias, New Jupiter, hell, most of that sector."

"So if he's such a big shot, why play hop-on with a smuggler? Why not go first class on the next liner?"

The captain's eyes narrowed. "Why don't you?"

Xander and Jacob glanced at each other. Jacob could see the doubt in Xander's eyes. Apparently, so could Bennet.

"Listen," he said. "These corporate types are always playing their little spy games. For all we know, this guy's offering Mixel the plans for BiCo's new toaster oven design. Secret meetings, takeovers, headhunting for new executives—they get off on all that stuff."

"I know all about it," Xander muttered.

Bennet glanced down at his watch. "So do you want to go or not?" he said to Jacob with an annoyed look. "This suit's paying me enough for four passengers. Between that and the cargo, I'm going to make a killing either way, so don't do me any favors."

Jacob could feel Xander bristle beside him.

"I don't know, Jacob," Xander muttered, looking over at him. "What do you think?"

Jacob looked back to the shadows where the stranger had last stood, trying to get some sense of him, but nothing came. All he could feel was that odd sensation of comfort that had reappeared with the captain. He shook his head.

"I'll be okay," he said at last, trying to muster all the confidence he could. Xander snorted.

"Fine," Bennet said. He pulled a small data pad from his jacket pocket and took the gold card Xander proffered. "Your boy will have to bunk with the crew. I'll be giving up my quarters to the suit and moving into the first mate's cabin. I grew up listening to Silas's snoring. A few weeks won't kill me."

He slipped the card into a slot on the pad and was about to key in the payment, when, glancing over at Delaney, who stood nearby, her arms wrapped tight about herself, he hesitated.

"Listen," he said, his eyes softening. He looked back to Jacob. "You said you wanted to be a cabin boy? Tell you what, you help out when I ask you to and the rest of the time you stay out of sight, and I'll give you half fare. An even hundred. What do you say?"

"Okay," Jacob said.

"All right," Bennet said. He tapped a few keys, then handed the card back to Xander. "Just put in a good word for me to Kala," he said with a wink. Before Xander could reply, he turned back to Jacob. "We're about finished with our business. So say your good-byes, then, and come aboard."

He turned and started to walk away, when Xander stopped him.

"If anything happens to him, I'll be coming for you. There's nowhere in the galaxy you'll be able to hide."

Bennet shook his head, then gave a quick salute before disappearing into the hangar.

Seeing the look on Xander's face, Jacob spoke up.

"I know you don't like it, Xander, but I'll be okay. I can't explain it, but I think this is supposed to happen."

"Did you have a vision about it?" Delaney asked, coming over.

"No. Nothing like that. I just can feel it. There's something about the captain. I feel safe around him."

"Then, that's good enough," she said. "Right, Xander?"

Xander looked down at the blindfold covering her eyes and sighed. He handed over the pack Jacob had loaded up that morning. His clothes, a few books Xander had given him along with the stunner and the whistle that had once belonged to Xander's son—it was all he owned.

Xander handed him the gold card. "There's still two hundred thousand left on the card. Just don't lose it, for chrissake."

Jacob looked down at it in awe. "I don't need this," he whispered.

"You may, Jacob," Delaney said. "We want you to have it. I want you to have it."

Jacob looked over at Xander. The man nodded.

"Thanks," Jacob said, slipping the card into his pocket, "for everything."

Xander put a hand on his shoulder. "Be careful out there,"

he said. "Stay on the ship. Before you know it, you'll reach Teiresias. Easy."

Jacob nodded. He suddenly felt very tired.

*Not the best way to start a trip,* he thought. But it wasn't the thought of everything that lay ahead of him that exhausted him. It was everything that lay behind. Harmony, the Foundation, Mixel—as much as he hated leaving Xander and Delaney, he would be glad to leave the rest. Yet when he thought about what had brought him to this point, it seemed so much like a dream, like one of Xander's books.

"I still can't believe that all this is happening," he said. "Yesterday morning everything was normal. I never would have guessed I'd be leaving this way."

"Listen, Blinder, there's only one real constant in the universe, and that's everything changes. Nothing stays the same."

"I thought I'd learned that back in Harmony," Jacob said. "But being with both of you, I guess I forgot."

Delaney reached out and pulled him close. He could feel the warmth of her body, the softness of her clothes, her skin.

"Just remember when you're out there that we'll be thinking about you. Always."

She released him and pressed a small metal object into his hands. He looked down at her sounder sitting in his palm.

"This way a part of me is always with you," she said.

"I'm glad to have it," he said. "Take care of each other," he said, looking over at Xander.

Xander nodded. Jacob could see the sadness in his eyes.

"Well, this is it," the soldier said. "You've got a long trip ahead of you. I hope you find what you're looking for. You deserve to."

Jacob smiled. "Don't worry," he said, giving them both

55

one last hug. "I'll be back. I've seen it in my dreams."

He turned and headed toward the hangar.

He paused at the threshold, allowing himself a look back. Xander waved once. His other arm was now around Delaney's shoulders, who stood silent, still, and smiling. Her head was elevated slightly, as if she were staring up into space through the fabric of her blindfold.

*They're safe now,* he thought, stepping through the gateway.

He could feel himself shed his fatigue as he approached the ship, could feel it fall away as the hangar bay doors closed behind him. He was ready.

# PART TWO
## The *Odessa*

# CHAPTER SIX

Legs curled up against his chest, Jacob huddled by the port-hole, watching the golden star draw near, then pass away. It was the third day, and Jacob had long since grown accustomed to the speed with which the closest stars came and went, each one swifter than the last as the *Odessa* ripped steadily faster through space. The endless clouds of stars had been still the first day, shining points scattered on the dark plain, like a reverse image of the flower-dotted grasslands of the world he'd left behind. But as the ship's speed climbed in preparation for the break into otherspace, even the distant stars had begun to drift.

"Still not bored, eh?"

Jacob tore his gaze away. It was Dobson, the oldest member of the crew, a grizzled man whose patchwork of tattoos never failed to draw Jacob's stare. Dobson slept in the bunk above his own. Actually, Jacob was sleeping in Dobson's bunk: he'd switched to give Jacob the window.

"I've looked out it enough, believe me," was all the man had said when Jacob thanked him.

As ship's engineer, Dobson spent most of his time in the back half of the ship, listening to, adjusting, and coaxing along the complex, powerful machinery upon which so much depended. When he wasn't working, he could usually be found lying on his bunk listening to music, or sitting at a table in the tiny mess hall sipping coffee. He spoke little, but he said more to Jacob than any of the other seven crewmen. In fact, he seemed to be just about the only one who didn't mind having Jacob around.

"They're moving faster," Jacob said, gazing back out the window.

Dobson nodded. "Another few days, those stars in the distance will be racing right past. The close ones will be little more than blurs."

"Then what?" Jacob asked.

"Then we break through. To otherspace."

"What's that?"

Dobson laughed. "Guess you've never been offworld, after all." He shrugged. "It's just otherspace. The place between the wormholes."

"Oh," Jacob murmured.

"Don't know what a wormhole is, do you," Dobson teased.

"Not really."

"Wormhole's a path into otherspace. A shortcut, see? Go in one side, come out the other, only you might be ten thousand light-years away from where you went in. Can't get anywhere in space without them."

"So where are they?"

The man shrugged. "Here and there. As far as we can tell, they're pretty rare. The ones we know of were discovered by accident. And only a few of those actually take you close to a habitable star system. The rest end up out in the middle of nowhere. Some people think wormholes are all over the place, just waiting to be uncovered, but nobody really knows. Space is an awfully big place."

"Sounds hard to get around."

"It would be, if it weren't for breakers. Just about any ship these days that travels between systems has got one. It's a special drive that opens up a temporary wormhole in space. Long enough to make the trip, at least."

"How long *does* it take?"

"Depends on how far you want to go, really. And how fast you're going when you break through. Seconds, minutes, hours—it's all relative. When you're in otherspace, it doesn't seem like it takes any time at all—or it can seem to take an eternity. Or both. Or neither."

"I don't understand," Jacob said.

"Don't worry, you will. What matters is that you're where you wanted to be. And a journey that would take too many lifetimes even at break speed has been turned into merely weeks or even days. In the meantime, just keep on enjoying those stars while you still can. The novelty wears off."

"What's that one?" Jacob asked, pointing to an enormous red sphere glowing fainter than its smaller companions in the middle distance.

"That there's a red giant, all bloated and fat like an old man dying. He won't be around for long."

"Have you ever seen a star die?"

"Not one of them red buggers. They take forever to go. But I've seen plenty of the smaller ones go supernova. A pretty sight."

"Not sad?"

Dobson chuckled. "Sad for anyone nearby. But don't mourn the stars. Plenty more being made. Besides, we're nothing to them. Our lives are like the blink of an eye as far as they're concerned."

Jacob nodded. From space he could sense their cold majesty—even the small points in the distance—better than he'd ever been able to on Nova Campi. But their coldness, their distance, didn't bother him. He loved them for their beauty, for their independence, separated from others of their kind, burning with a fire of their own.

Xander had told him once that space could be the loneliest of places. Jacob could understand why, could even see it on some of the faces of the men on board, but he couldn't feel it. Not yet, anyway. If anything, it was the opposite—as soon as they'd made orbit, he'd felt a sense of peace, of comfort, like when Captain Bennet was around. He'd clung to the porthole, watching the orbital platforms, cargo ships, and passenger liners shrink as the *Odessa* began to pull away, watching Nova Campi shrink, become just another orb floating against the massive bulk of Duna, finally watching the ringed gas giant itself contract until it was just another point of light in the blackness.

Then there was only space—a world of darkness with little to disturb it but the scattered stars, the distant plumes of galaxies, the gaseous nebulas of color that blossomed and faded as the hours passed. And there he was—warm, safe, with nothing but the universe to gaze at, the view always changing yet always the same, the sounds of the ship throbbing close about him, the cabin lights dimmed.

The takeoff had been surprisingly gentle. The *Odessa* had drifted up out of the hangar on its float jets—just larger versions of the engines that sped the tiny floaters from place to place above the surface. Gripping the edge of his bunk, Jacob could see Mixel Tower from across the way, could see

Melville spread out around the mighty black pillar. And he could see the other ships below in their separate bunkers— some smaller than the sleek *Odessa*, but most larger. It surprised Jacob. On walking into the hangar, he'd been amazed at the size of the ship, a blunt-nosed vessel of dull metal several times larger than Xander's house. Its wings extended from a pair of thrusters and were themselves tipped with a second set of thrusters. But in spite of the *Odessa*'s enormity, after a quick burst of speed and some brief shuddering as the vessel broke through the atmosphere, Jacob could see that all the traders' ships—Bennet's included—were dwarfed by the corporate cargo and passenger liners waiting in orbit.

No matter how big the *Odessa* appeared on the outside, however, the inside seemed to belong to a much smaller ship—dark, narrow passageways, small quarters, cramped cabins and galleys. Besides the cargo bays, only the bridge seemed to offer any sense of room to move around. But Jacob had seen the room only once, during a cursory tour of the ship just before takeoff. And while Captain Bennet hadn't explicitly forbid him from coming on deck, he'd made it clear that Jacob wasn't welcome there.

"Don't mind the captain," Dobson had told him afterward. "He just doesn't like kids."

Jacob soon learned that the engines took up much of the ship. Dobson brought him down to see the maze of machinery their second day in space.

"Why is it all so big?" Jacob asked, looking around.

"Takes a lot to send this much weight a trillion miles through space. That's what most otherspace ships are—one big engine with a little box of people strapped to the front."

"So where's the breaker?" Jacob asked.

Dobson nodded and motioned him over to a panel on the wall. He entered a code into the pad and a section slid open like a drawer, revealing a block of machinery.

"It's smaller than I thought," Jacob said, staring down at the bundle of circuits and wires.

"Doesn't look like much, but it's worth the whole rest of the ship put together," Dobson replied. He reached down and pressed a button, releasing a glass tube. An oblong, bluish crystal lay suspended inside, its myriad sides cut with symmetrical precision.

"It's beautiful," Jacob gasped, watching it sparkle and gleam as it slowly rotated within the tube.

"That crystal's what powers the drive. Without it, there's no breaking through. Pretty little devils, aren't they? Unfortunately, they burn out after a few trips. Then you got to replace them. And they're not cheap, either. In fact, they're getting more expensive all the time. I hear whispers that there's a shortage, that we're running out. That's why the real wormholes, the permanent ones, are so valuable."

The glass tube sank back into place with a gentle touch from Dobson. He closed the breaker and went back to work.

Jacob watched him work for a while—adjusting dials, putting his ear against the conduits, opening panels and examining the mass of wires. At one point the tattooed engineer shook his head.

"What's the matter?" Jacob asked.

"She's picked up a little hiccup. Happens now and then. Shouldn't be any trouble."

A twin pair of stars now sailed by the porthole as Dobson climbed into the top bunk with a groan. Jacob stared in wonder at the two brilliant spheres that reminded him so much of Delaney's eyes. The ones she'd given up for him. He'd been trying not to think about Delaney or Xander the last few days, had tried thinking only about the ship and the stars, about the world he was heading for.

"How much longer before we reach otherspace?" he asked.

"Another few days," Dobson answered from the bunk above. "We could break through now, but at this velocity we'd only jump a little ways. To go as far as Teiresias, we'll need top speed. At that point we'll break through, come out on the other side, and then there's a day or two of slowing down. 'Cause as fast as you're going on your way in, that's how fast you're going coming out. Slow down too fast and you'd just split apart."

"That's a cheerful thought," Jacob murmured.

"Space is a cold, cheerless place."

"You don't seem to like it much."

"I've been out here for nearly thirty years now. Ten of them with Bennet and his brother. I made my peace with it a long time ago. I just know it for what it is. That's how I've been able to last this long. Space isn't for everyone. But as far as liking goes? I like my job, I like my mates. That's enough."

"Do you like Bennet?" Jacob asked.

"Captain's a good captain. The *Odessa*'s a good ship. Both the best I've ever worked with."

"You don't mind being a smuggler?"

Dobson snorted. "We don't care for that term. We're traders."

"But isn't what you trade against the law?"

"We deal in unofficial goods. Things that for whatever

reason have been made temporarily unavailable through normal channels. Keep a low profile, avoid anything nasty, and there's no trouble really. The corporations use us—hell, need us—as much as we need them. Who do you think buys all our goods?"

"Then why are they illegal?"

"People like to pretend they're moral, upright, honorable. Makes them feel special. As long as they can wink at their own indiscretions."

"Hmm," Jacob murmured. Hearing Dobson, all he could think about was Harmony and Truesight. The Blinders were like everyone else—it was all just a matter of degree.

"You almost sound disappointed," Dobson said. "The business isn't that romantic. And none of these guys are what you would think of as criminals—they're just hard-working spacers who want to be left alone. It's the pirates you need to worry about."

"Pirates?" Jacob said. He'd read about them in one of Xander's old books.

Hearing Jacob's voice, the engineer laughed. "That's right. Those bloodless parasites will do anything to get their hands on a ship. They've gotten worse lately. A real problem in some sectors. If the corporations would stop fighting one another for a few minutes and get together, they could probably wipe the bastards out."

"Have you ever had to fight any?"

There was a pause. "Couple times. It's not any fun. Just leave it at that."

The man's voice having suddenly taken on an edge, Jacob let the subject drop. Months with Xander had taught him when to back off.

A few minutes later, Jacob heard the familiar sound of

Dobson's snoring, a light rhythm just audible over the susurration of the engines. He turned back to the window and lost himself once more to the darkness.

As the stars began to spin ever faster, Jacob also began to find a new rhythm. Though he was still drawn to the world outside the porthole, the desire for some other kind of company started to grow within him. He spent less time curled up on his bunk by the window and more time in different parts of the ship.

When they weren't working, eating, or sleeping, the majority of the crew could be found in the lounge. Packed with couches and padded chairs, the room had one whole wall comprised of a video screen that endlessly ran movies and shows from all over space. But Jacob tended to avoid the place. It was too loud in there to talk to anyone, and the flashing video images brought back too many memories of Melville. He spent most of his time in the mess hall, talking with whoever came in for a drink or a meal.

Though the crew was never unkind to him, they tended to ignore him at first. It was as if he wasn't even there. It reminded him of being back in Harmony—those days he'd spent walking amid the Blinders, oblivious to his presence.

But as the next few days passed, Dobson's fellow smugglers began to warm to Jacob, chatting with him at mealtimes, even teasing him a little over his newness to space. They were curious about his books—already several had been passed among the men. A few even spoke of trying to acquire some at the next port of call.

Most of all, they loved the music. Jacob had come into the mess hall one day to find most of the crew gathered for dinner.

Two of the men—Malcolm and Eric, a pair of techs who maintained the ship—were playing a tune on a couple of guitars while the other four sang along. Even Silas had joined in. Oddly enough it was a song Jacob had often heard in Harmony—one his father had liked. After getting over his initial shock at seeing the pierced and painted men bellowing some ancient Earth song at the top of their voices, Jacob slipped back to his quarters and returned with his whistle. Soon he was playing along, the men dropping out one by one to listen. At first Jacob was nervous, but he could see by their faces that they were impressed. The two guitarists broke into another tune and Jacob followed, improvising to the chord changes. Soon everyone was clapping along and laughing. Then Captain Bennet walked in.

The room went silent. Jacob could see the men glance sheepishly at one another. Bennet showed no sign of anger. If anything, he had a slightly bemused look on his face. But the tone in the room had changed so abruptly, even Jacob felt guilty.

One by one the men started to rise from their tables and drift out, Silas last of all, mumbling about the duties awaiting them.

Bennet began laughing.

"Hey, don't let me stop the show!" he called after them as they headed for the door. "I love a good tune as much as the next guy. And the kid's quite a soloist!"

As the door closed behind Silas, Bennet's laughter abruptly ceased. He turned and regarded Jacob somberly, the diamond in his ear glittering as it caught the light.

"Looks like the crew's taken quite a shine to you."

Jacob didn't reply.

"Well, don't get too cozy. We'll be reaching Teiresias before you know it."

He turned and headed out the door. Jacob followed him.

"When will we be there?" he asked, tailing Bennet down the corridor.

"Soon," the captain barked, picking up the pace so that Jacob almost had to trot to keep up. "We'll be breaking through sometime tomorrow. After that it should be just another day or two."

"When do you want me to start helping?" Jacob cried. "I'd like to make myself useful."

Bennet pulled to an abrupt stop, causing Jacob to nearly run into him. They were now just outside the bridge. The man turned to face him.

"You've been very helpful," the captain said.

"But I haven't done anything!" Jacob said. "I've spent most of my time just sitting on my bunk looking out the window."

"Exactly," Bennet said, smiling as the door whisked open behind him. His smile faded. "Let's face it, kid, you're just along for the ride. Try to remember that."

He gave a quick salute, then stepped through the doorway and disappeared.

But for the rest of that day and the next, whenever Jacob encountered any of the other crew, they'd give him a quick grin and compliment him on his playing. Malcolm—a tall man with black spiked hair and blue-and-red-striped skin— even asked Jacob if he would teach him how to play.

The captain's attitude didn't bother Jacob. The man was pleasant enough, if a bit standoffish. It wasn't anything worse than what he'd had to deal with those first few weeks with

Xander. In fact, Bennet was far more agreeable than Xander had ever been, lacking the soldier's moodiness, the dark cloud of pain that often retreated but never fully went away.

If anything, Bennet always seemed relaxed, as if he knew exactly what he was doing at every moment, as if nothing bothered him at all. The few times Jacob got to see him with the crew, he studied the man carefully, watching every gesture, trying to absorb every sign of surety. More than anything, Jacob loved the sense of safety he felt in the captain's presence. He knew nothing could go wrong as long as Bennet was near.

All in all, Jacob would have enjoyed the trip completely if it weren't for his fellow passenger, Folgrin.

"Is that his first or last name?" Jacob asked when Dobson told him. They were alone in the lounge, Jacob watching Dobson touch up one of his tattoos with an ink cutter.

"Don't know," the engineer replied in between pen zaps. "That's just what they call him. Doesn't matter to me. I don't imagine I'll have much need to address him."

Jacob was on board for two whole days before he'd even caught sight of the pale-haired man sitting in the corner of the mess hall, wearing the same black suit he'd been wearing back at the hangar on Nova Campi.

For the most part, Folgrin remained secluded in Bennet's quarters, even taking his meals there. No one seemed disappointed.

But every once in a while Jacob would be in the mess hall, having lunch with Dobson or joking around with one of the crew, and he would suddenly notice the businessman sitting in the corner—as if he'd appeared out of nowhere—watching him with his strange eyes. They would exchange glances for a

70

moment before Folgrin's lips would curl into the slightest grin. Then Jacob would look away, fighting off a shiver at the image of those black eyes glistening with reflected light.

"What is it with those eyes?" Jacob asked the navigator Timlin one day after Folgrin had left.

"They're just contacts, probably loaded with enhancements."

"But they cover up his whole eyes. They're so black."

Timlin shrugged. "Some of the suits have taken to wearing them. Supposed to give them an edge in negotiations. The whole poker face thing."

"What's that mean?"

"Never mind. It's like it hides their soul. Not that most of them have one."

Lying in his bunk the night before the break to otherspace, Jacob was inclined to agree. There seemed to be something hollow about the man. Maybe it was those contacts that made him seem so blank, almost inhuman. Or maybe it was the fact that Jacob still didn't know what the man's voice sounded like, having never heard him speak.

As always, it was warm in the ship. But as he tried to fall asleep, Jacob wrapped the thin blanket tight around himself, as if it might somehow help drive the memory of those eyes from his mind. Between that and the anticipation of tomorrow's jump, Jacob was restless. For the first time since leaving, he felt that the *Odessa* couldn't reach Teiresias quickly enough.

Before Jacob even opened his eyes, he knew Folgrin was standing over him, could feel the chill radiating beside him, a presence as cold as space.

71

He opened them, anyway.

Sure enough, there the man stood, looking down at him with that same taut smile.

Jacob began to call for Dobson, but stopped himself. The bunk above him was gone. Taking a quick glance around, he realized all the bunks were gone but his. He was alone with Folgrin.

*So I* am *dreaming,* he thought. The realization, though not enough to warm him, was enough to keep him from struggling. Not that it would have mattered. Jacob suddenly realized he couldn't feel his arms at his sides or wiggle his toes. He was paralyzed from the neck down.

A *clever trick,* he thought, looking for the needle in Folgrin's hands, but both were thrust in the pockets of the man's suit coat. As if he could read Jacob's mind, the man shook his head, his smile widening.

"What do you want?" Jacob cried.

Folgrin got down on his knees beside Jacob and leaned in. Now the poison had worked its way up, freezing Jacob's head so that he was forced to gaze into those black eyes as they drew closer and closer, until they were only inches away.

As they continued to draw near, Jacob saw a point of light appear in each eye. They were stars. They came and went, only to be replaced by another set and another, then pairs, then sets of four, five, six, a dozen, hundreds, each set swirling by faster until they became streaks of light shooting out from a central black hole.

Folgrin was so close his face was now nearly touching Jacob's, his eyes yawning portholes like the one Jacob had spent so many hours gazing through. The cold was excruciating. Though Jacob couldn't feel it, he knew the skin of his face was freezing, hardening, cracking, ready to break apart at the slightest touch.

And then he was falling into the eyes, falling into space with the stars shooting by. The man was gone, the ship was gone. It was just darkness and streaks of light.

The sensation of falling stopped. Jacob felt something solid beneath him once more. He looked down to see his hands gripping the grusker's hair.

*I've been here before,* Jacob thought.

He looked up. Sure enough, the planet loomed before him. A moment later they were falling toward it. They entered the atmosphere with a roar, and the grusker bellowed in pain as the flames began licking off its horns and tusks. Jacob could feel his skin begin to thaw. Somehow he wasn't burning.

Looking down he realized the grusker was gone, replaced by the painted metal of the *Odessa*. He was riding the head of the ship as it hurtled toward the surface.

They had passed through the atmosphere. Orange sky and clouds surrounded Jacob. He looked over his shoulder in terror to see Folgrin advancing toward him from the back, the ship disintegrating behind him in a shower of debris with every step the man took.

Jacob turned back around to see Bennet standing there, the sun shining on him, his figure bright against the dark surface of the planet, oblivious to the wind roaring around them as the ship fell.

"Get in there!" Jacob screamed. "You've got to pull the ship up, save what's left of it!"

Bennet shook his head sadly.

"Sorry, kid," he called back. "There's no turning her around!"

He took the diamond from his ear and handed it to Jacob. "It's the best I can do," he said. Then he jumped into the air and was swept away.

"No!" Jacob screamed as he watched him disappear.

He glanced over his shoulder once more. Folgrin had nearly reached him. By now, there was almost nothing left of the ship.

The man suddenly froze, his smile dying as his black suit flapped in the wind.

A wave of joy rose as Jacob looked down at the diamond in his hand. Maybe it could save him after all. At least from Folgrin.

But the joy was short-lived. Turning back around, Jacob realized it wasn't the diamond that had killed Folgrin's smile but the planet's surface. A hundred yards below and closing fast.

# CHAPTER SEVEN

The first thing Jacob noticed on waking was the stars. At first he thought it was just the dream still clinging to him, the fear making the stars somehow colder, less brilliant. But it only took a few moments at the window to make him realize what was wrong—though they burned as brightly as ever, they no longer raced by with the same sense of urgency. The ship had slowed.

An ear to the wall confirmed it—the engines throbbed at a lower frequency. If it weren't for the fact that Jacob had spent a lifetime learning to discern the minute pitch differences between people's sounders back in Harmony, he might never have noticed. But there was no doubt about the change.

It was early still for anyone to be up, but he wasn't surprised to see the bunk above him empty. No doubt Dobson had noticed the change as well. If Jacob had to guess, the sound of the engine slowing had likely woken the man from a dead sleep.

Aside from Dobson and Kendrick—the ship's pilot now on bridge duty—most of the smugglers still lay in their bunks fast asleep. Jacob threw on some clothes and stumbled sleepily from the cabin. The ship's main lights were still down as well. Like the crew, they would remain dormant for another thirty minutes before going dayside. It was the only way for anyone to have any real sense of diurnal rhythm, since it was always night in space.

He thought of heading down to the engines to see what Dobson was up to, then changed his mind and made for the mess hall. He was thirsty and still rattled from the dream—a stimulatte was called for. Timlin had introduced Jacob to the energy drink—a blend of sweetened cream, fruit, and synthetic stimulants—a couple of days ago. Most of the crew, with the stubborn exception of Dobson and Silas, preferred it to coffee.

From around the bend he heard some voices, low and anxious. He glanced around the corner in time to see Bennet and Dobson emerge from the mess and head for the bridge. Forgetting his thirst, he followed them, sticking to the shadows as they made their way toward the front of the ship. Though they weren't arguing, Jacob could detect the tension in their voices as they spoke.

"I know, Captain. I know," Dobson muttered at one point.

Just before the bridge, Jacob was surprised to see them pull up and come to a stop before a doorway. It was Bennet's own quarters, now occupied by Folgrin. They exchanged a few more words, which Jacob strained to hear. In the dim light, he watched as the captain nodded, then reached up and knocked on the door. Jacob slipped down the corridor a few yards closer and ducked into another doorway.

The door whisked open and out stepped Folgrin, fully dressed, his hair combed.

*Does he even sleep?* Jacob wondered.

Bennet spoke first.

"Looks like our trip's going to be a little delayed."

"What's the problem?" Folgrin demanded. It was strange to hear his voice for the first time after so many days of silence. It was smooth but intense, as if every word were given equal weight.

"Engines have got a few hiccups. They're having trouble getting up to speed. At least the kind we need to get to the other side of the Rim."

"Can't you fix it?" Folgrin said, turning to the engineer. Jacob could hear the irritation in his voice.

"Sure, I can," Dobson said. "But I need a few things first. Things I don't have on board. We need to find a starport."

"Then find one," the businessman said, "and be quick about it."

"We're working on it," Bennet snapped.

Folgrin turned back to him. "This shouldn't have happened at all, Captain. You assured me your ship was up for the journey."

"The *Odessa*'s a fine ship. These things just happen."

"Fine. I'm willing to accept that. Just remember what's at stake. We both have jobs to do. And if I can't get mine done, then you pay the price."

"Like I said, don't worry about it," Bennet murmured. "No big deal."

Folgrin shook his head. "So can we break to otherspace or not?"

Dobson nodded. "I think so. Only problem is, there's not too much within range at the speed we've got now. The farther I try to push it, the more chance of an error. Then you're stuck in the middle of nowhere. Or worse. I think I can get us to Maker's Drift without too much risk."

"Never heard of it," Folgrin said.

"It's a small outpost," the captain explained. "Stopover for the short ships heading to Nova Campi and a few of the other colonies this side of the Rim."

"Will it have what you need?"

"It should," Bennet replied.

Folgrin snorted. "Fine. And Captain," he said as Bennet and Dobson turned to leave. "Whatever it is you need to get—buy two. I don't want any more delays."

The news spread quickly among the crew. By the time breakfast was over, everyone knew what had happened and where they were going. Jacob listened to their rumblings with a growing sense of dismay.

"What's wrong with Maker's Drift?" he asked Lewis, the ship's cook, as the man gathered up the dishes.

"What's right with it? That's the question, kid," Lewis replied.

"It's bad luck, that place," added the gunner Branson.

"Well, why?" Jacob asked.

"It's a small world," Timlin said, having just come from the bridge. "A drab, cold planet. It's not owned by any corporation—Mixel set things up a while ago, then bailed for greener pastures."

"You mean Nova Campi?"

"That's right," said Timlin. "That and a few other colonies out this way. There's rumored to be a whole group of habitable planets beyond this edge of the Rim ripe for the picking. Good worlds are hard to come by. That's why Mixel holds so tightly to Nova Campi, hoping it's the first of a whole slew of new settlements under their control. But Maker's Drift—it's a failed world. A dead world."

"Aye," said Branson. "She's got a starport, but any ship worth its salt won't stop there unless it's got no choice. It's a rusty, run-down hole of a town. A real rat's nest. And then there's the barren lands, where the witches live."

"The what?" Jacob cried. He'd heard stories of witches growing up in Harmony, tales to scare the little ones mostly. One told of a group of blind witches who shared a single magic eye. It could look right into your soul. But those were just silly stories. "You're joking," he said when they smiled at his reaction.

"Oh no," Lewis said, growing quickly serious. "All kinds of strange folk have made their way to Maker's Drift over the years. Escaped convicts, witches, anarchists, you name it. Anyone with a reason to hide. 'Course, no one really knows how many there are—or if they're still even out there—once they head into the wilderness, no one hears from them again."

"You mean they just disappear?" Jacob asked. "A whole group of people on a small planet?"

"I hear they're cannibals," Kendrick muttered.

"Probably all ate each other," Malcolm said.

"No, the planet's haunted," Eric broke in. "There's an entire civilization buried under the surface, and they're none too happy to have a bunch of human beings crawling on top of them. That's why Mixel really pulled out. I read a whole story about it."

*They're pulling my leg*, Jacob thought. But looking around, he could see the grim looks on their faces, could feel the fear hovering in the room like the cold mist that some-times gathered over the lake near Xander's.

"Don't worry about witches," Timlin said. "Or anything else on Maker's Drift. Captain'll probably make you stay on board, anyway. We'll be in and out of there before you know it."

"I'm not worried," Jacob said, trying to sound brave. "Besides, I don't believe in that stuff."

The men all glanced around. A couple murmured to one another.

"Believe it, kid," Branson said. "There are a lot of freaks in the universe. You must know—you're from Nova Campi, aren't you? What do they call that group living out in the middle of nowhere?"

"The Blinders," Jacob said, looking down. His heart started pounding.

"Aye," Branson replied. "My brother used to make deliveries to another one of those groups on Allston. A stranger bunch you'll never find, he says."

"They don't hurt anyone," Jacob said. *Except themselves,* he thought. An image of Martin Corrow, the high councilor, rose before him. Seeing him, Jacob could feel that sick pit in his stomach open all over again.

The overhead lights suddenly turned red, casting everything in a dark ruby glow. Jacob was about to ask what had happened when the door whisked open. In came Silas with Folgrin behind him.

"All right, everybody," Silas barked, "to your posts. We break in ten."

The crew scrambled to their feet and began to file out. Jacob rose and started to go with them when Silas took him firmly by the arm and pulled him aside.

"Not you, kid," the man said.

"But I was going to go down to the engine room where Dobson is," Jacob said.

"Dobson's got plenty to worry about without having you there. Captain wants you and Mr. Folgrin, here, in the lounge. Follow me."

They left the mess and made the short trip next door. Silas led them in and gestured to one of the several cushioned chairs facing the screen wall.

"Buckle yourselves in," Silas said. "The *Odessa* usually breaks smooth, but you never know."

"How long will it take?" Jacob asked.

"Seven minutes to go. Then we break. Then we come out. Then it's over. Think you can handle it?"

Jacob nodded, blushing. Silas saw his look and his face softened. He gave Jacob a wink, then turned and headed out. The door whisked shut behind him, leaving Jacob alone with Folgrin.

Jacob glanced over, but the man had already settled into one of the comfortable chairs toward the back of the room. Jacob slowly made his way to the opposite side of the room, hesitating before finally picking a seat in the front row. He wished he could have taken the back and kept Folgrin in front. Without looking behind him, he sat down and fastened the seat belt built discreetly into the chair.

"You seem nervous, Jacob," Folgrin said. "Don't like breaking through, eh?"

Jacob didn't respond. He kept his face forward, focusing on the screen ahead of him, with its massive display of space. Pumped in directly from an external camera attached to the ship's nose, the crisp image essentially turned the wall into a massive picture window.

"Don't worry," Folgrin said. "I hate it too. I remember the first time I went through otherspace. Felt like I was dying."

81

Again, Jacob remained silent. But he was sure he could feel Folgrin's eyes boring into the back of his head, as if they could dig right into his brain and read his innermost thoughts.

"You know," the man continued, ignoring Jacob's silence, "they say it basically *is* like dying. What we all will feel when we die. God, I hope not. But maybe. If so, I've died a hundred times. I still hate it, only now instead of being just terrifying, it's boring, too. Hard to imagine. Yet I always come back. The one good part." His voice drifted along to that same steady flow. No humor, no emotion, cold and powerful like the stars.

After days of not hearing Folgrin speak, Jacob suddenly wished he would just shut up.

"I've never been to otherspace before," Jacob murmured.

"So I've heard," the man replied, his voice finally shifting in an uptick of interest, sending goose bumps along Jacob's arms.

A single long tone sounded, and the red lights flickered blue for a moment before going back to red.

"See you on the other side, Jacob," Folgrin said, just as a hum of music washed through the cabin, a distant chord, ethereal and faint. Before he could ask about the sound, a flash of light exploded in his eyes.

It took a long time for Jacob to realize he had stopped breathing. For a moment he was convinced his heart had ceased beating too, the silence was so intense. Even the engines seemed to have stopped. He was sure he had frozen, gone numb like last night's dream.

*Maybe I'm dead,* he thought. *Maybe Folgrin was right.*

Though he wasn't sure, he did know one thing—he was blind. But it was a different kind of blindness from the one he'd lived with most of his life. It was white rather than black,

82

a pure saturation of light. Jacob preferred the dark—it wasn't painful, unlike the blankness that now sent brilliant pain shooting up into his head. It was as if he could see the light entering every blood vessel in his eyeballs, tracing a path backward into his brain, like electricity traveling along wires all the way back to their source, coursing back through the vast network of neural pathways that received the light, burning everything in its wake.

The pain faded, and very slowly Jacob began to see the world come back to him.

It started with shadows, rough shapes that broke up the solid field of white. For a moment he thought he glimpsed the figure of the strange boy who had come twice to him in his visions. It was the only time he'd inhabited a world so blank, but soon the shades turned solid, became the chairs and walls around him, took on color and dimension.

He gasped, never having felt so happy to breathe in air, even the stale, dry ship's air. He could feel his whole body loosening, breaking free from the invisible web that had held him.

He was bathed all in light. It was coming from the screen. The wall that moments before had shown the darkness of space punctuated by the onrushing stars was now just a single mass of light. Jacob stood up, wavering slightly on his feet a moment before making his way over to the screen. He reached up and touched it, dazzled by the brightness that made him feel lightheaded, as if he were in a dream.

For a long time he stared. And the more he stared, the more the wall changed. He began to realize the white wasn't uniform. There were specks of darkness that spattered across it in strange patterns, like static on an empty video screen. It was as if he were looking at a field of stars so cluttered they had taken up all of space, layer after layer of stars folded one over the other, as if every moment of time had been frozen and kept, superimposed upon the moment before it, only to be covered up by the next for as long as time had existed and ever would exist.

Jacob cocked his head, focusing on any sound besides his own breathing, but the ship was still. Even the engines were silent.

*So this is otherspace.*

He hadn't thought it would be like this—so ethereal, so light. He hadn't expected to be able to move around, to feel so free. In spite of the mild disorientation and the initial wave of pain, there was something comfortable about it, familiar, as if he'd somehow been here before, as if he almost belonged here. Folgrin was wrong—being in otherspace wasn't like dying, it was just a different way of being alive.

He turned to see Folgrin staring at him, his black eyes glistening from the screen's brightness.

"You were wrong," Jacob challenged, mustering as much courage as he could. "This isn't that bad."

Folgrin didn't respond. He just continued to stare. At first Jacob thought he'd finally managed to shut him up, but the longer he watched, the more he realized that there was something strange about the man. He seemed so stiff, so lifeless, a statue.

"Folgrin?"

Still no response. His heart pounding, Jacob left the screen and crossed over, coming as close as he dared.

Folgrin remained frozen. Jacob came even closer, waved his hand in front of the man's face just to make sure, but the man never flinched, never even blinked.

Jacob reached down and touched one of the chairs. It moved. He thought of touching Folgrin, but the thought made him shiver. He turned back to look at the screen. It still flickered and glowed. He pulled away, knowing he could get lost in the staring, the way he used to at night in the woods below Xander's, where he would spend what seemed like hours gazing into the flames.

Jacob shook his head, tried to shake out the heaviness, the strangeness. How was this possible? How was he able to move about in otherspace while Folgrin sat paralyzed? A fresh wave of dizziness rose from the back of his head. Once more, he felt as if he were in a dream.

*Maybe I am*, he thought.

He went up to the door. To his surprise, it opened. He'd half-expected to be greeted by nothingness, as if the universe outside the lounge had been reduced to the white blanket of otherspace, but the corridor looked unchanged under the red overhead lights.

He made his way to the bridge. Sure enough, there was Captain Bennet, his brother Silas, Timlin and Kendrick, all in the same state of suspension, eyes toward the windows before them, bathed in the same white light. Jacob took a few moments to survey the bridge, then moved on to other parts of the ship before returning to the lounge.

In spite of the giddy warmth coursing through him as he wandered the ship, there was an edge of darkness to this world he found himself in. Stopping outside the lounge, he suddenly realized why—it reminded him too much of being back in Harmony, of being alone though surrounded by others, trapped in a state of indifference by their inability to perceive him. The old haunted feeling returned. In other-space, he was a ghost all over again.

He took a deep breath and went through the doorway. Folgrin was still there, still staring with those dead eyes. A sudden thought entered Jacob's mind, setting his heart pounding once more.

*What if he can see me after all? What if they all can?*

It hadn't occurred to him before. They may be stationary, but how did he know they couldn't see? What if they were still conscious, watching him from behind frozen eyes, wondering how he alone could move?

Glancing over at the screen, he started at the sight of the dark spot at its center—a circle of pure black that was quickly growing, pushing away the white. Jacob was disoriented for a moment, but the blackness became familiar as it grew. Sure enough, he could soon see the distant points of light set amid the darkness.

He scrambled for his seat—the *Odessa* was about to leave otherspace.

He hardly felt a thing coming back. It was like returning from one of his visions—the slightest bump deep in the mind, a tremor of the eyes as they readjusted to the here and now. Blinking, Jacob looked around the cabin as the red lights switched off and the ship lights returned to dayside.

*Maybe it was just a vision after all,* he thought. *Maybe I just dreamed the whole thing.*

It seemed logical, but it didn't feel right. The pain, for one thing, had certainly been real. He could still feel echoes of it in his aching eyes. And in spite of the dreamlike sensation of otherspace, there was a different quality to it than his normal visions—a feeling that rose up from within rather than something that lingered outside of him, pressing on all sides the way it usually did.

"Back again," Folgrin murmured. It was strange to hear his voice so thin and shaky.

Jacob turned and looked behind him for a moment, watched Folgrin as he shook his head and rubbed his eyes, as if awaking from a long sleep. The man glanced at his watch.

"Ten minutes. Not bad. Enjoy the ride?"

"It was okay," he replied, turning away.

There was silence behind him. Once again, he could feel Folgrin's eyes digging into his back. He glanced up at the wall screen. A pale brown orb had appeared in the distance. Dozens, perhaps hundreds, of dark shapes hovered against its light.

"What are those?" Jacob asked.

Folgrin snorted. "Asteroids. That must be Maker's Drift on the other side. Idiots brought us in too far away."

"Maybe that was the best they could do," Jacob offered, hearing Folgrin unlatch his harness. He turned once more to watch the man rise and begin to storm out.

But at the threshold, Folgrin suddenly stopped. He gave his head a slight shake, as if waking from a daydream, then slowly turned and regarded Jacob for a moment, his eyes narrowing. Jacob wanted to shrink down behind the seat and disappear—it had been bad enough when he was facing away and could only imagine the withering stare.

Then, without a word, Folgrin turned and left the room, leaving Jacob alone, terrified and wondering at what the man might have seen.

The particular fear was short-lived, however. Turning back to the screen, Jacob gazed once more at the dull planet now grown slightly larger in size, then started. He jumped up from his seat, went to the wall, and placed his fingers against the image of the approaching world, as if trying to feel its actual surface, as if he could push the floating asteroids aside.

He had seen this world twice before in his dreams, the last time just a few hours ago when he'd ridden a disintegrating *Odessa*—the same ship that was carrying him now—straight down into its surface.

# CHAPTER EIGHT

Pausing just outside the bridge, Jacob could sense the argument by the tone of the muffled voices on the other side of the door. He'd made his way slowly to the front of the ship, feeling the tingle in his spine grow stronger with every step. A sense of dread lay heavy over him, prickling along his arms, across his chest, and up into his head. His eyes felt the force of it most of all, already weakened and raw from the journey through otherspace. Stepping up to the threshold, he raised one hand to knock, only to have the door open to the sight of Bennet and Folgrin standing toe to toe on the bridge. Folgrin seemed his normal self—cold, smooth, tense, like a trap wound up tight, waiting to release. But for the first time since starting their voyage, Bennet's laid-back demeanor seemed to have been put aside. Even his hair, normally pulled back into a ponytail, lay loose and wild about his shoulders.

"I told you before, these things happen!" Bennet fumed.

"That's not exactly reassuring," Folgrin snapped back. "I'm beginning to wonder about your competence, Captain."

"That asteroid field is nothing. I told you we can just go around it. Given the circumstances, you should just be thankful we're in as good shape as we are."

"Again, not much of a consolation. I can only wonder what's to come next."

Bennet's face darkened an even deeper shade of red so that it nearly matched his beard. Jacob glanced around the room at the bewildered looks on the faces of the crew. He could sympathize. Even the normal wave of ease that always washed over Jacob in Bennet's presence seemed to have been diluted by the force of Folgrin's withering glare.

"You'd better leave the bridge," Bennet said. "We've got a lot of work to do."

The lights suddenly flickered. Jacob could hear the engines dip for a moment before rising again. Folgrin raised his eyebrows.

"No thanks. I'll stick around. Looks like things are getting interesting."

"I'm sorry, you misunderstood," the captain replied, "it wasn't a request. Go back to your quarters. There's a nice bottle of scotch in the cabinet by the bedside. Help yourself to a drink. I'll let you know when we're there."

Folgrin shot back a reply, but Jacob was no longer paying attention. He was focused instead on the image of the planet hovering in the broad window before them. The *Odessa* had risen above the asteroid field and was skimming its surface, leaving an unbroken view of the planet. Once again, the memory of his dream returned, bringing with it a fresh wave of fear that not even Captain Bennet's presence could mollify.

"Captain, we have to turn around!" he shouted. Before he knew it, the words came tumbling out of his mouth.

Everything stopped. All eyes were upon him. Bennet's already angry stare deepened as he noticed Jacob for the first time, while Folgrin regarded him with cold interest.

"What is this kid doing on my bridge?" Bennet growled. Silas frowned and started toward Jacob.

"I'm sorry, Captain," Jacob murmured. "I shouldn't have—"

"I think we should hear him out," Folgrin broke in, drawing an even darker glare from Bennet. Silas hesitated as Folgrin turned to Jacob.

"What is it, Jacob? Why should we turn around?"

Jacob could see Folgrin watching him intently. A slim smile appeared on the man's face.

"Well?" Bennet demanded, breaking the long silence.

Jacob didn't know what to say. He just knew he couldn't tell the truth. Not now, not with Folgrin gazing at him with that awful, probing stare. Besides, what choice did they really have? From the sound of things, they couldn't just turn around and break back into otherspace.

An alarm saved him, a series of sharp tones followed by a blinking light from one of the consoles.

"We've got a ship ahead, Captain," Timlin said, swiveling back in his chair.

"Let's see it," Bennet said, turning from Jacob and Folgrin, his voice suddenly firm and neutral, in command.

The view on the middle section of the window suddenly zoomed in and down. A glowing box of superimposed light appeared on the screen, highlighting a dull metal shape drifting below them along the top of the asteroid field. As the screen continued to zoom in, Jacob could see what appeared to be a ship similar in shape to the *Odessa*. But something was different. It seemed to hover at an odd sort of angle, its thrusters and portholes all dark. Smaller objects trailed behind it, floating a short distance from the tail. At first, he thought they were smaller craft, but as the view closed in, he realized they were pieces of debris.

"Looks like a dead one," Bennet said. "Can you ID it?"

"I'll try," Timlin said.

There was a long pause. With everyone's focus on the view screen before them, Jacob eased toward the door.

"Got it," Timlin said. "It's a trader. A small one—the *Miranda*. Went missing three months ago."

"Any life signs?"

Timlin shook his head.

By now Jacob had reached the door. As the image continued to zoom in even more closely, Jacob noticed a series of dark score marks across the *Miranda*'s hull.

"What are those marks, Captain? What happened here?" Folgrin asked, echoing Jacob's own thoughts.

Bennet didn't reply. "Kendrick, let's pick up the pace a bit. More power to the engines."

"You got it," the pilot replied.

"Captain," Folgrin continued, "I demand that you tell me what's going on here. What happened to that ship?"

Jacob was about to flee when the captain turned to Folgrin.

"Pirates," he said with a faint smile as the lights faded and flickered a second time. "That's my guess, anyway. Now, unless you have any further demands, you can retire to your quarters and leave me to run the ship."

With that, he turned back and began issuing orders to the men on the bridge.

Folgrin didn't move right away, but it was enough for Jacob, who slipped through the doorway and down the hall. The last thing he heard before the door closed behind him was the sound of Bennet's voice, disturbingly calm.

"Better tell Branson to warm up the gun."

\* \* \*

Jacob was running so fast, he bumped right into Dobson as the man came through the engine room hatch and fell backward onto the ground.

"What's got into you?" Dobson said, reaching down and lifting Jacob up with one enormous hand.

"Pirates!" Jacob cried, trying to catch his breath.

"What?" Dobson cried.

Between gasps, Jacob related what he'd seen on the bridge. When he'd finished, Dobson shook his head.

"Don't worry, Jacob," he said. "That wreck's three months old. Whoever did it is long gone."

The ship gave a slight stutter. The lights flickered for the third time. Once more, Jacob could hear the hum of the engine dip before rising back.

Frowning, the engineer swore under his breath.

"Dobson," Bennet's voice—small and digitized—called out from somewhere. Dobson raised his left wrist, pulling up his sleeve a few inches to reveal a gold bracelet.

"Here, Captain," he said, speaking to the bracelet.

"What the hell's going on back there?"

"Trip through otherspace put a real strain on the engines. Just a few power fluctuations. Nothing serious."

"Well, get it straightened out," the captain's voice crackled. "We're making a run for port and I need all the power we can get."

Dobson glanced down at Jacob for a moment, his frown growing.

"I'm on it," the engineer replied, heading back toward the engine room. He paused in the doorway and turned back to Jacob.

"Like I told you before, don't worry. You'll be okay," he said. "Now go get me a sandwich. I'm going to be a while."

Before the door had even whisked shut, Jacob turned and ran back toward the mess hall. It suddenly felt good to have something to do, even a small task.

The overhead lights suddenly went out, and the floor lights came on as the ship went from dayside to power-saving night mode. The darkness caught him unawares, and turning a corner, he ran into yet another figure. This time he didn't fall. This time the person caught him, held him firmly by the arm. He didn't even have to look up to know who it was. He could feel it in the coldness running up his arm.

"Hello, Jacob," Folgrin said, the same cold smile from before spreading across his face. "You're in quite a hurry."

Jacob looked away. "I-I am," he stammered, feeling his arm growing numb. "In fact, I have to go—"

"Not so fast, Jacob," the man broke in, tightening his grip. "Let's have a talk. It's a good time for a talk, isn't it? So much excitement on the ship. Everyone so busy."

"But I really do have to go to the mess and—"

"Excellent idea," Folgrin interrupted again. "Let's go."

The man turned and led Jacob down the corridor toward the dining cabin. Soon they'd reached the doorway. Folgrin glanced both ways and, seeing no one, dragged Jacob into the room.

The mess was empty, its lights dim. Lewis had finished clearing the tables from breakfast. Folgrin released Jacob's arm. Before Jacob could make a move to get away, the man put a hand against his chest and pushed him up against the wall, then held him in place with one finger. It was only a finger, but Jacob felt as if he were pinned to the wall with a steel rod.

There was a long silence as the man regarded Jacob, as if seeking something. Jacob just stared back and tried not to panic, tried to keep his heart from racing right out of his chest. Captain Bennet hadn't been afraid of the man, neither should he.

"You moved," Folgrin said.

"What?" Jacob cried, gasping against the feeling of pressure on his chest. Glancing down, it looked as if Folgrin were barely touching him.

Jacob felt his heart start to pound even harder. *He can't hurt me,* he tried telling himself. *Not here. Not now.*

"I'm not scared of you," he managed to say.

Folgrin shrugged. "If you say so. But back to the matter at hand. You moved. Back in the lounge, when we came out of otherspace. You were in one chair before. Then, when we came out, you were in a different chair."

Jacob suddenly remembered Folgrin's double take on the way out of the lounge, the strange look he'd given him, and realized with horror that he must have returned to the wrong seat in haste.

"I don't know what you're talking about," Jacob said.

"I almost didn't notice it at first," Folgrin continued, as if he hadn't even heard Jacob. "Just chalked it up to normal otherspace distortion. Very clever," the man added as if he were talking more about himself than Jacob.

Jacob was about to repeat his denial, then paused. Somehow he knew it wouldn't make any difference.

Seeing his silent hesitation, Folgrin laughed.

"So how'd you do it, anyway?" he asked. "What's your secret?"

"I have to go," Jacob whispered. "Dobson needs me."

He started to turn. Folgrin pushed him back against the wall, this time harder, all five fingers of his hand spread out against Jacob's chest, as if poised to pluck out his heart. He leaned in close, so that Jacob could see his own face reflected in the black pools of the man's eyes.

"Tell me your secrets, Jacob. I want to know all about you."

Jacob felt himself weakening, growing faint. He felt as if he had no energy to speak. But if that was so, then why did he feel the stories, the dreams, the truth about himself rising up?

As he opened his mouth for the words to pour out, an explosion shook the ship.

Jacob felt himself being thrown forward and to the right. He could see the look of shock on Folgrin's face as the man was lifted into the air along with him, falling backward away from him over a table.

Jacob hit the ground rolling, bringing his arms up around his head as chairs tumbled over him. Coming to a stop, he saw the ship lights turn red, just as they had less than an hour ago when they'd broken through otherspace. But this time, Jacob knew there was no breaking through. This was something different.

Pushing a chair off of him, Jacob struggled to sit up. There was a pain in his side where the chair had struck him, but he didn't seem to be badly injured.

Folgrin wasn't so lucky. Peeking above the overturned table, Jacob could see the man lying on his back. Whether he was unconscious or dead, Jacob couldn't tell. A large cut ran across his forehead. Blood covered his face, staining the trimmed edges of his white-blond hair. His eyes were closed, and Jacob's first thought was how different the man looked without those black orbs gazing at him. Folgrin seemed somehow smaller, less frightening. His second thought was of the high councilor. A sharp memory rose up—Delaney's father lying at his feet, blood welling from his head where Jacob had struck him—making Jacob dizzy as he struggled now to get to his feet. It hadn't occurred to him until this moment how much alike the two men were, how much they both unsettled him.

A second explosion rocked the ship. Jacob bumped up against the table, but this concussion was less severe.

*We're under attack.*

He'd been so shaken by the first strike, the thought hadn't entered his mind until now.

He bolted for the door, pausing only to take one look back. Folgrin hadn't moved. The wall screen showed the planet still before them, so large now that it filled the entire screen but for a patch of black space in one corner. A red streak zoomed out in front, flying away from the *Odessa*, a missed shot from whoever was attacking.

Jacob ran back down to the engine room, passing Malcolm and Eric along the way. The men said nothing to him as they went by, their grim faces focused on their duties.

Jacob reached the doorway to the engine room as a third explosion shook the ship. The red lights dimmed several times as Jacob hit the release button beside the door. It took several tries before the door finally opened. A cloud of smoke rolled out, dark, acrid, accompanied by a strange smell that made Jacob think of electricity. His eyes began to water, and he coughed, waving the plume from his face just as Dobson appeared, a mask covering his head. Seeing Jacob, he pulled up and stripped off his mask. His face was covered with sweat.

"We're being attacked!" Jacob cried.

"I know, kid," Dobson said with a smile. "Did you bring me my sandwich?"

"What?" Jacob shrieked. "No, I couldn't. I tried, Dobson, but Folgrin wouldn't let me. He held me against the wall and tried to get me to tell him, but I wouldn't tell him." Jacob was yelling now, trying not to cry.

Dobson's face grew dark. "It's okay, Jacob. I was just kidding. Listen, the best thing for you to do right now is to just stay—"

Before he could finish, another blow struck the ship, throwing both of them against the starboard wall. The lights flickered, and this time an alarm began to sound. Swearing, Dobson grabbed Jacob by the arm and began marching down the hall.

"It's the pirates, isn't it?" Jacob cried, shouting to be heard above the alarm.

"Aye. They're trying to cripple us. Get us to stop so they can board us."

"They're going to come here?"

Dobson shook his head. "Captain'll never let the likes of them touch his ship. He's making a run for the surface."

They turned into the crew's sleeping quarters.

"Grab your things," the man said.

"But—"

"Hurry, now."

Jacob reached under his bunk and pulled out his pack. His whistle, clothes, and books, the stunner Xander had told

98

him to keep—he was grateful now he'd stored everything in one place.

Before Jacob could ask any questions, Dobson grabbed him once more and continued toward the midsection of the ship.

Partway down the corridor, they pulled up before one of several small hatches lining the wall. Jacob had noticed them before but never known what they were. Dobson punched a code into a pad beside the hatch. The door whisked open, and the engineer shoved Jacob inside.

"Escape pod," the man shouted. He pointed up. Jacob looked up to see a red light above his side of the hatch. "When that goes green, release the pod. Switch is to the right." Jacob glanced down to see a yellow lever to the right of the door.

"We're going to crash," Jacob cried, not bothering to form it as a question.

"We might," Dobson called back. "We're nearly in orbit now. Be hitting the atmosphere soon."

"Stay with me!" Jacob pleaded.

"Got to get back to the engine room. Don't worry, I'll see you soon."

Before Jacob could say another word, the hatch closed. Dobson was gone.

Jacob glanced around at the pod, a tiny sphere with enough room for maybe four adults to squeeze together. It was quiet, the sound of the siren barely discernable through the thick hatch doors.

A bright flash from behind made Jacob spin around.

Through the porthole he could make out the attacking ship in the distance. It looked smaller than the *Odessa*, but not much. A volley of red streaks erupted from the ship's guns, larger versions of the plasma bolts Xander used to take down gruskers. Jacob braced himself as they raced in. Two passed below the wing, missing, but the third struck the thruster not far behind where he was situated. There was a shower of sparks as particles of the *Odessa* flew off into the darkness.

But they were fighting back. The *Odessa* fired a return volley, two of the blasts striking the pirate vessel, causing it to veer left and disappear behind the ship, out of Jacob's view.

A moment later the darkness faded, brightening into a thick orange mist. They were entering the atmosphere.

*We got away,* Jacob thought.

It started with a tremor, the slightest shaking as they hit the atmosphere, barely distinguishable from the normal vibrations of the ship. Within seconds it grew worse. Glancing out the porthole, Jacob could see a thick column of smoke trailing from the *Odessa*'s thrusters as it broke through the cloud bank. Something was terribly wrong.

Then it was impossible to see out the window as the shaking took over. He tried looking for a harness, but it was too late. All Jacob could do was hold on as tightly as possible to avoid being smashed against the inside of the sphere. The escape pod's lights had gone out, leaving nothing but an orange haze shining through the porthole behind him and the glow of the red bulb over the hatch, weaving so violently with the shaking of the ship that it had become a red line arcing back and forth, tracing a jagged series of streaks.

Jacob wanted to close his eyes and surrender to the shuddering violence, but he held on, focusing on the red arc weaving before him, waiting for it to turn green the way Dobson

100

said it would. He had to watch. It was his duty.

*How did this happen? How did I get here?* he wondered.

Ever since breaking through to that strange world of other-space and coming back, life had been one surreal shadow, an accelerating nightmare as fantastical as his nightly visions. And now—this blurry world dominated by the changing color of a single light upon which so much depended.

As the shaking grew even worse, Jacob began to be convinced that this was in fact a dream, a vision from afar. It was someone else's life he was watching, a life he could never even have imagined if it weren't for his developing powers.

*But how can this be a vision?* he thought. *I can't even see properly.*

All he wanted was to escape.

A changing of the light brought him out of his trance. He glanced up above the hatch. The dancing arc was green. It was time to leave.

Forgetting Dobson, Bennet, Silas, the rest of the crew, forgetting Folgrin, forgetting how he'd gotten on board or even where he had been going, Jacob forced his right hand to let go of the handle to which it had cemented itself and reach toward the yellow switch, itself a blur. It was only inches away, but it seemed to take forever for his hand to make the trip, as if the shaking had slowed time itself.

Finally he reached it, could feel the lever come within his grasp. It was time to say good-bye to the *Odessa*. He pulled the lever.

Nothing happened.

It took a moment for Jacob to grasp the fact, to understand that nothing had changed. The ship was still going down. He was still going down with it.

He flicked the switch again, and again. Still nothing.

*It's broken,* he realized. *Everything's broken.*

It was his last thought as the shuddering smeared all sight, as the roar of the plummeting ship penetrated the pod's steel hull, making thought impossible. He could only close his eyes and let himself fall.

# PART THREE
# Maker's Drift

# CHAPTER NINE

A gray flower drew into focus, sharpened against the blur of yellowed grass around it. It was the first thing Jacob saw upon opening his eyes—gray petals curling and drooping like an old woman's hair thrown back, a brown stalk with leaves so withered it seemed impossible that such a plant could produce so delicate a flower, even one so colorless, all gray and brown but for a single dot of crimson at the center of its head, like a tiny pool of blood.

It was so different from any kind of flower he'd ever seen, the blossom of an alien world, both beautiful and somehow frightening.

He struggled to sit up, then stand. His body ached. Pain shot through him from every direction, making it impossible to locate its source.

He turned around in a circle, dizzy, wavering. He was in a clearing, the tall grasses yellow, the trees at the edges leafless, gray like the flower at his feet. It was as if all the color had been drained from the world. It was like his visions. But this wasn't a vision—there was too much pain.

Jacob spotted the escape pod ten yards away, dented, its porthole cracked, its hatch open. Had he opened the door? Had he crawled out or had he been thrown?

A dark plume of smoke rose from beyond the nearby trees. It must be the ship. Or what was left of it. The pod must have ejected after the crash to put him so close. Any earlier would have put him a hundred miles away at least.

A sharp pain made him gasp and cry out. For the first time, he looked down at himself. There was blood on his clothes, but from where he couldn't tell. And then he saw his left arm, saw it drooping like the petals of the flower, bending like rubber, as if the bone between his hand and his elbow had been removed.

For a moment he could only stare at his broken arm, grossly swollen and bruised. It was just another part of this strange place, another piece of the unreal world he couldn't quite understand. He reached down and tried to lift it, detached and curious in his shock. He could hear himself scream before the darkness rushed in again.

There was no flower this time, only grass, as the sound of an explosion brought him back.

He sat up again, more slowly this time, careful not to look at his throbbing arm. It didn't seem like he had been out for long—a few minutes perhaps: The blood on his clothes and skin still glistened red.

The explosion had come from the wreckage on the other side of the trees. He could see a fresh plume of black smoke mushrooming into the orange sky. Doing his best to ignore the pain, he stumbled through the trees toward the plume.

The woods were open, and he passed quickly through to a larger clearing on the other side. He paused at the edge of the trees and gasped.

The *Odessa* lay in two pieces. Its front section remained

mostly intact, though crumpled, its nose buried in the ground, while the hind section lay fifty yards away with broken wings, nearly split in half and burning.

Jacob guessed that the explosion must have come from the tail section, where the engines lay. As if in answer to his thought, another blast erupted from one of the wing's thrusters, sending out a shock wave that reached Jacob from a hundred yards away.

Stretching out in a straight line behind the ship lay a trench of upturned earth, rocks, and trees that disappeared over a ridge a quarter mile away. Bennet must have raised the nose of the ship enough to keep it from crashing headfirst. But it hadn't been enough to save the *Odessa*—though Jacob could make out the pieces of the ship, they were all blackened and broken, spiked with twisted shards of metal and glass.

Jacob stumbled toward the ship, the fear of what he was about to see cutting through the strange cocktail of pain and shock that numbed him.

He found the first body rounding the corner of the front section. It was facedown, badly burned, to the point where Jacob couldn't recognize it, though from its length he guessed it was Malcolm. He had felt corpses before in Harmony at the final passing during funerals and had even seen the remains of one of his own people in the grass during his exodus across the plains. But that had just been bones. This corpse—still very much the figure of a man in spite of its smoldering—was far worse. He gasped and looked away, only to spot Timlin nearby. The navigator was facedown, but Jacob recognized the tattoos with which Timlin had adorned his arms and legs.

Jacob turned and headed away from the front section of the ship. He'd seen enough. He wanted to find Dobson, but at this point anyone alive would be a welcome sight. Maybe those in the tail section had fared better.

Making his way through the smoke, he crossed the littered ground between the two halves of the ship, his shattered arm hanging limply at his side. He risked only the quickest glance at it, then looked away, sickened by the swelling.

Nearing the tail section, he was surprised at the size of the ship. He hadn't been on board too many days, but he'd forgotten about the hold—a large compartment that ran along the belly of the craft, occupying nearly half of its interior. The corridors and decks he'd traversed—now on fire from the explosion—comprised only the top half of the ship. Boxes and crates spilled from the cargo hold, many broken themselves, spilling their own contents in odd mockery of the ship that had carried them.

He didn't spot anyone else before Dobson. Most of the crew must have been either on the bridge or other parts of the front section, or lost in the explosion. Jacob wouldn't have found him at all if he hadn't heard a groan from behind a piece of sheet metal. Lifting it with his one good arm, he was overjoyed when Dobson turned and looked at him, smiling briefly in spite of the blood coming out of his mouth. But Jacob's joy quickly turned to anguish as he looked down to see the man's lower half pinned beneath a piece of machinery. Looking at Dobson's face, as pale as a dying star, Jacob could tell there wasn't much time left. Suddenly, he felt like he was back in Harmony all over again, gazing at the ashen face of the grower, the man's leg mangled by a harvester gone amok. Only this time, there was no alarm to signal, no one to turn to, no one to help.

"I'll get help. Don't worry, you'll be okay," Jacob said. He knew he shouldn't say it—it wasn't true, either part—but it was the only thing he could think of to say.

Dobson shook his head. "Stay," he gasped.

Jacob nodded.

"Would've made it," the man whispered a moment later. "Explosion caught me as I was about to climb down. Of all the luck."

Jacob nodded, thinking about his own luck. But it wasn't luck—it was Dobson putting him in the pod, getting him out of harm's way.

It didn't take long. Toward the end, Dobson's breaths came quick, shallow, and then stopped altogether. It was a strange feeling watching the man die. More than anything, he felt peaceful in spite of the sound of nearby flames and the sight of blood trickling down the corners of Dobson's mouth, though the realization brought a flush of shame when he looked into the man's empty eyes. Still, he couldn't help feeling that he'd been witness to an important moment, a sacred moment, one larger than either of them.

"There you are," the voice said. Its normal smoothness was shaken.

Jacob turned to see Folgrin standing a few yards away. His suit was torn in several places, and his face and hair was blackened by soot so that he appeared little more than a shadow. Only his teeth stood out, hovering and white, as his face broke into a grin.

"None the worse for wear, I see," he added, before glancing down at Jacob's arm and wincing distastefully. "Except for that. Hurts, does it?"

"Where are the others?" Jacob demanded. Between

Dobson, his arm, and the surreal landscape of the wreckage, he was suddenly in no mood to deal with the man.

"Mostly dead. I think I heard some voices coming from what's left of the bridge, though if anyone did survive, it would be a miracle."

"*You* survived," Jacob spat.

"I certainly did. Captain's quarters remained remarkably intact. I'm a lucky one. Just like you. Once again, you find a way to surprise me. Now, let's go."

Seeing him start toward him, Jacob pulled back.

"Go where?"

"Away from here."

"But there may be survivors. We can't just leave them!"

"Won't take those pirates long to figure out where we went down. They'll be here any minute to gather what's left—including us."

"No," Jacob said. He marched past Folgrin and headed for the bridge section. "I'm tired of listening to you. I'm tired of seeing you. I'd rather deal with a hundred pirates than you."

He'd gone only a dozen steps when a wave of electric pain shot up his left arm as Folgrin grabbed him from behind, the man's hand squeezing Jacob's broken arm above the elbow. Jacob screamed as he felt himself being dragged away from the *Odessa*'s remains.

"Foolish boy," Folgrin snarled. "For someone who's supposed to be so smart, you're awful stupid. Let's get out of here."

Able to muster little more than a whimper, Jacob barely heard him. His head was spinning now from the pain in his arm as they headed toward the trees.

"Hey!" a voice shouted from behind them.

Folgrin whirled, pulling Jacob around with him, making him cry out as another spasm of pain shot up his arm.

It was Bennet's brother, Silas. Like Folgrin, he was covered in soot. Only his synthetic arm gleamed, its gold unblemished by the crash, the fingers weaving in agitation as the man strode toward them. A metal pipe three feet long was in his other hand.

"Let go of the boy," the first mate growled.

"Sorry, Silas," Folgrin shouted back. "This scene is about to get even nastier than it already is. We can't be around for it. I'm too important. So is the boy."

"We've got some injured men up front. Your help is needed. Boy needs that arm looked after, as well. Besides, don't look like he cares for your company."

"I don't!" Jacob cried out. "Help me, Silas! He won't let me go."

Silas glared and started forward again, his fingers little more than a whirl.

Folgrin drew a stunner from his coat pocket and pointed it at Silas. The man took a few more steps, then pulled up, a look of confusion creeping over his face. It seemed as if he were looking past them.

"Don't come any closer, Silas," Folgrin said. "Go back. Take care of your men. I'll take care of Jacob."

Silas opened his mouth to speak, but the words never came out as the streak of light flashed over Jacob's shoulder and passed through Silas's midsection, the plasma bolt cauterizing as it left a hole larger than Jacob's fist. Silas looked down in shock, then dropped the pipe and sank to the ground.

"No!" Jacob screamed.

111

Folgrin cursed.

Jacob glanced back to where Folgrin was staring. In the distance loomed three dark shapes closing in fast over the tree line. Floaters. Several more streaks of plasma flew by. One came so close, Jacob could feel the heat against his face as it zipped past.

"Come on," Folgrin said, grabbing Jacob's good arm this time.

"No!" Jacob cried, pulling away. He didn't care anymore. The crash, Timlin, Malcolm, Dobson, now Silas—it was all too much. All he knew was that he didn't want to go anywhere with the man now trying to drag him toward the trees.

"Stop fighting me!" Folgrin shouted. For the first time, Jacob could see him losing control.

And then Jacob was falling back onto the ground. A piercing howl filled his ears. For a second he thought it was his own, but as he looked over to see Folgrin writhing on the ground, clutching his arm, he realized something terrible had happened. Sure enough, glancing down Jacob saw Folgrin's severed hand still clinging to his own arm, the wrist burned black along its edges.

He brushed it off in horror and stumbled to his feet, holding his broken forearm against his chest with his other hand, and ran toward the woods, more plasma bolts streaking past his head. He had to get away. From all of them.

Before he knew it, he was plunging into the trees, ignoring the branches that whipped against his face.

He ran and ran for what felt like miles, not noticing where he ran, not caring as he crossed streams and meadows, stumbling over ridges and through ravines. For a long time he ran on adrenaline, on fear, as if the only way he could ever feel safe again was to put more and more distance between himself and the crash site.

Eventually, his adrenaline ran out. It happened so suddenly, stopping him short as he stumbled into one last clearing. It was as if he'd run so fast, he'd left a part of himself behind, and it was only now catching up, crashing into him, making him dizzy, so that his head spun and the trees danced in circles at the edge of the clearing. He dropped to his knees, fighting the wave, then fell to the ground, feeling himself plunge into darkness for the third time that day. The last thing he saw before passing out was another one of this world's strange gray flowers, staring at him with its crimson eye.

# CHAPTER TEN

The sound of humming brought Jacob back. A quiet tune in a woman's voice, floating to him through the darkness.

For a moment, Jacob thought he was home. Not at Xander's house, but back in Harmony, nestled in a warm blanket in the underground house, his mother hovering nearby, singing. He'd dreamed of being back in Harmony before, in the days before Delaney had left Mixel. But those had been nightmares. This was no nightmare, though the song he heard was haunting, and Jacob knew that if it had words, they would be sad ones.

It was no dream of any kind, in spite of the song and the smell of withered bulbs that reminded him of home. He could remember the real nightmare he'd just lived through only too well, a surreal plunge into a world from which he'd barely escaped. The crashing *Odessa* had not only stranded him on Maker's Drift—it had carried him over a dark threshold to another kind of world where death was everywhere. He shuddered at the thought of those burned and broken bodies that only hours before had moved and breathed, had spoken to him, had looked at him with bright eyes, at the memory of Dobson fading, of seeing Silas meet his sudden, violent end, all in the span of a few chaotic moments. But the sudden realization of his own close brush with death—the fact that he could just as easily have met the same fate as any of those men had things only gone a little different—made him shake most of all.

He'd made it through, spared but damaged. How badly, he couldn't say. All he could feel was the pain in his lower left arm—a dull, gentle throbbing.

He kept his eyes closed for a while, taking in his surroundings through the senses that had defined the boundaries of his world for the first thirteen years of his life. He could sense that he was in an enclosed space. He could feel his broken arm was wrapped in something tight. The woman was old; he could hear it even in her humming. And underneath was the smell of smoke. It wasn't pungent like the smell of burning zephyr back on Nova Campi, but it wasn't like the acrid stench of the wreckage from which he'd escaped. It was wood smoke, and it was close—he could hear the crackling of a fire nearby, which puzzled him. Who would dare light a fire inside?

There was another smell as well, an aroma of spices and cooking that finally made him open his eyes.

It was dark in the house. The place was small—smaller than Xander's, perhaps even smaller than the earth home he'd grown up in. But this cottage wasn't made of earth. He could see the wooden beams of the low ceiling running above him, could see the arched timbers running from the beams down into the posts, dimly lit by the flames of a fire burning in a recess set into the nearby wall.

He was lying on a couch of some kind, covered in thick blankets up to his neck. He drew his right arm out and, pulling the blankets aside, realized his clothes had been

115

removed. His body had been cleaned of the mud and blood, and his shattered arm lay encased in a plasticast from the elbow down. The cast's smooth synthetic wrap seemed in odd contrast with his surroundings. The wooden ceiling and walls, the woolen blankets, the stone enclosure for the fire, the iron pot suspended over the flames—it was the kind of world he'd read about in Xander's most ancient books.

"Awake again, I see."

Jacob turned to see the woman rocking in a chair among the shadows. He pulled the blankets back over him and sat up, resting his broken arm on his lap. Though it still ached, it didn't hurt to move it.

"I was awake before?" he asked.

"Oh, yes," she said, chuckling as she rose from the chair. "When Chester first brought you in. Though you hardly made any sense at all. I'm not surprised you don't remember."

"Where am I?" he asked.

"Somewhere safe," she replied.

She came around the back of the sofa and into the light. Her hair was white, tucked back into the folds of a plaid scarf around her head. She was old but not frail. Jacob could tell by the way she walked—slow, graceful, with purpose. Her voice, too, was rich in age and wisdom, not the withered croaking like many old women he'd known in Harmony. Her skin was wrinkled, but her face was full, her eyes light and dancing as they caught the flames of the fire.

"I need to get back," he said. The idea of returning to the wreck, of having to risk a run-in with the pirates or—just as horrible—with Folgrin again made his stomach turn. But the idea of being stranded suddenly seemed far worse. He glanced about the room for his clothes, but they were

116

nowhere to be seen. "I have to get back to the ship and find the captain. He'll know—"

"Hush," she said, coming over to him. "Chester checked the wreck. He found no other survivors. There is no going back."

Jacob lay back and closed his eyes against the tears now welling to the surface as the words sank in. In spite of his efforts, he could feel the drops squeeze from the corners of his eyes and trickle down along his temples.

"What'll I do now?" he whispered, more to himself than anyone.

"For now, nothing. Don't worry. The future isn't going anywhere without you."

Wiping the wetness from his face, he took a few deep breaths and tried to forget, tried fighting back the waves of panic that rose as he imagined himself forever stuck on this dead world far out in the darkness of space, cut off from the rest of the universe.

Her humming helped. She'd pulled a chair up close and had renewed the song. He followed its melody until his heart no longer raced and the sickness in his stomach began to settle.

"How long was I out?" he said at last.

"A few hours. Enough for us to get that arm reset and for you to get your wits back. Enough for me to check the bones."

He was about to ask her what she meant, when she rose abruptly and took a wooden bowl from a nearby table. Using a long ladle, she filled it with soup simmering in the iron pot. Its aroma made his mouth water. He watched her take a small bottle down from the mantel and add a few drops to the steaming bowl.

"Medicine," she said, seeing the question on his face.

Jacob remembered Xander giving him "medicine" the first time he'd taken him back to his house. It had turned out to be whiskey. He wondered if this was the same.

She sat back down beside him and began feeding him, one spoonful at a time.

"I can do it myself," he offered.

"Nonsense," she said.

Feeling the warm liquid—somehow salty, sweet, and tart all at the same time—slide down his throat, he suddenly felt too tired to argue.

"You just rest," she continued. "Chester will be back soon. He's gone to wash your clothes."

Between the warmth of the soup, the fire, and the blankets, he could feel himself growing sleepy again. But it was strange, the warmth. It almost seemed to be coming more from within, creeping from his stomach out into all his limbs, so that even his broken arm seemed to throb a little less.

"I'm Jacob."

"Morag," she said in return.

She began humming again as she fed him. The warmth had reached his head now, like a rising tide, setting his mind afloat. He could feel his eyelids growing heavy.

"You sleep now," Morag said, taking the bowl away at last. "As for me, I must consult the bones again."

"Bones?" Jacob murmured. His voice sounded faint and far away. "What does that mean?"

"They are the bones of my mother, and her mother, and her mother before that. They talk to me. They tell me what I want to know."

"Oh," Jacob said. Then, in the midst of his drifting, a memory appeared, rolling in like a wave that lifted him for the briefest moment.

"You're a witch," he whispered, trying to cry out the words but feeling them sink like stones even as gravity seemed to strengthen its hold upon his limbs. Suddenly, all he could think about were the crew's stories of people disappearing, the rumors of cannibalism, madness, witchcraft. And now here he was, saved from the woods only to be made a feast of. A feast for witches.

She laughed. "I've been called worse," she replied, removing the scarf from her head.

The room was getting bright all of a sudden. *But it isn't day yet,* he puzzled, suddenly forgetting his fear, leaving it in the flow. He could see lights bobbing in the air and wondered how it was possible to feel so light and so heavy at the same time. The lights now gathered together, hovering above her, bright colors dancing. Everything was dancing in the room, weaving to the rhythm of her floating white hair.

"Don't fight it, Jacob," she whispered, her eyes almost all light now. "That which was broken must be mended. This will help you start again."

She turned to the fire, picking up what looked like a leather sack with two wooden handles and a short mouth attached, and began working the handles, humming that same haunted song as she did so, filling the bag with air and pumping it into the fireplace, making the flames leap, causing the embers to glow brighter as the room dissolved into haze, a fog that wrapped Jacob in warm brightness, covering everything from sight.

Jacob went home that night, opening his eyes to a dream. He was back on Nova Campi, on a hill outside Melville with its sparkling towers, clean against the green fields around it.

Then he was in the city, though he didn't how he'd gotten there.

The streets were nearly empty, quiet as he traveled down the central boulevard. But as he walked, he kept passing people whom he knew—Kala, LaPerle, Xander's friend Karl, the smuggler Raker who'd given them the tools they'd needed to rescue Delaney from Mixel Tower, others he'd met on various trips to the city. They all smiled at him as they walked by. Some of the smiles, like Kala's, were warm. Others were sad, or amused, or regretful. LaPerle's was cold, almost a sneer, like Folgrin's. No one spoke to him. In fact, he realized there was no sound at all, not even the echo of footfalls. He could feel nothing either, though he knew he was walking. He had no sense of smell, no sense at all but sight.

He had left Melville, was at the shore of a lake. It was his lake, the one near Xander's where he'd learned to swim, where Xander had rescued him. And Xander was there with Delaney on a blanket near the water's edge. The well-heeled teens, the boys and girls who first welcomed him, were there also, waving to him before going back to playing in the sand, batting the golden ball around as before.

He walked over and sat down beside Xander and Delaney. They gave him warm greetings, mouthing words he couldn't hear. Delaney still had her jeweled eyes. They burned with the glow of sight. For what seemed a long time he stayed on the blanket, gazing out over the water.

"I will stay here forever," he said.

But the words, like a thunderclap, shattered the silence, sending a shock wave out over the water, and the next thing he knew, he was far off, over the ridges, away from the groves of zephyr and on the plain, heading east, back to Harmony.

It was then Jacob realized he wasn't alone. He could sense someone with him, someone at his heels, moving when he moved, stopping when he stopped, a shadow in the corner of his eye, though every time he turned, no one was there. But he knew. By the flicker at the edge of sight he knew he wasn't alone and hadn't been the entire journey. Stranger still was that it didn't seem to trouble him.

He looked down to see bones woven into the grass, untrammeled by the gruskers, the remains of the fellow Blinder he'd encountered on his flight from Harmony. The skeleton looked so clean compared to the burnt remains he'd spied just yesterday. He wondered what his follower thought of the lonely bones.

And then he was back, first overlooking the colony with its surrounding fields busy with bent workers or grazing flocks and herds, then among its streets once more. He didn't like being back. The faces seemed blurry. There were no smiles for him, not from the neighbors he recognized, his classmates, his best friend, Egan. Worst of all, he realized they couldn't have seen him even if they hadn't been blind. Where their unseeing eyes had once been were nothing but empty sockets.

There was but one exception—the man, tall, his dark hair and beard streaked with gray, waiting for him in the square. Martin Corrow, Delaney's father, smiled at Jacob with a sinister grin, his solitary eye winking in recognition. Jacob avoided his gaze, shied away from the high councilor's outstretched arms and fled.

He was running up a ramp, toward the council house, the great chimes swaying but silent. The entrance gaped, waiting, as it always had, to swallow him up. But the opening was no

121

longer dark like before. It shone pure white, opaque. He glanced at the ledge above. The great orange feline he'd once seen in real life and had spoken with many times afterward in his visions was there, but he was no longer staring at Jacob. His eyes were closed, his head was down—either sleeping or dead.

Jacob passed through the entrance, broke the plane of light and now found himself suspended amid the blankness.

He gazed around, trying to make sense of where he was in a world made all of white. The disorientation was complete—no sense of up or down, no sense of depth or distance. All he knew was that he was moving. There was no wind roaring in his ears, but he could feel himself being pulled by a powerful force, traveling at great speed and distance. He couldn't tell if his companion was with him or not, but like before, it didn't matter. None of it mattered. He just was.

*Otherspace,* he thought. It suddenly seemed so familiar. He was in otherspace. That same heady feeling as before, the same distortion of time and space, only with no ship, no crew, no Folgrin.

Looking back, he wasn't sure how long he'd traveled. He remembered what Dobson had told him about time in otherspace. It was as if, without a physical point of reference to connect to, time had lost its meaning.

A black dot appeared in the distance before him, an impossibly tiny point that grew quickly, expanding so that it became the dark at the end of the tunnel.

And then he was out, back in the world. But not his world. Glancing around at the leafless trees, the gray flowers, he suddenly realized he was on Maker's Drift. He wandered through a meadow, passed through a copse of trees to yet another meadow where a small cottage perched at a bend in the stream. He could sense his wandering partner once again and turned. This time, the follower didn't move.

It was Morag. She looked tired, but she smiled and gave him a knowing nod.

"Now you know," he said. He winced, the words thundering in his ears.

"I know," she said, her own voice but a whisper. She walked past him into the house.

He followed her, opening the door to darkness. He paused only a moment to look at the stream glinting in the sun as it tumbled over the rocks, then he turned inside, back into the darkness.

# CHAPTER ELEVEN

Jacob opened his eyes and sat up. Transformed by day, the cottage seemed larger in the light, with a staircase in the far corner that he hadn't noticed before.

There was no sign of anyone. He thought of calling out, but something in him resisted breaking the silence. A fire burned in the fireplace before which his clothes lay draped over a wooden rack, drying. The blood and dirt had been washed from them. He moved gingerly at first, pulling the blanket aside and standing. But he felt stronger than he had expected to and was surprised by his lack of soreness.

His clothes were dry enough, and so he put them on, careful of his arm, which still ached slightly when he moved it. The swelling seemed to have gone down, though it was difficult to tell through the cast.

There was a thick slice of buttered toast on a plate, along with a cup of dark tea. Both were cold, but he stuffed the bread into his mouth and chewed it as quickly as he could, suddenly ravenous, before washing it down with the tea.

After he finished, he went to the door and looked through the window. A beat-up old floater hovered in the yard near two piles of firewood—one split, one not. Between the piles lay an ax, its head half-buried in a large block.

124

He went outside and took a few steps before freezing. A familiar sensation ran up his spine—a tingling that left him cold. It was different from the feeling of danger, the feeling of being watched that had plagued him those last days on Nova Campi, but he knew there was something strange about the place. Then he recognized it—the stream nearby, the trees, the meadow—and turned.

Sure enough, the cottage was the same. He'd just visited it in his dreams, had returned here at the vision's end, following Morag inside. Only, Morag was not inside. Not in real life.

A familiar noise in the distance caught his ear. He hurried around the side of the cottage to the back, following the sound. It was coming through the trees beyond the stream, nearly blending with the sound of running water. He stepped across a line of stones that formed a bridge to the other side and discovered a short path through the trees. Coming out at the other end, he paused at the sight of the sheep.

It was a small herd. Twenty, thirty animals in black and golden coats of thick wool grazing among the dried grasses. And there was Morag in their midst, a switch in hand, guiding a select few toward a nearby barn.

A man was with her. He appeared about her age, his beard white. But like Morag, he seemed full of vitality as he helped her guide the sheep.

Seeing Jacob, he paused to wave and smile, then whistled to Morag. Jacob waved in reply as Morag left and came toward him. She seemed so ordinary compared to last night amid the dancing lights and haze, amid the humming and shadows.

"So you're still alive, I see," she said, coming up to him. "Not boiled in a cauldron?"

He blushed and looked down to the ground. She chuckled.

"Ever seen sheep before?" she asked, changing the subject.

Jacob nodded. "We had them back home. They were just white, though."

"That's right," she said. Before he could puzzle over her words, she took him by the hand and led him into the field.

"Chester!" she called. The man waded through the herd and came over.

"Yes, dear," he said.

"Husband, Jacob here knows sheep. He can help you bring them in. I'll go in and get supper ready. When the milking's done, come."

"Supper?" Jacob cried, glancing up at the angled sun. "But it's morning!"

"Late afternoon," she said. "You had a powerful sleep."

She turned and disappeared through the trees. Chester watched her go, then turned to Jacob with a smile.

Jacob hesitated. "I've never actually worked with sheep before," he said.

"Don't worry," Chester said, his voice soft, kind. "They pretty much bring themselves in."

He handed Morag's switch to Jacob and went back to work. Jacob quickly discovered he was right—it took very little persuading to get the dozen or so sheep in need of milking into the barn. Chester showed him how to coax the rich milk from the udders, then set to work. It took Jacob a little practice, but soon he was squirting milk into the bucket with his one good hand.

"How's the arm?" Chester asked, nodding toward Jacob's cast.

"Better," Jacob said.

"A nasty break that was. All purple when I found you in the woods. You're lucky, though. Morag's a skilled healer. And with that plasticast, you'll be well enough in a day or two."

"Thanks for saving me," Jacob said. He hesitated. "You went back, right?"

Chester nodded.

"There wasn't anyone alive?"

Chester shook his head. As sad as it made Jacob to learn that Bennet and the rest of the *Odessa*'s crew were gone, he couldn't help but feel a sudden wave of relief—at least he'd never have to see Folgrin again.

"How did you find me, anyway?"

"Morag sent me out. Her mothers' bones told me where to go."

"They really did?" Jacob said. "How is that possible?"

Chester shrugged. "It's her gift. Don't ask me to explain it. Lucky for you, it just is," he said. "'Course, those damn bones send me out to the woods nearly every other day. For every time they're right, I can think of a dozen times they're wrong. No disrespect," he added, leaning down to pat the ground. He glanced back at Jacob and winked. "A small price to pay for living with a witch, my boy."

He watched Jacob turn red and laughed.

They returned just as the sun was setting to discover a delicious aroma wafting through the house.

"Lamb shanks," Chester said. "Morag's specialty. You're a lucky guest indeed."

Morag ushered them to the table and served them in turn. They all ate in silence. The way the rich flavors of the dish combined with the tenderness of the meat was beyond anything Jacob had ever tasted.

When they'd finished, Chester stoked the fire with the same device Morag had used the night before—which Jacob learned was called a bellows—then put the kettle on for tea.

"Morag," Jacob said, watching the flames rise in the dusky house, "why is everything so . . . I don't know . . . so old here?"

Morag laughed. "You're not referring to Chester and myself, I hope."

"I mean your house. The wood, the fire, even the bowls and the plates. It's like something out of a storybook."

"Storybook," Morag replied with a friendly snort. "Speaking of old. I'm impressed you know of such things, Jacob."

She paused, gazing into the flames.

"Chester and I prefer the old ways. Don't misunderstand me, technology has its place, such as the starship that brought us to Maker's Drift years ago. We couldn't have done without it. Our floater takes us to the port for whatever supplies we may need. And that cast on your arm there—much better than an old wooden splint. But we follow the ancient ways as much as possible simply because we like them better, not because they are better. They please us. There's magic in them, you might say." Her eyes seemed to flash.

Jacob thought of life in Harmony. He supposed it wasn't so far from this, even with the sounders, the finders, the pathminders, the ghostbox. Of course, the way everything was always breaking down in the colony made the place seem almost more primitive than this. There had always been a feeling of desperation under the surface of Harmony—that there wouldn't be enough food, that something would go wrong and leave them in need. It wasn't a matter of whether people liked it or not, it was just the way it was. He had only fully realized it after escaping. In spite of the similarities he felt between this place and Harmony, he didn't sense that desperation here.

"I'm sorry I called you a witch before," he said, glancing over at her. "It's just that the men on board the ship told me Maker's Drift was full of them."

"Did they now?" Morag quipped. "What else did they tell you?"

"That criminals and cannibals lived here too. And that anyone who entered the barren lands disappeared."

Chester chuckled.

"Did you hear that, Chester? Cannibals!" Morag said. She turned back to Jacob. "Don't believe anything spacers tell you, Jacob. They're the most superstitious fools in the galaxy. On the other hand, none of us in these parts go out of our way to dispel the rumors. We like our peace and quiet, that's for sure, and if the stories keep people away, that's fine with us."

"So there *are* others?"

"A few here and there. And some of them are a bit rough. The real bad ones don't last long, though. We all look after one another. The rest of the time, we mind our own business. And I can assure you, none of us are cannibals, convicts, or even witches, for that matter."

She laughed. "I suppose I have a few witchy ways about me," she said, smiling at her husband. "I'm actually a healer by trade. But most of the time I commune—with the bones, with this planet. That's my true calling."

"The crew told me that Maker's Drift was a dead planet, that it was haunted," he said. "But you talk as if it were alive."

"The truth lies somewhere in between, I suppose. I

129

dragged poor Chester with me long ago to settle in these barren lands. I was called to this world, Jacob, this old, old world, to live and wait and listen. You see, Chester and I believe in the ancient powers, the powers of the earth. Silly stuff, some might say. But it works. Here, especially.

"My mothers' bones like this planet. That's why they brought us here and told us to stay. There *was* someone here once before us. A people. They're gone now—have been for a long, long time. But they add their voices to our mothers' and help us with our charms. And in return, we listen so they are not forgotten."

Jacob shivered. He could feel his heart pound, listening to her speak, and the feeling returned, the one he'd had back on Nova Campi. As if someone was watching, someone was listening. The watchers this time weren't men, but something else entirely.

"Of course, you know the nature of this world," she said, her eyes suddenly piercing him. "You've already tasted of its power."

A chill ran down his spine as the memory of last night's dream rose to the surface.

"What do you mean?" he demanded.

"Why, you have the gift, dear. A bit of magic, just like me. It's in the way you see things. You know what I mean, Jacob. Don't pretend otherwise."

Jacob looked away from both of them toward the fire before finally turning back.

"You came to my dream last night, didn't you," he said.

Her eyes lit up. She rose from her chair and came over to him.

"Oh, no, Jacob," she said, kneeling down to take his

hands. "I have a few charms, I've learned to elevate my senses, my intuition, but I have no such powers."

"But I saw you last night," Jacob protested. "You followed me all the way to Nova Campi and back. It was really you, not some part of my dream like the others."

"Yes, it was really me. You showed me everything. It was an amazing journey—one of the highlights of my life. But I didn't come to you, Jacob. You came to me. You pulled me into your dream and took me with you. I thank you for the gift."

Jacob pulled his hands back and looked away. Morag nodded and returned to her chair.

"I wasn't trying," he whispered. "I've never done anything like that before. I don't know how it happened."

He couldn't understand why Morag seemed so pleased. How could anyone enjoy having their consciousness invaded? Then he remembered—it had already happened to him. Twice. The boy had visited him twice.

Morag laughed. "I know your troubles. I've seen your life, my poor, dear boy. But everything—the troubles, the joys—they've all made you what you are, in every way. Don't be ashamed of your magic, Jacob," she said.

"You used that word before," Jacob murmured. "There's no magic, Morag. It's just how I am, the way my brain developed. It's just the way they made me."

"One person's science is another's magic," Morag said, shrugging.

Jacob glanced over to where Chester sat, watching intently, his face half in the dark, half-illuminated by the fire. He gave Jacob a quick wink.

"It was such a strange dream," Jacob said, at last. "Different from the others."

"It was no ordinary dream, for certain," Morag agreed. "Perhaps it was the eyeblood. I added it to your broth last night."

He remembered now seeing her add drops from the small vial above the fireplace. "What's an eyeblood?" he asked.

"A flower that grows around these parts. One of the *only* flowers that grow around here. It's mostly used as a sedative, but it's been known to have a slight hallucinatory effect in some people."

Jacob recalled the silver blossom with its crimson center that he'd seen upon first awakening from the crash. But the memory was a dim one, clouded by pain, a distant recollection from another age.

"But I don't believe that's why you had the vision you had," she continued. "There was a purpose to it. Just like there is a purpose for your being here in the first place."

Jacob thought about everything that had gone wrong to get him to this place he was never supposed to be. All the pain, all the stupid tragedy and death. There was no purpose to it, but he kept the thought to himself.

"I've heard of journeys like the one you had last night, Jacob. Rare ones."

She paused as Chester rose and tossed two pieces of split wood into the fire.

"You know, they say a person's life flashes before their eyes when they're about to die."

Jacob stirred, thinking of his vision—the movement, the people—it was a journey through his life, a kind of summation, only in reverse. But he came back. At the end, he returned to where he'd started.

"Are you trying to say I'm dead?" he joked.

But Morag, for once, looked totally serious.

"Do you feel dead, Jacob?"

He shivered in spite of the warmth coming from the nearby fire. He wanted to laugh, shout, do something to break himself from the cold grip now embracing him.

"No," he whispered. "I'm alive."

He was glad he said it. He suddenly felt like it needed to be said, as if he had to convince himself.

"Good," Morag replied, nodding and smiling once more.

"But I feel different. Something is different."

That part certainly was true. And it wasn't just the crash's aftermath. Ever since leaving Nova Campi, or rather, ever since his trip through otherspace, he'd felt different, as if the world had lost an edge of its realness. Maybe that was a little taste of what death was like.

"Different," Morag said. "Always different. Always changing, that's for sure. And you are different, Jacob. Special. I could tell that right away. Even before you came into my dream. The bones said so."

"Good thing you have those bones," Jacob murmured.

Chester burst out laughing. Morag scowled, but only for a moment.

"Maybe you did die, Jacob," she continued. "And you just came back. Different. Changed. You joke, but I felt it last night. There's a power in you, growing, evolving, waiting to be discovered."

Jacob shook his head.

"There are some things I can do, things I can see, but I don't understand them. They come and go. I can't control them. That's why I was on the ship. I was on my way to Teiresias to meet some people who could help me figure it all out," he said. He looked down at his arm. "Then all this happened. Now, who knows."

Morag and Chester gave each other a quick glance.

"Maybe *we* can help you figure it out," she said.

She nodded to Chester, who rose and went over to a wooden chest at the back of the room. A moment later he returned to the fire with something in his arms.

"What is that?" Jacob asked.

"Chester's bagpipes. Smallpipes, he calls them. There are more ways to make the journey besides drinking eyeblood. For me, it's Chester's playing. He made those pipes from the wood of this world's trees. An old, hard wood. And I've strengthened them with my own charms. They sing like no others."

Jacob had studied most kinds of instruments back in Harmony in the school's music library and had heard of bagpipes, though not of this kind. No one in the colony played them, but he'd listened to recordings. Their sound—exotic, wild—had always caught his ear like no other instrument.

The pipes came in two pieces. Chester took one part and slipped it under his right arm before tying it to his waist with a belt. He lifted his arm a little and gave it a pump. Listening to its hiss, Jacob realized it was just like the bellows they used to set the fire blazing.

The second part consisted of several wooden shafts, beautifully carved and polished, tied into a black leather bag. One piece had finger holes, much like his whistle. Another connected to the bellows. The others, three drones of varying lengths, were grouped tightly together, converging in a single stock that tied into the bag.

Chester took the bag under his left arm and hooked the

connector to the bellows under his right. Then he began to pump. Jacob watched the bag as it filled with air.

"Just relax and listen to the music, Jacob," Morag said, lighting a stick of incense from a candle on the table.

"What's going to happen?" Jacob asked.

"That's up to you, boy. The pipes are charmed with the strongest magic I could find. My best readings come when Chester plays for me on dark nights like these. Sometimes, I just end up hearing some good tunes. But other nights . . . well, hopefully you'll see. Just let yourself go. I'll come along if I can."

He wanted to ask her more questions, but before he could open his mouth to speak, Chester began to play.

Jacob caught his breath. On the recordings he'd heard in Harmony, the pipes had had a piercing, commanding timbre that had made his hair stand on end. These pipes seemed to be a different instrument altogether—quieter, softer, and lower in tone, like the sound of water falling over the smooth stones of the stream beside the cottage. He understood, now, why Chester called them smallpipes.

Watching Chester's fingers work the chanter, Jacob felt his eyes begin to well. Though there'd been music on board the *Odessa*, it was nothing like this. All he could think of was Delaney, of how she'd played for them every night, how he'd watched her fingers as they moved across the keys. He'd hardly thought of her or Xander over the last few weeks. The realization struck him hard. Delaney, Xander, his mother and father—he missed them all. He missed his old life, mourned the loss of it. Maybe Morag was right. Maybe a part of him had died along the way.

The chanter's song was a slow, graceful air, and as sad as

135

it made him, the tune warmed him with its beauty. But it was the drones that really did it—the notes converging in a single hum, a single chord. Their purr reminded him for a moment of Harmony, of the gatherings in the central square as the entire colony's sounders came together.

The humming drones, the wafts of incense, a full belly. All these combined to weave a heaviness that fell about him. He could feel himself getting lost, moving beyond his sorrow and his longing for home, moving beyond the moment.

He wasn't alone in this. Chester was lost in his playing. Morag's eyes were half-closed, the pupils rolled back so that there was nothing but white beyond the slits. It would have unsettled Jacob had he not felt so tranquil, so removed from the present.

There was a slight shift in perception, a lifting sensation. Jacob realized his eyes had been closed and snapped them open. Everything was as it had been a moment before— Chester still played, his whole body working to the rhythm, Morag still sat withdrawn—only now the color had gone out of the room. It was the old familiar blueness of his visions. But the visions had always brought glimpses of the possible future, or of a present somewhere else. As far as he could tell, he hadn't gone anywhere in time or place—it had remained one continuous stream. So why had the world gone blue?

A glimmer caught his eye. He turned toward the fire-place. The fire was gone, replaced by a tiny sphere of white light that hovered where the flames had curled a moment ago. He stared, transfixed, as the tiny orb, no bigger than his fist, began to grow and brighten.

He felt a sudden urge to investigate the burgeoning light and struggled to rise from his seat. But he was frozen, bound to the chair by a weakness in his limbs, a numbness he hadn't felt since Folgrin had come to him in his sleep and frozen him where he lay.

He glanced over at Morag. Her eyes were open now, staring at him with wonder and intensity.

"Go to the light," he heard her say, though her lips never moved.

*I can't*, he thought.

But he knew he must. So with every ounce of strength he had, he lifted an arm from his lap, then the other, used his arms to lift himself from his chair and begin the long walk toward the light that now seemed to fill the fireplace.

He dragged himself past Chester, who still sat oblivious to anything but his playing, and reached the hearth. Slowly, he raised a hand and stretched it toward the glow. He was but an inch away when the door opened with a bang, and a gust of wind ripped through the house, snuffing out the light. . . .

"Morag! Chester!"

Jacob opened his eyes and gasped. Chester had stopped playing, Morag had risen from her seat, and the light in the room had returned to normal. Both were staring at the young man in the open doorway struggling to catch his breath.

"What's wrong, Connor?" Chester asked.

"Father just came back from hunting. He and my uncles were near the ship that crashed," the young man said.

His eyes turned to Jacob.

"They found someone. Another survivor."

# CHAPTER TWELVE

The headlights on the floater were so dim, Jacob could hardly make out where they were going as Chester guided them through the mist and between the trees, trailing the quickly fading light of Connor's floatbike up ahead. From the black sky a light rain now fell. Jacob kept feeling its drops as the canopy's force field blinked on and off, the motor throbbing with each fluctuation of power.

Sitting in the backseat behind Morag and Chester, Jacob tried to steady his nerves. He'd been in a daze for the first few minutes of the trip, still caught in the aborted vision, still entranced by the glow of the growing orb.

But his stupor soon dissolved as the significance of Connor's words began sinking in. *A survivor.* His first thought was a member of the crew, but it was quickly replaced by another, more terrible notion. What if it was Folgrin now waiting at the neighbor's farm? What would his new friends do when the pale-haired man insisted on taking Jacob with him to Teiresias? Jacob couldn't figure out what Folgrin's interest in him was, but he could guess. And now he was going to be stuck alone with the man, without even the crew to protect him.

Morag glanced back with a strange look and caught his eye. She turned, reached out, and took his hand.

"You're shaking, boy," she cried out. "What's wrong?"

When Jacob didn't reply, Chester spoke up.

"The survivor," he said. Morag looked back at Jacob and raised her eyes.

"You're afraid of who it might be," she said. "Don't worry, Jacob. No harm will come to you if you're with us. We may be old, but Connor's family is tough."

Jacob nodded and mustered what smile he could.

Soon they pulled up before a large wooden house, weathered but square and solid like the barn beside it, its shingles darkened with rain. There were several vehicles nearly as beat-up as Chester and Morag's parked in the yard, including Connor's floatbike and a wheeled cruiser like Xander's.

Connor's father, an enormous, bearded man named Sol, came out onto the covered porch as they emerged from the floater and hurried through the rain. Chester guided Morag by the arm across the muddy ground, while Jacob carried her supplies.

"Thanks for coming, Morag," Sol said in a booming voice. "Heard you'd already helped one, figured you wouldn't mind treating another."

"Not at all," she said as they mounted the steps, passed through a doorway, and stepped into the kitchen. "Sol, this is our friend, Jacob."

Sol reached out and took Jacob's hand. "Welcome," he said.

"Thanks," Jacob answered, trying not to wince at the crushing force of Sol's handshake.

"What's the patient's state?" Morag asked, taking the bag from Jacob.

Sol shrugged. "Not great. Looks like he's been shot. Can't say how bad. He was pretty delirious when I found him. By the time we got him back, he was out. Still is."

"Let's have a look," she said. She started following Sol into the next room, then paused.

"Coming?" she said to Jacob.

Jacob hesitated as everyone turned to face him. Seeing the look of expectation on Morag's face, he shook himself and followed, his heart racing as they passed into the darkened room.

A small lantern cast its feeble light from across the room, while on an old couch the man lay asleep.

"Bennet!" Jacob cried in relief.

At his words, the captain stirred for a moment but didn't open his eyes.

"Not the one you were afraid of, I take it," Morag murmured.

"No," Jacob said. "That's Captain Bennet. The *Odessa* was his ship."

"Poor thing." She went over to the man and, pushing aside the blood-encrusted strands of hair, put her hands on his face, then felt down along his body, pausing over his abdomen where the clothes were stained red. She pulled aside his torn shirt and examined him carefully.

"He's lucky," she said. "The bullet passed right through him. He's got a nasty infection, though, and some plasma burns to boot. But he'll be all right."

She opened her case and began pulling out supplies—bandages, an IV, hypodermic sprays, and med patches. After nearly two days in Morag's antiquated home, Jacob found it strange to see her working with such equipment. She lit a foul-smelling candle, then set to work.

"Best get some sleep, young one," she said, observing the look on Jacob's face as she set up the IV. "I'll be tending to him for a while."

Jacob nodded. Seeing Bennet's pale face and wounds had suddenly made *him* feel pale and woozy, though he couldn't understand why. He'd seen far worse just yesterday. *Maybe that's why,* he thought. Maybe yesterday's trauma still had its hold on him. Maybe it always would. Regardless, he was grateful to leave the room.

He went back out into the kitchen where Chester and Sol sat quietly talking over a cup of coffee.

"Can I get you something?" Sol asked.

"No, thanks," Jacob said. "I just want some fresh air."

He pushed aside the screen door and went out to the edge of the porch. The rain had stopped and the sky was clearing fast. He watched the clouds move aside, hurried by a breeze that rustled the grasses and trees. Listening to the wind's sound, feeling it as it blew cool against his face, he would have almost thought he were back on Nova Campi if it weren't for one thing.

The sky was different. For a long time, he gazed up into the dark night absent of any moon and marveled at the alien patterns of the stars. He wondered if they were the same ones he'd seen on Nova Campi, made new by the changed perspective of a separate world, or if they were entirely different stars.

Suddenly sleepy, he lay down on the porch swing beside him and let himself rock back and forth to the chains' creaking rhythm, his eyes still on the stars. Maybe Xander was out there right now, looking up at those same points of light from his deck.

*Everything changes. Nothing stays the same.*

They were among the last words Xander had spoken to him less than two weeks ago. A wave of bitterness washed over him now as he struggled to make sense of them in the wake of everything that had happened. Were they words of warning? Of consolation? An expression of plain truth and nothing more? All Jacob really wanted to know was where he belonged, what he was meant to do, to be. But if Xander's words were true, then how could he ever find out for sure?

*Everything changes. Nothing stays the same.*

Over and over the words ran through his mind, as if by repeating them he could make them less terrifying, less sorrowful, somehow turn them into a comfort to warm him in the cold darkness of the night.

The red light of morning was coming into the sky when Jacob stirred at Chester's prodding. He sat up slowly, pulling off the wool blanket with which someone had covered him in the night.

"The captain's beginning to stir. We thought you might want to be present."

Jacob rose and followed Chester inside and into the parlor where Bennet lay. Seeing the captain bandaged and no longer pale, Jacob felt a wave of relief. The man looked battered and scraped now, his clothes dirty as Jacob's had been after the crash, but he still seemed commanding even in sleep, the diamond stud in his ear catching the light like one last morning star. Bennet would know what to do.

"He responded well to the antibiotics," Morag said, rising from a chair in the corner, her face tired. "He'll be good as new soon enough. Speaking of which, how's the arm?"

Jacob glanced down at the plasticast. The swelling seemed to have nearly disappeared and he was able to wiggle his fingers without pain.

"Feels okay."

"Good," she said, taking a sip from the steaming mug in her hand. "With the medicine in that plasticast, even bad breaks heal quickly. Another day or two, you can remove it.

142

Your arm will be even stronger than before."

A few minutes later, Bennet opened his eyes and sat up with a wince. Seeing Jacob, he gave a quick look of surprise before managing a weak smile.

"You," he said, pushing his hair back behind his shoulders. "You're alive."

Jacob smiled back. "So are you," he replied. "Thanks to Morag, here."

Bennet turned to the old woman. "I appreciate it."

"My pleasure," she said. "You're lucky Sol and his brothers found you when they did. The bacteria on this world works quickly. A few more hours would have done it."

"I've always been lucky," Bennet quipped, but the smile he flashed died almost as soon as it appeared. He glanced over at Jacob. "Who else is with you?"

Jacob shook his head. The captain looked away and cursed. For a minute he just sat there, turning back only when Chester came into the room with breakfast.

"Take me to the *Odessa*," Bennet said as the old man set the tray down on a small table beside him.

"Nonsense," Morag broke in, her voice firm. "You're still weak. A day or two of rest is what you need. Then Chester can take you back to the wreck or to the port or wherever you want to go."

But Bennet only shook his head and, reaching out, grabbed hold of Chester's arm.

"Please," he said, his voice no longer sharp in command but full of pain. "Please take me to my ship."

Jacob was about to follow Chester and Bennet—now dressed in a set of spare clothes—down off the porch steps when Morag stopped him.

143

"Good-bye, Jacob," she said.

Hearing the finality in her voice, he turned to her in amazement.

"What do you mean?" he replied. "We'll be back in an hour or two."

She shook her head, glancing past him at Bennet climbing gingerly into the back of the floater.

"I know his kind," she said. "He won't return here. He'll be wanting to get to port, to get back out into space. To move on."

"Oh," he whispered, following her gaze to where the captain now sat, head in hand, wounded. Jacob turned back to see her watching him now, her face suddenly serious.

"You could always stay here on Maker's Drift. Stay with me and Chester."

He hesitated, glancing back at Bennet. "I'm sorry," he said at last. "I can't."

She smiled and took both his hands. Her eyes sparkled once more as they had back at the cottage.

"I know, dear. Your quest calls you. It's really just beginning. And your fate is with him," she said, nodding toward Bennet. "The bones told me so before. But I wanted to make the offer, anyway. A selfish hope."

"Thank you, Morag," Jacob murmured.

"Don't look so glum," she said. "You have much excitement ahead of you."

"I'll miss you," he said. It had been less than two days, but somehow it felt much longer.

She leaned over and kissed his forehead, then rubbed the spot with both thumbs, her eyes closed. He could hear her murmuring words.

"Too bad I didn't bring my bones," she said, opening her eyes and smiling. "I could tell you how this all turns out."

Jacob laughed. "Why spoil the fun?"

He gave her a quick embrace. But when he turned to leave, she stopped him one last time.

"Remember the light you saw in the fireplace?" she said, drawing him close. "When Chester played. Remember?"

Jacob's eyes widened. "You saw it too?"

Morag nodded. "Keep looking for it. It's important, I think."

"I will."

"Good, then." She stepped away from him with a smile, pausing in the kitchen doorway.

"I'll see you in my dreams," she said, then disappeared.

After two days, the wreck of the *Odessa* still smoldered. They could see it as they drew near, a sickly column of black smoke rising above the trees.

Chester brought them down at the edge of the clearing, not far from where Jacob had escaped into the woods, and then the three of them proceeded with heavy steps, letting the captain take the lead.

They came across Silas first. Jacob stood by as Bennet stared quietly down at his brother, frozen in place. The body had changed in the two days since he'd last seen it—it had stiffened, looked somehow less human, less like Silas, and therefore somehow less horrible. Only one thing stood out.

"Bastards wouldn't even let him keep his arm," was all Bennet said before moving on. Sure enough, the first mate's synthetic forearm had been removed at the elbow.

Jacob glanced around, compelled to look for the severed hand he'd brushed away in horror those last moments before fleeing. To his relief it was nowhere to be seen.

For the next twenty minutes, he and Chester followed

Bennet numbly as they picked through the wreckage, listening to the captain's swears grow louder with the discovery of each new body. Soon all eight of the crew had been accounted for. Only one person remained missing.

"Where's Folgrin?" Jacob wondered aloud.

"Maybe he survived," Bennet said. "Wouldn't put it past the weasel."

Glancing around, Jacob was stricken by a momentary fear that the man was watching from somewhere nearby. The panic quickly passed. If Folgrin had survived, he would have likely been found by Sol and his brothers or else was long gone by now. But the idea that the man with the hollow eyes was still out there somewhere, possibly alive, gave Jacob chills.

Chester remained mostly silent during the affair, offering a few words of solace as he helped the weakened Bennet gather the bodies together in a section of torn-up earth. Limited by his arm, Jacob did as much as he could, fighting back his fear and revulsion each time he helped lift another body.

Two of the corpses were unfamiliar. Jacob pulled away at the sight of the plasma burn holes riddling the pirates' torsos.

"Managed to get one before they overwhelmed us," Bennet said, staring down at the bodies. "Branson got the other, I think."

"Should we bring them over with the others?" Chester asked.

Bennet kicked one of the pirates in disgust.

"Leave them for the raptors. Or whatever it is they have on this hole of a world."

Soon the crew was all laid out, side by side in the trench. Chester retrieved a pair of shovels, and he and the captain set to work. Before long a mound of dirt and rock lay over the

146

bodies. They covered it with a few torn pieces of hull to keep the scavengers away.

"Not great, but it'll have to do," Bennet said. "I've known men who've had worse."

When it was done, Chester sang a quiet song of farewell before the mound, then withdrew to the floater. Bennet sat down before the pile in exhaustion, while Jacob stood beside him. For a long time, neither of them spoke.

"I'm sorry about your brother," Jacob said at last.

Bennet nodded. "He always had my back."

"I'll miss Dobson," Jacob said. "If it wasn't for him, I might not have made it."

"He was a good man too. All of them were. Most of the time, anyway," Bennet added with a bitter smile.

Finally the captain rose and began combing through the wreckage once more, looking for whatever was left of value. Jacob could see that the pirates had done the same. Most of the cargo that had spilled out over the crash site was gone.

While Bennet poked around, a sudden thought occurred to Jacob.

"I'll be right back," he called to Chester, then slipped through the trees in the direction he'd first come upon the wreck. Soon, he spotted the escape pod, still in the tiny clearing with its door open, and searched it, hoping the pirates hadn't gotten to it first. To his relief, he found his pack still inside, its contents undamaged. He shouldered the bag and headed back to the wreck.

Bennet was waiting by the burial mound, a pack of his own hanging from his shoulders stuffed with what he'd managed to gather from his quarters.

"So what now?" Jacob asked.

Bennet turned to him with an intent look, as if he were

147

suddenly seeing Jacob for the first time.

"The old man, here, will take us to the port."

"Do you think we'll be able to find another ship?"

Bennet snorted. "To buy? Not likely, even if I had any money."

"But what about what I gave you? And Folgrin? I thought it was a lot."

"It was."

"So what happened to it?"

Bennet gestured at the wreckage all around them, his face darkening.

"It was all invested—the cargo, the ship, the supplies. Now everything's gone," he snapped. "Any more questions?"

"No," Jacob murmured, looking away.

Bennet sighed. "Look, don't worry about it. It was my job to get you to Teiresias, and that's what I'm going to do."

"Your job was to get Folgrin to Teiresias," Jacob shot back. "I was just along for the ride, remember?"

Bennet hesitated.

"Right," he said at last. He pushed past Jacob and headed for the floater, muttering under his breath. "You can come with me to one of the hub worlds, then," he called back. "From there you should be able to get to Teiresias. Easy."

*Easy,* Jacob thought, glancing back at the strewn pieces of ship as he followed behind. *Just like this was supposed to be.*

They climbed into the vehicle, Jacob in the front seat beside Chester, Bennet in the back. The floater groaned its way into the sky, just managing to clear the treetops, and pulled away. Jacob turned to see Bennet leaning over the backseat, chin resting on folded arms, watching as what was left of the *Odessa* disappeared from sight.

# PART FOUR
## Bennet

# CHAPTER THIRTEEN

The spaceport on Maker's Drift was as tiny and rundown as the ships it served. There were a few towers nearby, but their windows were mostly dark. The bright colors and sounds that flitted through Melville were missing here. Most of the action seemed focused on a handful of bars not far from the landing bays, filled with drunken spacers playing games or fighting one another, or else hunched drooling before loader screens, their passive faces bathed in the small screens' light. Jacob was suddenly very glad to have the captain close at hand as men of various stripes sent quizzical looks their way. He wondered if the pirates who had destroyed their ship were among the mangy crowd. If the captain thought so, he didn't seem to show any sign of it as he quietly asked around for the chance to get the two of them offworld.

For two days they slipped between the bars before an opportunity arrived in the form of the *Caber*. A rusty old tramp freighter, nearly half the size of the *Odessa*, the *Caber* worked a regular run ferrying supplies between Reynard, the closest of the populous planets on the border between the Core worlds and the Rim, and a host of smaller, more out-of-the-way stations, including Maker's Drift. Its captain, an old man named Krill with long white hair, had lost one of the crew—a man who served as both pilot and navigator—and was desperate for a replacement, having been stranded onworld for a week.

"How'd you lose him?" Bennet had asked.

"Just lost him," Krill muttered in exasperation. "Said he was going out for a drink first night we got here. Haven't seen him since. We need to leave this place—crew's getting antsy, and I don't want to lose any more of them to this snake pit. You can do the job, then?"

Bennet nodded. "Till we get to Reynard. You shouldn't have any trouble finding someone else there. But the boy comes with me. I'm training him, you see. He can help."

"Why not," Krill said. "Tell him not to breathe too much and you've got a deal."

To Jacob's surprise, Bennet never mentioned the *Odessa*.

The *Caber* was cramped and smelly, and it creaked so loudly as it rose through the atmosphere that Jacob was afraid they were never going to make it to orbit. But before long they had broken through, and Jacob was just happy to be back in space and under way.

Besides Krill, there were only two other men and a woman on board. Logan and Ben were both equally disheveled and a bit lazy, while Willow—who served as the ship's engineer—seemed to prefer the company of the machinery to any of her shipmates. They were all friendly enough but much quieter than the crew Jacob had traveled with on the *Odessa*. They all bunked together, including Bennet and Jacob, in a single cabin. Only the captain had his own quarters. Though Bennet didn't complain, he was somber and withdrawn the first few nights, so that the others soon left him alone.

The *Caber's* engines were so old and in such disrepair that, despite the engineer's best efforts to coax as much power as she could from them, it ended up taking them nearly a month to reach Reynard.

It was one of the longest months of Jacob's life—hours spent in a quiet, dark room trying to gaze out a tiny porthole so dirty the stars were nothing but blobs and blurs of dim light. So many times he wished he could reach through the walls of the ship and just wash the window.

What made it bearable was Bennet. After a week of brooding, the captain began to emerge. One morning, Jacob looked up from his bed to see the man standing over him.

"Hey," Bennet said. "I need you on the bridge."

Jacob had only been to the bridge twice. A low-ceilinged room illuminated by a few holographic control panels, it was no bigger than the crew cabin. Maybe smaller—there were only three seats jammed in between the dated banks of equipment.

"What's wrong?" Jacob asked, sitting up. A creaking had developed in what he guessed was the cargo hull beneath the main deck. The noise had woken him from sleep several hours earlier, and he'd been listening to it with growing alarm all morning.

"Nothing's wrong," the captain barked. "You agreed to help out, and I'm keeping you to the bargain. You do remember our agreement, don't you?"

"Of course!" Jacob replied.

"Good, then," the captain said, grinning as Jacob jumped up from his bunk. "Time for you to start your lessons."

"You mean you're really going to teach me to fly a ship?"

Bennet laughed. "Not exactly. We're going to start you off slow. You need to learn to find your way around out here before you bother trying to go anywhere."

Krill glanced over from his chair as they came onto the bridge, then stood up with a grunt.

"You've got the bridge, Bennet," he mumbled. "I'm going for a nap."

He passed by them and left through the still-open door.

Bennet snorted. "Now I know why he was so desperate for a new pilot. Saves him from having to actually run the ship."

"Does he do that a lot?" Jacob asked.

"More than he should. Even this far out," Bennet said with a shrug. "I think the guy's a loader. Saw a screen in his quarters not long after we came on board. Has a little bit of that dead look at times too. Poor guy. Probably saw something on a load-trip years ago and has been looking for it ever since. That's usually how it goes."

Jacob remembered the ghostly faces of the people lost in the glowing loader screens in Raker's bar back in Melville, remembered how Xander had shivered, refusing to tell him about the one time he'd tried it.

Bennet collapsed into Krill's worn seat with a sigh.

"Then again," he said, glancing around, "if I had to captain a ship like this, I'd probably be a loader too."

"It's not that bad," Jacob murmured, still standing by the doorway.

The captain nodded. "True enough. Just spoiled by the *Odessa*."

"How long did you own the *Odessa*?"

"Five years. And I was her first mate for another five years before that. 'Course I didn't own her alone. Silas and I bought her together from the previous captain. The old guy was ready to get out of space and get his feet on the ground. We'd both been with him for a while, and he liked us. Gave us a good deal. Almost had the thing paid off."

"How come you ended up being captain?"

Bennet shrugged. "Silas didn't want to be. I did. It's just the way it worked out."

He paused for a long time. "It's just the way it worked out," he said once more, then shook his head. "Have a seat."

He gestured to one of the two chairs in the front. Jacob sat down. Bennet pulled the other chair up beside him, and for the next two hours showed Jacob the navigation computer, demonstrated how to chart a course through the ever-shifting maze of stars. To both their surprise, Jacob caught on quickly. The maps, the numbers, the pathways—it all made sense, as if he could visualize the pattern in the air before him and feel his way around and in between the charts.

"A natural," Bennet said, nodding his admiration. "Takes some guys weeks just to pick up the basics like that."

After that, Jacob spent more time on the bridge, learning little bits here and there. He liked it because it helped break up the lonely monotony of life on board a ship where there weren't even light changes to indicate the passage of time, and because, for the first time in a long time, he actually felt useful. Most of all, he liked it because he got to spend time with the captain.

Pleased by Jacob's quick progress, Bennet seemed to open up more with every passing day. For hours, with the rest of the crew withdrawn to their quarters, the captain would entertain Jacob on the bridge with stories of tight escapes, close calls, and rich payoffs. He would tell jokes and describe all the different places he had been. Jacob remembered Bennet saying he didn't like kids, but it suddenly didn't seem

155

to matter. In fact, what Jacob liked most was that the captain didn't treat him like a kid at all—at least not on the bridge. No one—not even Xander—had ever done that before.

It was strange. In some ways, the captain reminded Jacob of Xander. Both were strong, with that sense of confidence that he always felt he lacked. They made everything look easy, everything seem simple. But in other ways they were strikingly different. As much as Jacob loved Xander, there was always an edge to the man, moments when Jacob felt like he had to tread carefully or risk waking the demons sleeping beneath the surface, though knowing they existed—and knowing that, in his own way, he helped keep them at bay— made him feel as close to the former soldier as he ever had to his own parents. Maybe even closer.

Bennet was easier: less moody, less prone to anger, despite the occasional burst of sarcasm. Still, it wasn't always easy. During Jacob's time on the *Odessa*, Bennet had always seemed unflappable, a man of drive and purpose. But the crash had diminished him: Some days found him listless, indifferent, as if he hardly noticed the world around him. At times like this, Jacob almost missed Xander's moody temper—it was better than this dispiriting apathy. Only on the bridge was Jacob sure to find the old Bennet, yet another reason why he looked forward to spending time there.

There was one thing, though, that puzzled him about the man.

"You've never asked me about why I'm trying to get to Teiresias. Or where I came from. Any of it," he said one afternoon. They were two days away from breaking through to otherspace and had finished a systems check in anticipation of the jump.

156

Bennet shrugged, quiet.

"You have to learn how to mind your own business in my line of work," he said at last. "Besides, what do I care?"

"I just thought you'd want to know," Jacob murmured, rubbing his arm as he turned back to the navigation panel. He'd removed the cast not long after leaving Maker's Drift, and though the bone had healed, it was still tender. "You've told me all kinds of things about your life."

Bennet sighed. "Okay, then. What's your story?"

"If you're not interested . . ."

"No, really. It's not like we don't have the time. Tell me all about Jacob . . ."

"Manford. Jacob Manford."

"Right, Jacob Manford. Go ahead, then," he said.

Jacob could hear the sarcasm in his voice, the thinly veiled resistance. It reminded him of being on the *Odessa* all over again. He suddenly wanted to leave the bridge, but that would only make things worse. Realizing there was no option now but to follow through, he began his story.

He told him about Harmony, about being a Blinder, about his sudden change and escape. He told him about meeting Xander and rescuing Delaney from Mixel, about the time they'd spent as a family. He even told the captain about his visions, about the strange powers that had emerged, and about the group of Seers he hoped would soon help him understand what he had become. After the man's strange reluctance, he wasn't sure he should. Even as he was telling Bennet, he wondered if it was a mistake. But he wanted to trust the man. Something inside even told him he had to, that it was vital.

"Quite a story," Bennet murmured, when he'd finished.

157

He seemed somber suddenly, distant. "A Blinder, huh? Never thought I'd meet one of those. And magic visions, no less."

"You don't believe me?" Jacob asked.

"Why not? I've heard stranger tales, I guess," he said at last, shrugging. "So how about using that magic vision of yours to see if you can find a way to get us to Reynard more quickly?"

"I'm trying," Jacob said, forcing a smile. "It just doesn't work. Not when I want it to, anyway. That's why I want to get to Teiresias. So the others can teach me how."

There was a long pause as Bennet looked down at the control panels. He flipped a few switches.

"So these people are friends of yours, huh?" he said at last.

"Well," Jacob said, hesitating, "I've never really met them, actually."

"Oh. But you know their names, right? You know how to find them?"

Again, Jacob hesitated. "No," he said, looking away.

Bennet snorted. "So how do you know you can trust them?" the captain asked. "How do you know they're even good people? What if they just want to use you?"

Jacob laughed, his embarrassment vanishing with the question. "Because I know they don't, that's all. They're waiting for me, waiting to help me. They're good people. I can feel it. The same way I could with you when we first met. I knew I was supposed to go with you, that you were going to help me. And here we are."

"Yeah, here we are," Bennet whispered, smoothing his beard.

They were quiet for a long time after that.

"Tomorrow's my birthday," Jacob suddenly said, more to himself than the captain. The realization had come upon him in the silence, and it startled him to think he'd almost forgotten. All growing up, he'd looked forward to his birthday, anyone's birthday. In Harmony, it was one of the only days when an individual was made to feel special.

"How old?"

"Fifteen."

"Fifteen, eh?" Bennet replied. He seemed to have regained his usual good spirits. "A good age to be for the first birthday out on your own."

"I hadn't thought of it that way," Jacob said. "Last year, I celebrated with Xander and Delaney. I wonder if they'll remember."

"Sure they will. That guy cares about you—I could tell by the way he threatened to kill me if I let anything happen to you."

Jacob laughed. "He certainly is protective. But it's important to have people watching out for you, right?"

Bennet paled, his smile faded. But only for a moment.

"I need a break," he said, standing up and stretching. "Time to get those lazy bums back here. It's their ship, after all."

Jacob watched him leave without a word, trying to make sense of the sudden change of mood. Then he remembered what Bennet had said after they'd buried his brother—that Silas had always had his back. His stomach sank. How could he have been so thoughtless?

# CHAPTER FOURTEEN

The following day, Jacob was in the navigator's chair, staring at the charting screen with its patterns of stars and byways, when Bennet told him to close his eyes. Before Jacob could ask why, the door swished open and the captain left.

The bridge faded to darkness as his lids lowered, but the points of light remained, floating before him.

*I've been looking at the stars too long,* he thought as he waited for Bennet to return. Between gazing out the dirty porthole and studying star charts, it seemed that they'd begun to follow him whenever he closed his eyes. Worst of all, he found himself constantly analyzing them, picking endless paths through the mazes with his thoughts the way he'd seen Xander thread needles whenever he needed to mend a piece of torn cloth. Only, a hundred needles needed to be threaded in succession through his star-filled mind.

He had learned a great deal over the last few weeks, and as much as he enjoyed it, it would be a relief to break through tomorrow morning. After that, it was only a couple days of slowdown. Then they would reach Reynard, and maybe his mind would give him a break.

The door swished open behind him.

"You haven't opened your eyes yet, have you?" Bennet asked.

"No," Jacob said. Was this some sort of test?

"Good," the captain said.

Jacob listened as the captain walked over and placed something on the workstation before him.

"Okay, open your eyes," Bennet said.

A small round cake lay before him on the panel, a flashlight sticking up from its center. The flashlight was on, its beam casting a glow onto the ceiling of the gloomy bridge.

"What's this?" Jacob asked, his face reddening.

"It's a birthday cake," Bennet offered. "Don't tell me you've never had a birthday cake before."

"Not really," Jacob said. "My mother usually made me pancakes for breakfast."

"Well, that's something, I guess. It's an old tradition where I come from. Normally they light a bunch of candles on the cake, then you blow them out and make a wish. Didn't have any candles on board—the flashlight will have to do."

"Do I still get to make a wish?"

"Can if you want. Never hurts," Bennet said. He looked around the worn bridge with a grin. "You might want to wish that we make it through otherspace in one piece," he added.

Considering the disquieting rise of creaking and groaning Jacob had been hearing all day as they crept ever closer to the necessary speed, it didn't seem like a bad idea. But in the end, it wasn't what he wished for.

*Please let me find them,* he thought, closing his eyes. *Let me find my place.*

"Okay," he said, glancing over at the captain.

Bennet nodded, switching off the flashlight and plucking it from the tiny chocolate cake—one of the few palatable items to be found in the ship's meager kitchenette.

He cut the cake in two, and for a few minutes they ate in silence.

"Engine rat," Bennet said at last.

"What do you mean?" Jacob asked.

"That's what I was doing when I was fifteen. I was an engine rat. That's what they used to call us—skinny little guys who could creep way into the engines when things needed fixing."

Jacob tried imagining Bennet as a teenager, covered in grease.

"So you were in space, too?"

"Yeah," Bennet said, laughing. "On a ship not much different than this. Maybe a little bigger. I'd run away from home the year before. Didn't get along with my father, you see. My parents had moved to Alterra when I was seven. It was just a frontier world back then, sort of like Nova Campi, and by the time I was around your age, I wanted nothing to do with it or them. I was gone for three years. When I came back, they were happy enough to see me—even my dad. They wanted me to stay. But it was too late. I'd already gotten my space legs. Some people are just born to it. So I headed out again. This time, Silas came with me."

He paused. A bitter smile crept across his face.

"And now, here I am. Right back where I started."

"We'll be on Reynard before you know it," Jacob said.

Bennet nodded, wiping the crumbs from his hands. There was a long pause.

"Thanks," Jacob said at last. "For the cake. For everything."

The captain shrugged. "Why not," he said with a smile. "So what did you wish for?"

Jacob paused. "Am I supposed to tell you?"

"Technically, no. But let me guess," Bennet quipped. "You wished to make it to Teiresias and find your friends."

Jacob reddened. "Well, that is my goal."

"Hey," Bennet said, "at least you have a goal, a purpose. That's better than me. I don't know what mine is anymore. Guess I need to find one."

"I'm really not that different from you," Jacob offered. "We've both been cut off from our old lives. Besides, I might know what I'm looking for, but I don't know how it's going to turn out. I just have to hope. You do too."

"Maybe you're right," Bennet said, his voice suddenly quiet. He shook his head. "I just want to go back. That would be my wish. Back to the way things were before."

"I don't," Jacob murmured. "Besides, you can't go back, no matter how hard you wish. No one can. Even I know that."

Bennet looked down at the controls. His earring flashed against the light of the navigation screen.

"Where did you get that?" Jacob asked, pointing to the man's ear.

"This?" the captain said. He reached up, removed the diamond stud, then handed it to Jacob. "Won it in a poker match a few years back. Got in on a big game—bigger than I had any business being in. Came down to me and some trader from Albion. He put this up; I put up the *Odessa*. Had nothing in my hand either, but I needed to sell the bluff."

"You bet your whole ship for a piece of jewelry?" Jacob cried.

"Well, it's not just any old piece of jewelry," the captain said, taking the stud from Jacob and putting it back in place. "It's actually a pretty sophisticated cloaker. Sound, image, movement, heat—it'll fool just about any kind of surveillance you can find. Renders anything within ten feet invisible to scanners. It's got a few other little tricks too. The thing's actually illegal in most systems. Of course, a lot of things are illegal in my trade, which is exactly why the little bugger's so useful."

Jacob remembered the feeling that had come over him the first time he'd met the captain—the feeling of safety, of relief, as if all the hidden eyes watching him had suddenly been closed. That was back in Melville, when Mixel probably was following his every move.

"Of course," the captain continued, "I wouldn't have really turned over the *Odessa*."

"Wouldn't you have *had* to?"

Bennet winked. "I had options. Contingencies. Always have a backup plan, Jacob. As soon as you think there's only one solution, one possible outcome, that's when you're in trouble. I always have another plan."

He glanced at Jacob for a second, then stared back down at the empty plate.

The door swished open, and Krill shuffled onto the bridge. He looked sleepy, though after Bennet's earlier comment, Jacob wondered if he'd just come from the load-screen. He dropped into his chair with a grunt, giving a quick scratch to his whiskers.

"Twelve hours to go. Then we make the break. You boys ready?"

"Aye, Captain," Bennet replied, looking over to Jacob with a wink.

"I'll bet you are," the old man rasped. "I don't blame you. Always good to get back to civilization, get your feet on the ground. Wish I could get back to stay."

"Why don't you?" Bennet asked.

"I don't know," Krill murmured, gazing around the bridge as if waking from a dream. "If there was a reason, I've forgotten what it is."

It took Jacob a long time to fall asleep. It was the ship that did it—the vibrations of the hull, the screaming of the engines as they made the final push, creeping their way hour by hour to the point where the *Caber* would have enough speed to travel the necessary distance through otherspace to put them in reach of Reynard.

It didn't seem to bother the captain. Though Bennet had come to bed long after Jacob had settled into his bunk, the man fell asleep right away, his light snoring barely audible above the noise.

"This isn't some padded luxury liner," Ben said when Jacob worried aloud after dinner.

"Don't worry," Logan, the other crewman, added. "Sometimes she's even louder. But we always come out the other side."

Jacob tried holding on to those reassurances as he finally slipped into sleep. But even when he did fall asleep, a part of him seemed to remain conscious, still listening to the engines, waiting for the cracking of the hull, the great explosion of noise that would be the final sound he heard.

At some point he realized he was dreaming. He was perched on top of the *Caber*, riding through space as he had done before in his dreams, this time sitting with his legs folded as the stars flew by. The ship was passing a nearby sun. Jacob could feel its heat along his left side, nearly burning his skin, as the darkness of space froze him from the right.

He had a guitar in his hands—it was the old instrument his mother had kept in the corner beside the piano. From

165

time to time he used to pick it up, strum it back into tune, and work out simple songs. Now, holding it, he found himself unable to play. All he could do was turn one of the tuning keys tighter, plucking the string as he turned, and listen to the pitch rise higher and higher as the tension on the string mounted. He knew he should back off, but his left hand wouldn't stop turning.

*Snap!*

The string broke with a sour twang. He set to work on the next one, slowly cranking it higher. It too broke. One after another he went through the strings until he was left with the smallest. He tuned it higher, higher, higher. His finger plucked the string, now tuned to a note so high it could barely be heard. For a long time he plucked the note, listening to its pitch as it drifted out into space. His left hand trembling, he closed his eyes and gave one last turn, crying out as the final string popped and fell away.

"Congratulations," a voice said.

Jacob opened his eyes to see Bennet standing before him, the bright light of the sun shining on one side of him, casting his other half in black shadow.

"But I broke it," Jacob whispered.

"You certainly did," the captain replied. Smiling, he took the diamond from his ear, reached down, and placed it in Jacob's hand.

Jacob stared at the jewel glinting in his palm. Suddenly, all was quiet. The engines' cry was cut off. The silence was as deep as the darkness of space. All he wanted to do was watch the diamond sparkle, but he knew he should thank Bennet.

He looked up. The captain was gone. Someone else was in his place.

Like Bennet, Folgrin was cast half in shadow, as if a line

had been drawn down the middle and his left side had been cut away. The remaining half was illuminated so that even his black suit seemed to glow with a brilliant sheen.

He gave Jacob the usual malicious grin, then reached down and took the diamond from where it rested in Jacob's palm. Try as he might, Jacob found himself unable to move. The silence had frozen him.

He watched in horror as Folgrin lifted the diamond and placed it where his left eye—now concealed in shadow—would normally be. It flared, a point of brightness in the dark that grew until it suddenly exploded, bathing Jacob in fire and light.

"Hey!"

Jacob's eyes snapped open. Bennet was standing over him, shaking him gently.

"Everything okay?" Jacob said, raising his voice to be heard above the engines. He pushed his blanket aside and sat up.

"I was going to ask you the same thing," the captain shouted back. Jacob could see the worry on his face. "Looked like you were having a nightmare."

"I'm fine," Jacob replied.

"Good. We're a few minutes from breaking."

"Already?"

Bennet shrugged. "I let you sleep in. You seemed pretty agitated last night. Figured you could use the rest."

Jacob nodded, trying to shake off both the dream and the sleep still wrapped around it.

"Krill wants me on the bridge with the others," the captain said. He hesitated. "It's going to be a little crowded there."

167

"I'll stay here," Jacob said.

"Okay," Bennet said. He gave a quick grin. "See you on the other side."

He waved, then left the cabin. A few minutes later, the ship's lights went red, just as they had on the *Odessa*.

This time, Jacob wasn't in a cushioned chair, nor did he have a large wall monitor to show him what lay before them.

But it didn't matter. Lying on his bunk, he could feel the wave of energy cross over him as the ship's drive initiated the jump, could feel the tunnel of light overtake him as the ship broke through to otherspace. He even thought he could hear the ghostly chorus of sound for the briefest moment, as he had the last time he'd entered otherspace on board the *Odessa*, but against the ship's roar he couldn't be sure.

This time there was only a brief moment of pain. He looked over at the dingy porthole. Sure enough, it was a bright disk suspended in the shadowy red half-light. As before, the silence was incredible. For a moment, Jacob pan-icked—the utter calm conjured the final moments of the nightmare he'd only just left. But as the pain moved quickly from his eyes to the back of his brain and then dissipated, he relaxed, luxuriating in the quiet.

He walked over to the outer wall of the cabin and pressed his palm against the porthole, spreading his fingers out so that the light shone bright between them. Jacob felt as if, with one little push, his hand could pass through into the dazzling stream beyond.

He turned and left the cabin, walked down the corridor—the light still streaming all about him—and passed onto the bridge. Like he'd seen on the *Odessa*, the crew of the *Caber* sat frozen, Bennet among them, some gazing ahead, others locked in a downward stare, their arms suspended in various positions. Once again, he was alone. But for some reason, it didn't bother him the way it had so many times in the past. He felt safe, wrapped in the light. He returned to the cabin and settled down before the window, wondering how long the silent stillness would last.

Looking through the porthole, he realized that, with concentration, he could begin to distinguish dark flecks against the light, just as he had the first time he was in otherspace. The more he concentrated, the more texture he began to see, as if the brightness beyond the walls of the ship was just a river of stars rushing by and everything was slowing down. All he had to do was work a little harder and he could make the river slow down even more, perhaps even stop.

And what would happen then? He suddenly wasn't sure he wanted to find out. He let go, and once more the tunnel reverted to a single sheet of light.

Lying back on his bunk, he shut his eyes and let himself fall into the sensation of movement. A tired calm washed over him now, a spent feeling as darkness replaced the light beyond his closed eyelids. But into this darkness the stars rose once again. It was as if he were gazing at one of the ship's navigation charts. Strangest of all was the sense that he knew exactly where he was amid the three-dimensional chart, where the tunnel was taking him, that he only had to reach out and pluck the distant point of light, no bigger than a grain of sand, and he would be there.

# CHAPTER FIFTEEN

It was Delaney's eyes that saved them.

After landing at one of the spaceports on Reynard, they quickly parted company with the *Caber*. Looking back at the quiet gaze of Captain Krill as they walked away, Jacob tried to figure out if it was a look of sadness that they were leaving, or one of jealousy that he wasn't going with them. Either way, he couldn't help but feel a pang of guilt.

Bennet, however, had no such compunctions.

"Thank God we made it off that heap," he said as they turned out of the hangar.

"It got us where we needed to go," Jacob said.

"True enough. But it took a lot longer than it should've. I just hope we're not too late."

"Too late for what?"

Bennet glanced down at Jacob. "Too late for you to find your friends. Didn't you say they were worried about being found?"

"I guess. I just want to get there," Jacob replied, trying to hide his disappointment. Pretty soon he'd be saying good-bye to the captain and heading back out to space, alone.

"Well, that's exactly what we're going to do."

Jacob froze. "You're coming with me?" he asked. His

170

heart started to race. "I thought this was it."

Bennet hesitated. "Listen," he said at last, staring down at the ground. "I've been thinking about it for the last couple days. I've got a buddy, a smuggler who works out of Teiresias. I was thinking about looking him up. I figure he can help me out till I get back on my feet. That is, if you don't mind the company." He glanced back up at Jacob.

"No," Jacob said, a wave of relief washing over him.

"Good, then," the captain said with a nod. "Just tell me you still have the rest of that money you were going to pay me back on Nova Campi."

Jacob smiled and pulled the golden card from inside his shirt. Through everything that had happened, he'd kept it safe.

A look of relief crossed Bennet's face.

"For once, my generosity has paid me back. That'll get us to Teiresias in style. After the month we've had, we deserve it. That okay?"

"It's okay," Jacob replied. After everything that had happened, he knew Delaney would want him to use the money this way.

Reynard dwarfed the more fertile Nova Campi, not only in size but in its population. Gazing around in awe, Jacob felt as if all of Melville could have fit in the starport alone—just one of three—in which Krill had left them. Stopping for lunch at a nearby tower, the two took a brief trip to the top to survey the landscape. The brightly lit domes, spires, and streets spread in all directions, beyond which Jacob could just make out the red sands of the planet's deserts.

"Where's the green?" Jacob asked. He found himself suddenly missing the plains of his homeworld. And in spite of the

171

textured beauty of the cityscape, even the dried grasses and bare trees of Maker's Drift would have been a welcome contrast to the sterile world with its dry, bitter atmosphere.

"Not much of anything on Reynard. But it's not what's on Reynard that's important, it's the wormholes above it. Ten in all, eight leading to within a day's travel of other systems, including Alpha Centauri—the largest and oldest system of them all, besides Earth's, of course. Reynard's one big hub, barren but breathable and convenient."

"I just can't imagine how many people must live here."

"Millions. But don't let it fool you—there's plenty of green space. See all those domes? Parks and gardens under most of them. Now, let's go find a ship."

They left the tower and took a train to the passenger port on the other side of the city. It took them an hour of waiting in line. Finally they were at the counter. Bennet booked passage for the two of them, then Jacob paid. It felt strange to hand his card over to the smiling woman behind the ticket counter. He'd never bought anything himself before, and he felt a momentary sense of panic as the sensor scanned his card—drawing down from the store of credit that had come from Delaney's eyes—as if he'd done something wrong, even though he knew he hadn't.

The stars outside the spaceliner shone bright as ever with the cabin lights turned down, but Jacob only half-watched them as they drifted by. Between the hours he'd spent studying charts on board the *Caber* and the weeks in space—with still three more days to go before they reached Teiresias—the view had become familiar to the point where Jacob now saw it in his sleep, dreaming almost every night of floating stars.

It was just as well. As it had on board the *Caber*, the vastness of what lay outside the large picture window made the smallness of the cabin more bearable. Or was it the other way around?

He glanced over at the twin bed across from him where the captain was sleeping. At least Jacob thought he was sleeping. Bennet seemed to drift in and out so often since leaving Reynard it was getting hard to tell. He hesitated, trying to decide whether to wake the captain or not. It was dinnertime and he was getting hungry. But he had promised Bennet he wouldn't leave the cabin without him.

"I know it's a big ship, but it's not like I can get lost or anything," he'd complained not long after they'd arrived on board the spaceliner a week ago.

"Never know who's on board a ship like this," the captain replied. "Plenty of sketchy characters heading this far out on the Rim. At least those in the lower decks. I don't want anything happening to you—not when we're this close."

Jacob had made the mistake of telling Bennet about the dark premonition he'd felt preparing to board the shuttle that would take them to the orbiting starliner. He couldn't help it—as they walked down the gate, the prickles along his spine had grown so intense he'd let go a cry without realizing it. Bennet almost had them turn around. But they'd already paid for the passage—if they didn't go, they'd be stranded.

Once on board, the wave had subsided, shrinking to little more than the usual gnawing of fear that had settled in two months ago back on Nova Campi. But Bennet had made him promise, and in the end, he'd relented.

In fact, though Jacob didn't want to admit it, he sensed what Bennet meant. Heading for their cabin after coming

173

aboard, Jacob had stuck close to the captain, gazing in wonder at the colorful crowds jostling and laughing as they all made their way through the wide, bright corridors of the *Justine*, a strange contrast to the dark, quiet, cramped interiors of the first two vessels he'd been on. Though there were plenty of men and women in expensive suits—likely BiCo executives returning from business offworld—they seemed outnumbered by the larger crowds of ordinary people, a mix of hopeful prospectors in search of the difficult but lucrative work in the planet's mines, lower-level BiCo employees, and even some tourists. There was an intense, almost festive energy among the crowd that both captivated him and made him wary.

Still, in spite of the restlessness that had begun to creep in over the last few days, the trip was far more comfortable than the month they'd just spent on board the *Caber*. In fact, the *Justine*—a mid-sized passenger liner—seemed luxurious in comparison. The cabin they'd booked was small but, like the rest of the ship, was quiet, clean, and odor free, with wooden furniture and soft fabric. Best of all, it was private. And now, here he was—nearly a week later—one day away from breaking through to otherspace for what would hopefully be the last time, at least for a while. But though his excitement grew each day he drew closer to his goal, he couldn't shake the uneasiness. It didn't make sense. How could something feel both right and wrong at the same time?

Maybe it was Bennet. The captain's usual good nature had begun deteriorating not long after coming aboard the *Justine*, while the moments of listlessness that Jacob had grown to dread back on the *Caber* began to multiply, threatening to overwhelm the shipless man now without even the menial bridge routine to keep him going. The rest of the time, he seemed nervous, distracted, joking less with Jacob than he had on board the *Caber*, as if he were somehow angry with him.

Yesterday had been the worst.

They'd gone to the dining hall that evening. Tired of room service, Jacob had convinced Bennet to spend some time away from the cabin. Getting out in the open—walking the concourses on the main decks, checking out the scattered groups of jugglers, comedians, and eclectic musicians, mingling among the bright crowds laughing and talking—seemed to help. Bennet's mood lightened for the first time in days.

They were at the table an hour later, eating their meal. Waiters darted back and forth amid the muted glow of the vast banquet hall, as the spotlight focused on a trio of girls singing from the stage up front. Bennet had grown somber again as his gaze shifted between the nearby tables and the passengers strolling by.

"What are you so nervous for?" Jacob finally asked.

Bennet managed a quick smile. "That feeling you got. You know, right before we came on board. Guess it's got me spooked."

"I told you, it's gone. As soon as we came on board, it went away," Jacob said. "Besides, I thought you didn't believe in all the visions, the premonitions."

"I didn't at first. Then it came back to me."

"What did?"

"On board the *Odessa*. On the approach to Maker's Drift, you burst into the cabin, told me I had to turn around. You knew we were going to be attacked, didn't you?"

Jacob looked down at his plate. "Not exactly."

"Yeah, well, whatever. You knew something was going to happen. So congratulations, you got to me."

"Well, stop it. You're making *me* nervous."

Bennet gave a quiet laugh. "Sorry."

Sensing his discomfort, Jacob tried changing the subject. "What do you think of the ship?"

Bennet shrugged. "Not bad. It's comfortable enough. Most of what you see is pretense, though—a veneer of class, and pretty thin at that. Strip it away, it's the same as any ship."

He paused, glancing up at the high, arched ceilings. Slowly revolving orbs meandered through the air above them, burning with a flickering glow, like giant versions of the candle flames Xander sometimes used to light the house at night.

"Still," he continued, "I used to think from time to time of giving up smuggling, taking a job on a ship like this. Maybe even get my own vessel to command. A nice boring life shuttling souls between the worlds. More comfort, more space, probably more money."

"Why didn't you?"

"Space is boring enough as it is. Why make it worse? Besides, Silas never would have gone for it—too rough for a ship like this—and there was no way I was leaving him or the others. Space is no place to be alone, no place to be without your friends. They're the ones that get you through."

A waiter appeared, as if from nowhere, and whisked away their plates almost as they were taking their last bites. Bennet raised his eyes.

"Quite the service. Going to miss that when we get to Teiresias?"

"I don't really like it. It makes me uncomfortable," Jacob said.

"Me too," Bennet murmured. He picked his napkin up

and began twisting it around first one hand, then the other.

They were both quiet for a minute.

"So what will you do if your friend's not on Teiresias?" Jacob asked.

"I don't know," Bennet murmured, his eyes flicking up to Jacob, then away.

"Will you try to get another ship?"

"I don't know," the captain snapped. His face had turned ashen. He wiped his mouth with his napkin and tossed it onto the table.

"But you must have a plan," Jacob said, suddenly remembering Bennet's earlier advice from the *Caber*. "You told me before that you should always have a backup."

"Yeah, well, maybe I do," Bennet said, his voice suddenly rising, drawing stares from a few nearby tables. "Whatever it is, it doesn't include you, that's for sure."

He stood up, started to turn, then hesitated. "I don't want dessert," he said, then walked away, leaving Jacob alone at the table, shaken.

"Captain?" Jacob now whispered from his bed, his voice barely audible above the *Justine*'s hum.

"Yeah," Bennet murmured. He turned his head and looked over at Jacob.

"Sorry about last night at dinner. I shouldn't have put you on the spot like that, not after everything that's happened."

"It's okay," Bennet replied with a quick smile. "I'm the one who should be sorry. What can I say? I'm not at my best these days. A captain without a ship's a pathetic sight."

"You're not pathetic," Jacob said.

Bennet looked back up at the ceiling and chuckled. "Thanks, kid."

"So tomorrow we break for otherspace?"

"Right. It'll happen around midnight, once everyone's gone to bed—most passengers prefer to sleep through it if they can. Eases the shift."

"But that leaves two whole days to slow down. It doesn't make sense for a ship like this."

"With the speed we'll be going when we hit otherspace, we'd need at least that—Teiresias is a long ways away."

"It doesn't seem like we're going that fast."

"Doesn't sound like it, you mean. The *Justine*'s quiet. But look at the stars, Jacob."

It was true—they were spinning by faster than he'd ever seen them go, even on the *Odessa*.

The captain sat up with a slight groan, then stood.

"I need a walk. You want to go for a walk? Maybe get a bite to eat?"

Jacob nodded. He got up and started to follow the captain out, then paused in the doorway after turning out the light. The cabin was dark but for the window, the window dark too but for a field of drifting stars. It reminded him of the charts he'd spent so long studying on the *Caber*, and he suddenly realized he could recognize the star patterns in the window. Sure enough, closing his eyes, he had but to shift the angle, rotate along a three-dimensional pivot and he could see it all, could see where they were going—a tiny point of light toward which the ship now headed. Around that point of light a world waited, just for him.

The cabin lights arose shortly after midnight, murky and red, making the engines seem somehow louder. The thrusters had been subdued, nearly silent, the entire voyage until about an hour ago, when they'd suddenly throbbed to life, as if with the final push to break speed they couldn't help but protest. Though it was still nowhere near the roar he'd felt on board the *Caber*, it was enough to keep him from sleeping—not that he'd been able to sleep anyway.

It was strange. The first time he'd entered otherspace, he was scared, not knowing what to expect. The second time, he was nervous, wondering how it would be different. Now he felt nothing but excitement, partly because of what was waiting on the other side, but mostly for the pleasure of the ride, the feeling of peace, of solitude and safety that had pervaded every part of him after the initial painful shock of adjustment. It wasn't just that he felt different in otherspace—it was the secret feeling that he *was* different, that it had somehow *made* him different. How or for what purpose, he couldn't say. He could only hope to find out. Maybe on Teiresias he would.

The chorus washed through the cabin, an echo of ghostly song, and he drew a deep breath. The noise faded as quickly as it had come and before he knew it, the cabin was bathed in white light from the window, nearly enough to overwhelm the red entirely. There was no pain at all this time, but he could feel the tingle in his forehead the moment the ship broke through.

He got up from his bunk, went to the door, and opened it. He hesitated on the threshold—he wanted to explore the ship in the freedom of otherspace, but he had no idea how much time he had. He thought back to his previous two trips into the strange dimension. How long had they lasted? Minutes, hours—he realized he couldn't remember. And this was a big ship. What if he got lost and couldn't find the way back in time?

It was night. Bennet was asleep—even if he weren't back, it wouldn't matter. Besides, he needn't go far.

The halls were empty, hollow in the ruby light. All the passengers were sequestered in their rooms. He set off down the corridor, his footfalls quiet amid the dead silence of the ship.

He reached the end of the hallway and started down the wide staircase that curved to the deck below, foregoing the elevators that most used to whisk between the levels of the ship. A brilliant shaft of luminescence from a skylight fell onto the stairs halfway down. He stepped into its glow and looked up. On board the *Caber*, he had slowed the speeding funnel of light. He wondered if he could do so now, if he could stop it altogether and linger in otherspace indefinitely. The thought sent chills down his spine.

Then again, maybe he wasn't slowing down the space around him at all, maybe he was simply adjusting to its speed, learning to see its textures and penetrate its depths, as if the fabric of otherspace were a giant sheet of stars folded untold times upon itself, and he had simply to learn to look between its folds.

He remembered the brook that flowed into the lake where he and Xander swam, remembered staring into it one hot afternoon last year, transfixed by its flow. It was the bubbles that had caught his eye, the myriad pockets of air formed by the churning water as it flowed over the rocks. He began watching them as they floated downstream, hurried along by the currents, and discovered that, by concentrating on a single bubble, the blurred movement of the surrounding water seemed to freeze in place and sharpen, move as a single mass. Taking up a flower, he had cast one petal in after another to the same effect until his eyes had grown tired from the focus.

Perhaps something similar was happening now.

He was about to test his theory when a flicker of movement appeared below. He snapped his eyes down in time to see the shadow disappear from sight.

His pulse began to throb in his ears. Resisting the urge to flee, he forced himself to continue down the stairs, trying to ignore the sound of his heart beating against the silence of otherspace.

*It was nothing,* he thought. *I just imagined it.*

He reached the bottom and stared down the hallway. From here, the interior of the ship opened on the left, so that the hallway was really more of a balcony looking over a court surrounded by shops, lounges, and restaurants. Another curved staircase leading to the level below lay at the opposite end of the balcony. At the sight of the empty walkway, Jacob was about to breathe a sigh of relief when a figure suddenly appeared near the far staircase.

The figure—no more than a dark shadow from this distance—drifted slowly to the top of the stairs before disappearing.

Jacob went to the edge and looked down. His heart still pounded heavy in his chest, and his hands gripped the balcony railing so hard they ached. He could see the figure on the curved staircase, a small shadow making its way down slowly, pausing on each step.

He was about to call out when it suddenly stopped and looked up at him, raising an arm in greeting. In silence, it turned and began making its way back up the steps toward him.

Panic washed over him. He had been detected. And

where could he run? Could he even hide? There was no Xander here, no Bennet waiting to protect him as long as they were in otherspace.

He was about to run anyway, when something stopped him. Why should he run? Why not meet a fellow traveler? Perhaps he could learn some real answers.

As his courage returned, so did the sense of peace he'd grown used to in otherspace. By now the figure had reached the top of the stairs and was drifting slowly toward him. Jacob left the railing, headed back up the stairs until he reached the shaft of light. He sat down under its glow and waited.

The shadow came around the corner and proceeded up the steps, and as it came into the light, Jacob gasped at the familiar smiling face.

"You!"

"Hello, Jacob," the child said. The purple robe with the gold embroidery was gone now, but the face was the same one that had visited him twice before—first in the depths of his fever dream almost two years ago, then just before leaving Nova Campi. But he'd never appeared so clearly as he did now, and though his voice still rang with an unearthly tone, as if many voices spoke at once, it no longer sounded distant or full of static.

"How did you get here?" Jacob asked. "Have you been on board this whole time?"

The boy shook his head. "This is just a projection, the same as before."

"But I'm not dreaming," Jacob said. "This is real life. At least, I think it is."

He glanced back up at the skylight, still lit by otherspace. Aside from the boy's presence, everything seemed normal.

"Interesting," the boy replied, his face flickering with curiosity. "You appeared to us just now, like a star bursting in the night sky. I had to see you, let you know how close you are after all this time."

Jacob nodded. "You sound clear. There's no distortion."

"We've been tracking your progress as best we can ever since you left, but it's been difficult. Now that the Foundation suspects our location, we have to be careful. We don't know what means they might have to find us. But you're very close now."

"I'm in otherspace right now. When we come out, I'll be only a couple days away." He hesitated. "Am I in danger?"

The boy gave a grim smile. "We're all in danger. The Foundation is hunting us."

Jacob hesitated. "I don't think anyone's following me. But I'm not sure. I sense something deep down, in the background. Something isn't right."

"We sense it too," the boy replied. He looked away briefly, then turned back. "I must go," he said.

"But wait!" Jacob cried. "I have so many questions."

"There will be time soon enough to answer them."

"But I don't even know where to go. How will I find you?"

"Don't worry," the figure said. "Just get to Teiresias. We'll find you."

# CHAPTER SIXTEEN

"There it is."

Jacob sprang from his bunk to the window as soon as Bennet spoke. The ship had completed its braking cycle and had come around so that Teiresias filled most of the window. Half of the planet, anyway—a sharp curve of darkness cut down its middle, making the planet seem nothing more than a green semicircle slightly gone to crescent, a large cap floating sideways in the darkness.

"One side's missing," Jacob joked as the *Justine* closed in on the planet.

"You won't see it, either," Bennet said.

"Why not?"

"It takes Teiresias as long to rotate once on its axis as it does to orbit the sun. So one side's always in the light, the other always dark."

"That's right. I remember Xander telling me."

"Makes for one long night if you're on the wrong side."

"'Some are born to endless night,'" Jacob murmured.

"What's that?"

"It's from a poem," Jacob said, "by William Blake. It was in a book my friend Kala gave me once: '*Every night and every morn some to misery are born. Every morn and every night some are born to sweet delight. Some are born to sweet delight, some are born to endless night.'"*

"Lovely," Bennet murmured. "A real pick-me-up."

"I was learning to read at the time," Jacob explained. "It stuck in my head. You reminded me of it just now. Or the planet did, at least."

"So which one are you?" Bennet asked, turning to him with a grim smile.

Jacob paused. "I can see," he said at last. "So it must not be endless night. What about you?"

The captain snorted. "I thought I knew. Thought I had it all figured out. Not anymore. Maybe I never did."

Seeing the look on Bennet's face, Jacob turned back to the window, continued to watch Teiresias expand as they drew closer.

"Have you ever been down there?" he asked a few minutes later.

"It's been a while, but I've made a few runs out this way. It's not too bad. Hot as hell, on the dayside. Pretty heavy vegetation—hardly a spot of bare ground to be found. Just trees everywhere you look. Cut them down, the stuff grows right back. All that sunlight, see? Thank god for floaters."

"But Xander told me it was a mining planet?"

"It is, on the nightside. That whole half of the world is all dead. No one really lives there. Just rock, ice, and snow. Perfect for mining."

"What do they mine?"

"Breaker crystals."

"You mean the ones ships use to go through otherspace?"

"Yeah. It's what's put Teiresias on the map."

The planet now filled the entire window. Jacob pressed

185

his face to the glass and glanced around. Even this far out he'd been able to see ships everywhere, blinking in and out of sight, heading to or from Reynard's surface or to one of the many massive orbital platforms encircling the planet. But so far, all the ships Jacob saw here seemed to be coming from and going to the surface along a single, defined corridor, as if there were an invisible road in space. Then, slowly, a series of specks emerged. Drawing closer, Jacob could see they were a line of ships in orbit, their silhouettes spread out in formation.

"What are those ships? They don't seem to be moving."

"BiCo gunships," Bennet said. "Now you know why I never came here much—not exactly a smuggler's paradise. They've got the planet pretty buttoned up. It's all about the crystals. It's how BiCo's made its fortune."

"Dobson told me they were expensive."

"That's right. And Teiresias is one of the only known sources. Unless you're lucky enough to be near a wormhole, you can't go anywhere without them. The other corporations are exploring like crazy, hoping for a new planetary supply so they can get a piece of the market. But for now, BiCo's sitting pretty. Hence, the shiny new gunships."

"Sounds like a good place to hide if someone's after you."

"As long as you don't give BiCo a reason for wanting to find you first."

"You sound like Xander," Jacob murmured.

"I'll take that as a compliment."


A wave of heat struck Jacob, making him gasp as he stepped off the shuttle onto the tarmac. The moisture in the air was palpable, combining with the heat so that Jacob felt he had to push more than move through the turbid air.

Shouldering their belongings, he and Bennet headed toward the starport's main terminal, a large structure of wood and glass. As shuttles and cargo ships lifted off from the hot pavement, others landed in their place or in the nearby bunkers that served as hangars. The port on Maker's Drift had been seedy and run-down; Reynard had been one continuous steel sprawl. Here, Jacob almost felt at home. Though smaller, and more organic with its array of wooden structures, Tendrille—Teiresias's main port city—was like Melville: bustling and tidy. And in spite of the waves of heat that washed continuously across the surface, it felt good to see green again, even if it was in the form of thick vines and waving treetops instead of rolling plains.

They passed through the revolving doors into the cool, dry air of the terminal. Crowds of people drifted by, many carrying packs like Jacob's and Bennet's, while others sat in chairs, talking quietly to absent friends through earbuds while they waited. Jacob started a little at the sight of the guards standing lazily near the exits or strolling in pairs between the gates, their long rifles hanging casually by their shoulder straps. Unlike the bustle on board the *Justine*, the crowd here was subdued, talking quietly or not at all. Jacob wondered—was it the guards or just the nature of the cool, open expanse? Then another thought struck him—there weren't many suits. In Melville, and even more so on Reynard, he'd grown accustomed to the sight of the corporate personnel in their shiny clothes. Most of the people around him wore drab-colored, loose-fitting pants and shirts, their hair cropped close or shaved off entirely, women as well as men.

"Mostly miners," Bennet said as they headed for the main exit at the opposite end of the terminal. "Finishing up their stint, ready for a break. Tough going on the dark side, I've heard. BiCo cycles them in and out pretty regularly."

An alarm sounded off to the right. A half dozen guards materialized around a group that had just passed by. Jacob stopped to watch as a member of the group got singled out and separated by several of the soldiers. One of the soldiers silently scanned him with a sensor, then nodded to the others. The others quickly marched the pale, shaken man off toward a side door.

Jacob looked up at Bennet. The captain nodded grimly.

"Like I said, BiCo keeps close tabs on their crystals," he said.

After stuffing Bennet's belongings into a rented locker, they left the terminal and headed toward the center of town.

"So where do we go now?" Jacob asked, slowing to a stop.

"I was hoping you would tell me that," Bennet replied, glancing around. They'd left the port and had entered a busy street full of shops and restaurants. "Let's get dinner," he said at last. "I'm starved."

"Okay," Jacob agreed, glancing up at the sky in confusion. The sun still hung high above them, but it felt like it should be a lot later. Then he remembered—it was always noon on this side of the world.

*Jacob.*

They'd gone only a few steps when the man's voice sounded deep within in his head. Jacob froze.

*Over here,* the voice sounded again, this time to the right.

Jacob gazed to the right. The street was crowded, but his eyes quickly settled on a heavyset man seated at a table outside a café. The man hovered over a drink, his hat pulled down low so that Jacob could barely see his face.

*If you can hear me, raise your right hand,* the voice said.

Jacob was so startled by the sound of someone else's voice inside his head, it took him several moments to comply.

"What is it, kid?" Bennet demanded, glancing in the same direction as Jacob.

*Don't answer,* the voice said as Jacob opened his mouth to speak. *In fact, just keep walking.*

Jacob obeyed, continuing down the street without a word. Bennet frowned, then followed.

As they walked along, Jacob could feel his heart pound. He had to make a conscious effort to slow down his steps, control his excitement, and not break into a run. During his visit on board the *Justine*, the boy had told Jacob they would find him, and now they had. Finally, after all this time, he was going to meet one of them, someone like him.

*Tell your friend not to worry,* the man's voice instructed. *Just turn right up ahead and go into the Mandrel. It's a spacer's bar. I'll meet you there shortly.*

"Come on," Jacob said. "I know where we're going."

They turned the corner. Sure enough, up ahead Jacob could see the sign for the Mandrel, its floating letters blinking meagerly above the street. Jacob led the captain to the entrance, then paused at the sound of rough voices coming from inside. For a second he had a flash of being back on Maker's Drift all over again.

"Care to fill me in on what you're up to?" Bennet asked.

"He said he'd meet us here," Jacob said, glancing nervously through the darkened doorway.

"Oh, right. *He,*" the captain muttered. "Guess I missed that."

Jacob didn't reply as he lingered tentatively under the glowing sign.

"Don't worry," he said, seeing Jacob's hesitation. "I know

189

this place—nobody'll bother you." He gestured toward the doorway. "After you."

It was early enough so that the bar was busy but not packed. There were a few stares, but most of the spacers ignored them as they settled into a booth along the far wall. Sitting across from each other, neither spoke as they waited. Jacob suddenly realized his time with the captain was finally coming to an end.

"Need a drink?" a gruff voice said.

Jacob looked up at the tall man standing over them. He massive bald head was tattooed with a green design. A matching green mustache trailed down both sides of his chin.

"No thanks," Bennet replied. "We're just waiting for someone."

"Fine," the man said. He leaned into the booth. "Got something for me, Captain?"

Jacob resisted the urge to pull back.

Bennet smiled. "Nothing right now, Gus. Sorry. I'll fill you in later."

The man broke into a smile. "Been a while since you've been in, Bennet."

The captain nodded. "Don't worry. I'm sure you'll be seeing plenty of me—for the next few days, at least."

The giant turned and headed back to the bar.

"Gus owns the bar. But he has a few side projects, as well."

"Let me guess—he's in the business."

Bennet laughed. "That's right. You catch on fast. Too bad you're settling down. You've got good instincts. And the way you picked up those controls on board the *Caber*—you would've made a good first mate."

190

"Why not captain?"

"Let's not get ahead of ourselves, now," Bennet shot back. They both laughed. It felt good to laugh after the earlier quiet.

A stocky figure suddenly slid into the booth beside Jacob. It was the man from outside the café. He reached up and removed his hat to reveal short brown hair and a pudgy face thick with stubble. He was older than Bennet, maybe Xander's age. But when he smiled at them, his eyes crinkled up, making him suddenly seem younger.

"Hello, Jacob," he said. It was the same voice Jacob had heard in his head a moment ago. It was a strange voice—slightly husky, yet surprisingly soft and high for such a large man.

"Hi," Jacob said. As the blood rushed to his cheeks, he felt he should say something, but he didn't know where to start. "You're a Seer, aren't you?" he said at last.

The man smiled. "I am," he said. *Though I used to be a Blinder. Just like you.*

Jacob returned the smile as the words flowed into his mind. He could feel his face pulling back into an enormous grin so that he knew he must have looked like a fool, but he couldn't help it. Now that he was finally hearing the words he'd waited so long to hear, he suddenly didn't care.

"So, who's your friend?" the man asked, nodding toward the captain.

"This is Bennet," Jacob replied.

"Captain Bennet," Bennet said, reaching one hand out across the table. The man took it in his own, and they shook.

"Avery Warrick," the man said.

"Good to meet you," Bennet murmured. Jacob could feel

191

the man's reticence wash across the table, seep into his own joy, and dilute it.

"You weren't followed, were you, Captain?"

Bennet's face darkened. He shook his head.

"Sorry for the secrecy," Avery said, seeing Bennet's reaction. "There are people out there searching for us. Jacob may have told you. You can't be too careful."

"Captain Bennet got me here," Jacob broke in. "I wouldn't have made it without him."

Avery nodded. "We're grateful, Captain. We've been waiting for Jacob for a long time. We were starting to get worried."

"Glad to help," Bennet murmured, gazing down at the table.

"We crashed on Maker's Drift," Jacob added. "The captain lost his ship. We were the only ones who made it."

"Then we're doubly grateful," Avery said. He shook his head. "I can't imagine what you've had to go through. I'm sorry."

"Me too," Bennet said, his voice barely audible above the din.

"Is there anything we can give you? We don't have much, but we'd be happy to help any way we—"

"No," the captain cut in. "I'll be all right."

Jacob pulled the gold card from inside his shirt and held it out. Bennet glanced down at it, then shook his head.

"Take it," Jacob said. "I won't need it."

Bennet paled. "That's good of you, Jacob. But you may need it yet. Or your friends might."

"Please," Jacob insisted. "You went out of your way to help get me here."

Bennet hesitated. He glanced over at Avery for a moment, looking as sick as Jacob had ever seen him.

"All right," he said at last. "But you have to take this." He reached up, removed the diamond from his ear, and held it out to Jacob.

"What?" Jacob said, looking at it in amazement. "I can't take that. It's too valuable."

"It's a fair exchange," the captain replied. "And it might come in useful where you're going. Lord knows it's saved my rear end a few times. Come on," he added as Jacob paused, "it'll be something to remember me by."

Seeing Bennet wasn't going to back down, Jacob finally slid the card across the table, then took the gem from the captain's hand and put it in his pocket.

"Thanks," he said.

Bennet looked over at Avery. "So, what now?"

"Meet me behind the bar in about five minutes," Avery replied. "There'll be a floater waiting. You can go out the back here. It's okay, the owner won't mind. Just follow the hallway."

"So you know Gus, huh?"

"He helps us get things we need. Hasn't let us down yet."

With a nod, Avery slid out of the booth and disappeared into the crowd.

They waited in silence. After a few minutes, Jacob stood up. He turned to Bennet to say good-bye, but the captain slid out after him.

"I'll go with you," he said. Without waiting for a reply he pushed past Jacob and headed toward the back. Jacob shouldered his bag and followed.

They headed down a corridor past a couple of offices, pushed aside the back door, and stepped into the alley, both blinking against the sun. A white floater with black stripes and an enclosed cab appeared at the end of the alley. Larger than most of the floaters Jacob had seen, it looked even more beat-up than Chester's.

Jacob hesitated, then turned to Bennet.

"Good luck finding your friend," he said. "You'll have a ship again soon. I know it."

Bennet shook his head. "Don't worry about me. Just take care of yourself."

"Okay," Jacob said. He stared down at the ground where their short shadows stood together, dark against the bleached pavement. He looked back up at Bennet. "Thanks again for—"

"Forget it," Bennet said, cutting him off. He glanced away for a moment. "Looks like your ride's ready," he said at last, his voice softer.

Jacob looked over at the floater. The side door was open. Avery Warrick leaned against the hood, waiting with down-turned brim.

"Don't suppose you want to change your mind?" Bennet said. "Take on a life in space?"

Jacob shook his head and smiled.

Bennet shrugged. "Didn't think so," he said. "But you'll be all right. Avery seems like he's got his act together. That's more than I can say."

Jacob shouldered his bag once more and took a few steps toward the floater. "I hope I'll see you again someday," he called.

Bennet nodded, smiling weakly in return, his face pale even beneath the sun's brightness.

Jacob waved, then turned and walked quickly toward the floater. He looked back one last time to see Bennet give a quick salute before disappearing back inside the bar.

"This all you got?" Avery asked, taking Jacob's bag and tossing it into the floater. "That's it," Jacob said.

"Good," the man said, nodding. "Good to travel light."

He leaned into the backseat and pulled out a heavy bundle of clothes, including a jacket thicker than any piece of clothing Jacob had ever seen.

"For you," Avery said, thrusting the bundle into Jacob's arms.

"To wear? But it's so hot out!" Jacob exclaimed.

Avery smiled and winked. "Not where we're going," he said.

# PART FIVE
## Teiresias

# CHAPTER SEVENTEEN

The world was night around the floater, with little to light the way. A distant moon—small, white—and the scattered clusters of stars provided the only illumination, enough for Jacob to make out the landscape below. The snow-covered terrain glowed faintly under the meager light, barren in appearance, as if the night had scrubbed it clean of life.

He shivered, as much from the frozen sight below as from the excitement building within him. And in spite of the floater's warmth, for the first time since leaving the dayside he thought of wrapping himself in the parka Avery Warrick had given him.

"Is it all like this?" he asked.

There were so many questions he wanted to ask Avery about the others: what they were like, what they did, what they could teach him. But he found himself holding back, suddenly shy and overwhelmed by anticipation, wary of seeming overeager, like a child. So he contented himself with asking other questions instead.

"All," Avery replied, reaching up to scratch his whiskers. "From the time you cross the terminator until you reach the other side."

The terminator was the line between light and dark, day

and night. Though it was less defined on the surface than it had been from space, with an area of twilight where the vegetation sent out its last creepers into the dim, it wasn't as stretched out as Jacob had imagined it would be. The border came and went with surprising quickness as the floater zipped along.

"It seems so dark," Jacob said, pressing his forehead against the window glass. "Darker than any normal night sky. Maybe because I know it's forever."

"Nightside isn't a friendly place. That's what makes it perfect."

"Perfect for what?"

"For hiding, of course."

The floater hugged the surface so closely, the ground beneath them was no more than a blur. They moved in a straight line for the most part, following the contours of the terrain. Occasionally, Avery would change course, pulling the floater right or left, ducking around a rocky spire or squeezing between a pair of narrow valley walls, sending Jacob's heart into his throat, causing him to clutch white-knuckled to his seat.

"Sorry," Avery said, ducking beneath an overhanging ledge of snow-covered rock. "I'm so used to it, I stopped being scared a while ago."

"Why don't you just go higher?"

"Good to keep a low profile. Even out here. Never know who might be poking around."

They jetted out over a precipice. The land fell away beneath them, plunging hundreds of feet below into a basin that spread off to Jacob's right. While Avery dipped to skirt the cliff wall just below the plateau's edge, Jacob looked out his window. He could make out the other side of the basin miles away. But it wasn't the vastness of the open plane below him that caught his attention, it was what lay on the other side.

"What is that over there?" he asked.

At the base of the far end lay a scattering of lights. For a moment, Jacob wondered if he was seeing a family of stars reflecting off a frozen lake.

"Those lights? Those are the mines. Or what's above them, anyway. There are mining stations all over this side of Teiresias."

"The crystals," Jacob said. "Bennet told me about them."

"That's right. Those lights you see are the surface units. They're like little towns. Only temporary, like the crystals. When those go, so do the people. That settlement's been going for about five years. Not bad."

"Are we going someplace like that?"

"You might say that," Avery said. "We found one about three years ago, not long after we got here. A small operation, abandoned some time ago. They left just about everything intact. Even left the power plant behind. We've fixed the place up. It's home, for now."

"Is it far?"

Avery smiled. "We've got a ways to go yet."

He began humming a tune Jacob didn't recognize. Jacob turned and looked back out the window. They'd left the basin and the mines behind and were now speeding across a series of snow-packed hills. In the distance, Jacob could see a dark mass on the horizon where there were no stars, as if they'd been swallowed up. As they got closer, the shape of a vast mountain emerged, its snowy flanks rising toward a sharp peak. Jacob gasped. Even from here, he could tell it was larger than anything he'd seen on any world.

"What is that?" he asked, pointing toward the mountain.

"Night's Head," Avery said. "Dwarfs everything on the planet. Rumor has it that there are more crystals there than anyplace else on Teiresias. But BiCo hasn't touched it yet."

"Why not?"

Avery shrugged. "They're waiting, I guess. But for what, I couldn't say. Who knows, maybe there's nothing there, and BiCo's just keeping the rumor alive to draw investors. All I know is that it's off limits to everyone."

The mountain grew as they came closer to it, then slowly diminished as they shifted away. He watched it until it finally disappeared from sight.

*Tell me about the captain.*

Jacob started at the sound of Avery's voice in his head.

"Sorry about the mindspeak," the man said. "We talk to each other that way sometimes. You'll get used to it."

"I can't do it," Jacob murmured.

"You'll learn. You'll learn lots of things."

"That's what I've been hoping for. Ever since the dreams began, the strange feelings, the visions—I've wanted to know what it's all about."

"That's good. Caolas will tell you everything. He's our teacher, the first one of our kind."

Those words. *Our kind.* After all this time, it was both strange and wonderful to hear someone say them and to know that it meant him, as well.

"So about the captain—it was odd. I couldn't read him. He just seemed conflicted, a strange bundle of emotions. What can you tell me?"

"There's not much to tell about Bennet," Jacob said. "I

202

needed to get off Nova Campi, and he was available. I was only on board his ship for a few weeks before we crashed. It was a strange trip. There was this other passenger, a man named Folgrin who showed up at the last minute. Some businessman who needed to get to Teiresias. He supposedly worked for BiCo, but I don't think so."

Jacob shuddered at the memory of the man's severed hand still clinging to him.

*You didn't like him,* Avery spoke in his mind. *You were afraid of him.*

"It's a long story," Jacob murmured.

*You can tell Caolas later. For now, don't worry. Though I don't like it. None of it.*

"My friend Xander said the same thing. But Bennet isn't like Folgrin. He helped me. He got me here, even after everything that happened. And he taught me things—how to fly a ship, how to chart a course in space."

*So you trust him, then?*

*Yes.*

Jacob looked over at Avery in amazement.

"Not bad," the man said, laughing.

A few minutes passed before Avery spoke again.

"So what's with the jewel?"

Jacob reached into his pocket and took out the diamond. It winked gently against the dashboard lights.

"It's some sort of cloaker. Bennet said it can shut out any kind of scan. I think it's true—back on Nova Campi, I felt like I was being watched all the time, but when I got close to him, the feeling went away."

"That could be useful," Avery said, nodding.

About twenty minutes passed in silence. Jacob glanced

203

over a few times at Avery. The man seemed to have pulled back into his own thoughts.

As they dove down in between the narrow walls of a canyon, Jacob hoped he hadn't pulled back too much.

"Nervous?" Avery asked.

Jacob tried mustering a smile. "I'm sure your flying is as good as anyone's."

The man broke out into laughter. "No," he said, "I mean about where we're going. About meeting everyone."

"A little," Jacob said. "I've been waiting so long for this day, and now it's here."

"And you're scared you won't like it."

"Maybe. Maybe it's more that it won't like me."

"Fair enough. Being a Seer can be scary sometimes. Especially early on. I remember when my sight first came in. I was older than you. Eighteen at the time. I had settled into my specialization—a listener of all things—and was getting ready to be matched with a wife. And then my sight came in. It was terrifying. Those were difficult days."

"And lonely."

"Lonely as hell. Six months went by before I left."

"Did you tell anyone?"

"No. I was a listener—I knew better than to speak up, I knew what happened to people like me."

"You knew others?"

"I meant just anyone who was different. Anyone who posed a threat to the order of things. A threat to Truesight."

Jacob could hear the bite of sarcasm in those last words. It was strange to think of Avery—a man who seemed so gentle, so in control—as a listener. In Harmony, listeners were feared more than anyone.

"There was someone, though," Avery said. "A man—Marcus. You'll meet him tonight. I'll never forget the first time we saw each other. It was at one of the Gatherings. I don't know who was more scared, me or him. But we got over it. And then we left. It helped to have someone else. Especially when the powers started to settle in. I feel bad for the ones who have to go it alone."

"What colony were you from?"

"Aldrich Station on Rigel. Oldest of the colonies. Only Robertson, the original settlement back on Earth, where the Foundation has its headquarters, is bigger. Most of us come from Aldrich. Hell, half the people in the colony are descendents of Francis and Jean."

"Is there anyone from Harmony?" Jacob asked, trying to keep his voice from shaking.

"Not too many. But there's a couple."

*I wonder if I know any of them,* Jacob thought.

*There is someone,* Avery said. *Someone special. Waiting for you.*

*Who?*

"You'll see," Avery said aloud. He glanced at Jacob and smiled with a wink.


The floater swooped down into a valley and sped for the far end. Jacob felt a moment of panic as the hillside rushed to greet them, but at the last moment, an opening appeared against the snowy face and the floater ducked inside.

Jacob's heart began to race as they settled down onto the floor. Aside from a few tiny blue and red lights scattered along the far wall, it was dark in the hangar.

"I'll take your bag," Avery offered. "Grab your new

clothes. You may want to wear the jacket—it's a little chilly."

"Where is everybody?" Jacob asked, peering through the windshield into the dark.

"Inside. Where it's warm."

They got out of the floater and headed toward the lights. Jacob followed as closely as he could, taking tentative steps through the shadows.

Avery was right. It was cold. Colder than anything Jacob had ever felt before—much worse than the damp bitter night on Maker's Drift or those chilled mornings he'd ventured into the grass on Nova Campi. He could feel it bite onto his cheeks, nip at his ears, sear his lungs as he pulled the coat even tighter around him.

His eyes were beginning to adjust now. He could see two other floaters like the one that had brought him here nearby, and an even larger transport—a hauler—against the far wall of the hangar.

"Follow me," Avery said.

As they passed through an opening into a dark corridor, the door sealed shut behind them. A dim light above the opposite doorway revealed a row of lockers on both sides of the hallway. Jacob gasped as a wave of heat suddenly blasted him from the grates beneath his feet. It felt good at first, but within seconds he was tearing off his jacket as the hot wind circled about the narrow space. Avery took his jacket from him, chuckling as he placed it and the thermal pants Jacob carried in an empty locker.

*A little insulation from the frigid nightside. Melts the snow quickly.*

"I'll bet," Jacob replied. He glanced around, trying to make out what details he could. "It's so dark in here."

"Don't worry," Avery spoke out loud. "You'll find a nice

change through that door. Go ahead, I'll follow."

Jacob went to the door at end of the hall and paused. There was no handle, no button, no observable way of opening it. He pressed a hand against its steel. Solid.

"So how do I open it?" Jacob asked.

"Look up above."

Jacob glanced up at the faint light encased in a lens of glass, gleaming down like an eye.

"It's locked. Our own form of security. There's no way in except through that scanner."

"So what's the magic word?" Jacob joked. "Should I say please?"

"You can say whatever you want," Avery said with a grin. *You just have to say it the right way.*

Jacob nodded as the words rang inside his head. He stared up at the point of light until he could almost see the invisible beam washing over him, feel its presence as it swept back and forth across his mind.

The heat still in the room, the light glowing in the dark, it all brought back flashes of his fever dream, of being back in Harmony, in the bunker, standing before the ghostbox as the fires closed in. The memory stirred a sudden panic within him. What if all this was a trap? What if he'd been lured here for some dark purpose? And here he was—alone, on the other side of space with no one, not even Bennet now, to save him.

*Stop it,* he scolded, closing his eyes. He took a deep breath, then looked back up at the light.

*Open. Please open for me,* he thought, trying to form the words in his mind as clearly as he could.

There was a click. The portal began to move with only the faintest whisper.

"Good, Jacob," Avery whispered from behind him, giving

his shoulder a gentle squeeze.

Brilliant light emerged from behind the sliding door. Jacob shaded his eyes, blinking against the brightness, as Avery guided him over the threshold.

Before he could see the space, he could sense it—the moist, warm air, the aromatic scent of vegetation. It was as if he'd stepped through some otherspace portal and into an underground forest. He uncovered his eyes and took his first look.

They stood in a hall, an enormous dome well over a hundred feet across. Trees like the kind he'd seen back in Tendrille grew in scattered groves, with branches and vines curling out and entwining themselves around rocks, the dome walls, and one another. Paths wandered between the miniature groves dotted with fountains and small pools. Most spectacular of all was the great light at the dome's peak, a brilliant orb so bright, Jacob could only glance at it for the briefest moment. Shedding light and heat, it seemed to hover over them like a miniature sun with a power of its own.

He suddenly realized they weren't alone. A group of men and women were tending to the trees and flowers. Seeing Jacob, they rose from their work and approached with warm smiles. A couple ran off, calling to others. Soon a crowd had gathered, nearly thirty in all—men, women, children, all smiling and whispering to one another.

Jacob hung back. The last time he'd stood before a group was two years ago in Harmony's central square when he'd faced his fellow Blinders for the last time. He could remember their blank gazes, their quiet fear, as the high councilor addressed them. In spite of his shyness, it felt good to be seen now. The blood rushed into his face as he turned toward Avery.

"Home at last," the man said, laughing. Wrapping an arm around Jacob's neck in a playful headlock, he raised a hand to silence the crowd.

"All right, everybody, let's give him a chance to catch his breath. The kid's come all the way from the other side of the Rim to join us. He's not going anywhere. Right, Jacob?"

"Not as long as you'll have me," Jacob said.

The group broke into applause. Jacob smiled his thanks as Avery raised his hand for quiet once more.

"It's on the late side, and I'm sure you're all as hungry as I am, so let's get supper started. In the meantime, I'll give Jacob a quick tour, show him his new home."

The group murmured their agreement and began to file off to the right, offering smiles and quiet words of welcome as they left. Jacob scanned the crowd, searching for the boy who had visited him in his visions. There were a few children, mostly young ones in their parents' arms, a couple closer to his own age, though none who seemed to match.

Then he saw her—the familiar face, watching him with dark eyes from the back of the crowd. He gasped as she broke into a soft smile and came toward him with tentative steps.

*Delaney?*

It was Delaney and yet it wasn't. The cast of the features was slightly different, as was the age of the woman's face. It was as if he were looking at an image of his friend filtered through a mirror of time and space.

The woman drew up before him and took his hands into her own.

"Hello, Jacob. It's a pleasure to see you at long last."

Jacob started, resisting the urge to pull his hands away.

"I know that voice," he whispered.

"Yes, you do. It's been five years, but you know it."

"Mrs. Corrow?"

Delaney's mother smiled. "Call me Clarissa," she said. She gave his hands a quick squeeze, then released them and stepped back. "You've grown up. You're almost a man now. Last time I saw you, you were only eleven." She held one hand out, palm down, near Jacob's chest. His boyhood height.

"But you're dead," he said.

She laughed. "I suppose I am, in a sense. We all are to those we left behind."

"But I touched you. I felt your face," Jacob whispered, remembering the cold feel of the flesh beneath his fingers. "At your funeral. It was my first passing."

"Martin was always one for details," she murmured with a wry smile. "I'm sure he put on a good show."

Jacob shivered at the thought of the high councilor.

"So what happened? How did you escape?"

"Why don't we save that story for later," Avery said, coming over. He put his arm around Clarissa's waist. "You'll be staying in our quarters. There'll be plenty of time to talk."

"Of course," Clarissa said. "I'll go help the others with dinner."

"We'll be there shortly," Avery said. He leaned over and gave her a brief kiss. She smiled with a sidelong glance at Jacob, then turned and left.

Avery watched her go, then took Jacob by the shoulder. His voice rose up in Jacob's mind.

*Okay, kid. Time to see your new home.*

# CHAPTER EIGHTEEN

"We call this the arboretum," Avery said, waving a hand through the air. "This dome used to house the core of the mine—where everything was processed. Took us a whole year to turn it into this. You can thank Marcus for that."

"That light up there—it's like the sun."

"It *is* a sun, of sorts. We took the old reactor—BiCo likes to use these mini-fusion furnaces for their small operations— and tweaked it a little. That was my little trick. That thing doesn't just light and heat the arboretum, it powers the whole place."

"How'd you learn to do all this?"

"Marcus and I spent quite a few years wandering around, doing odd jobs, picking things up here and there. We both seemed to have a knack for engineering."

He paused and looked around the dome before turning back to Jacob.

"You see, most everyone here has spent time on their own. I'm sure you know, it's not easy to start over. All of us struggled; some failed. Those of us who didn't did what we could to blend in, find a new way to live."

"So how did you find one another?"

"We didn't. Caolas found us. One by one, over time, we

came together. Some of us were waiting for a long time before we were found. I was one of the first, though. Finding a place to settle was the hard part—we spent the first years just moving from world to world, picking up people where we could, keeping a low profile. Then we came here three years ago. Caolas led us here."

"It must be good to finally have a home. To know you never have to leave."

A bitter smile crossed Avery's face.

"Never? We don't think that way, Jacob. We can't afford to and neither can you. We've been lucky so far, but we could be forced to leave this place tomorrow. Forever." He reached out and plucked a blossom from a low-hanging bough.

"But all this work!" Jacob cried. "Why bother if you're not going to stay?"

Avery shrugged. "Hope keeps you busy. Besides, it doesn't matter where we are as long as we're together, right? That's where hope comes from. And places like this."

Jacob glanced up at the bright orb hanging over them, then closed his eyes. Its heat reminded him of the other side of the planet, that feeling on his face when he first stepped off the shuttle. He could almost feel Bennet's presence beside him. He wondered what the captain was doing now.

A familiar noise suddenly caught his ear; he opened his eyes and smiled.

"Birds," he said, listening to musical calls pass between the nearby branches.

"Yes," Avery said. "Mostly species from Teiresias. But we have a few from some of our original colony worlds—Pollard, Albion, Rigel, of course. None from Nova Campi, I'm afraid. They need the open grasslands to thrive."

"It doesn't matter," Jacob said. "Just the sound of birds, any birds, is enough."

"Come on, I'll show you where the living quarters are."

He started down a side path to the left of where they'd entered.

"What's that way?" Jacob asked, pointing in the opposite direction, where everyone had disappeared.

"The dining hall and kitchen are in that wing, along with two or three common rooms for recreation. I'll show you them last when we head over for supper."

Jacob followed Avery down the path until they reached the edge of the dome. A large set of double doors stood open, revealing a wide corridor lined with glowing lights.

"We just followed the mining tunnels, converting them into a series of suites, nearly ten in all. A little bit of polishing here, some smoothing there, some basic wiring, and voilà—enough for everybody, with room to spare."

The corridor branched several times, with doors scattered along both sides of the hallways. Though the floors were smooth, the walls remained textured and uneven, curving over their heads in an arch. Strangest of all was the endless glitter, an array of sparkling flecks, particularly near the wall sconces, that shone along every surface of the tunnel, even the floor beneath Jacob's feet, shimmering like a cloud of stars.

"What is this?" Jacob marveled, stopping to touch a section of wall.

"Crystals. What's left of them, anyway. The ones large enough to use were carefully mined out. But there are always plenty of shards left along a vein."

"They're beautiful," Jacob murmured.

"We're in sunset mode right now. You should see them when the lights go down at night. They keep glowing for half the night. Don't even need the hall lights for the first hour."

They reached the end of a hallway and paused before the door.

"Here's where you'll be staying, at least for now."

The door opened. Jacob followed Avery inside.

The suite consisted of a common area, spare with just a few pieces of soft furniture and a pair of lamps. There was a bathroom and several bedrooms off a short hallway. Avery showed him his bedroom—small and square, occupied mostly by a bed. Jacob put his pack on the dresser and looked around.

"Sorry, it's a little small."

"No smaller than the ones I had before," Jacob replied as they went back out into the hall.

"Nadia's room is next to yours," Avery said. "She joined us a few months ago. You'll meet her at supper. And Clarissa and I are right across the hall, if you have any problems in the night."

"Are you a couple?" Jacob asked.

Avery's face lit up. "Two years," he said.

Jacob nodded. He hadn't known Mrs. Corrow well back in Harmony. Delaney had only recently started working with his mother shortly before her own mother died. *Disappeared,* he reminded himself. He had met her only a few times. He remembered her as being kind, remembered the voice, how it put him at ease, unlike her husband, who had made Jacob uncomfortable long before he had ever gained his sight. *Former husband,* he reminded himself again.

They left the suite, passed quickly down the sparkling halls back to the arboretum. Jacob could make out the faint smell of spices and cooking food coming from the opposite end of the dome. His stomach rumbled.

"Just a few more minutes," Avery said, seeing Jacob glance in the direction of the smells. "I want you to meet Caolas first. He's waiting."

They headed through the trees toward a different side of the dome, this one opposite from where Jacob had entered. They reached another set of double doors, though this time the doors were closed.

*We call this the sanctuary,* Avery said.

He glanced up at the scanner gleaming down from above the threshold. The door opened.

They passed into a large rectangular room with an arched ceiling and a door set into the middle of each wall. The room was dark, but as they entered, a row of lights brightened along the length of both side walls, setting the myriad crystals embedded in the ceiling aglow. Jacob drew his breath at the sight—it was as beautiful as the darkest night sky. He half-expected to see the flare of a ship's engines break amid the sparkling vault.

"There he is!" a voice cried out.

A man stood in the open doorway to the left. Shorter than Avery, though nearly as stout, he had a fleshy face topped with curled white hair and wore only a simple robe—purple embroidered with gold thread.

*At last, at last,* the man's voice clamored in Jacob's mind. *You're safe and here at last.*

He came over to Jacob, a smile on his face. Jacob could only stand and watch in confusion. There was something so familiar about the man, but he couldn't figure out what it was.

"Jacob, this is Caolas," Avery said.

"No introductions are necessary, Avery," Caolas said. He turned to Jacob. "And how are you, young man? So nice to see you again."

Jacob didn't answer. He was too busy staring. In spite of the white hair, there was a youthful cast to the man's face—the skin was firm, pink, unmarred by the wrinkles Jacob had noticed on the faces of people like Morag and Chester. But far more disturbing was the man's eyes—a pair of opaque orbs that seemed to stare emptily into space, as if they had frozen over and never thawed.

Jacob was about to ask him about his eyes when Caolas's words suddenly registered. A different question now sprang to mind.

"Have we met before?"

Caolas laughed, a loud laugh, infectious, one that made Jacob first start, then smile. He suddenly gasped as the image of the boy from his visions appeared in Caolas's place. He blinked and the image was gone, but in that brief moment Jacob realized—the smile, the face, it was the same.

"You," Jacob whispered. "You're the boy!"

"Yes," Caolas said. "I am the boy; the boy is me. And why not? When you're projecting yourself, you can appear however you like. For some reason, I've always found it easier to assume that form. Not that it's ever easy."

"It didn't seem it those first couple times. You broke up after a minute or so."

"Yes, well, when you're trying to speak to someone half-way across the galaxy, a little static is to be expected. The first time, especially—you were quite sick."

"That's right," Jacob replied. "The fever. It almost killed me."

216

"It was that fever that accelerated your powers. Before that you may have had inklings, but when the fever struck, your brain, your body reacted, and you changed. That's when I found you. Finding you was the easy part."

"I did have dreams before the sickness. Some of them came true. Or parts, at least. And after, there were even more dreams, and visions, all kinds of strange things. But it's slowed down over the last few months. And there's no sense to any of the things that happen to me. I don't understand it."

"You're still growing, still developing," Caolas cautioned. "Ups and downs are expected. You're so young, Jacob. Most of us didn't begin to see until we were well into adulthood. And the powers took even longer to emerge. We'll work it all out. Tomorrow it begins."

"Tomorrow what begins?"

Caolas laughed again. "Why, the training of course. Time is of the essence. In fact, I hope it's not too late. If only you could've come sooner."

Jacob looked down at the ground. "I should've," he said. "But it was hard to leave. Xander and Delaney were my family."

"Delaney?" Avery said, his eyes sharpening.

Jacob nodded, but before he could explain, Caolas spoke. "They still are your family, Jacob. But so are we now. We've all left people we love behind, some by necessity, some by choice. And though we would never desire to take their place in your heart, we do believe we have something to offer you that they couldn't."

"I know," Jacob said. "I'm glad to be here."

Caolas nodded, reaching out to grip Jacob's shoulder. "I can sense it. But you're tired, Jacob. Your spirit's tired—you've had a long and difficult journey to get here. We'll do what we can to make it worthwhile. Starting with a good supper."

He gestured toward the door, and they all left together.

They walked side by side through the arboretum toward the dining hall. As they made their way, Jacob found himself stealing glances at Caolas, beside him. The man stared straight ahead, his eyes and his head never moving. It seemed impossible that those clouded eyes could see, yet he never wavered.

As they neared the open doorway leading into the dining hall, Jacob could hear the clamor of voices, the rattling of dishes, the sound of laughter all mixed together. His nervousness returned with the noise of the crowd.

He was greeted warmly all over again. Nodding shyly to the smiling faces welcoming him, he followed Avery to one of the many packed tables. Beside an empty seat sat two boys and a girl. The two boys seemed a few years younger than him, the girl his own age. The boys were both dark-haired, with sharp little features that reminded Jacob of the grass-badgers that burrowed into the hillsides near Xander's house. The girl had short brown hair, amber eyes, and—Jacob realized with a start—a beautiful face.

"Jacob, this is Nadia," Avery said. The girl glanced up at him briefly and smiled, blushing as she did. "She's staying in our quarters along with you for now. She's a newbie, too."

He turned to the boys. "This is Trouble," he said, pointing to one. "And this is Even More Trouble," he added, pointing to the other.

The two boys stuck their tongues out at him and laughed.

"Desmond," said one.

"And I'm Eliot," the other chimed in.

"Twins," Avery explained. He reached down and grabbed

each one by the ear. "Now see here," he growled. Both boys froze, wide-eyed. Nadia giggled. "You go easy on Jacob. He's had a long trip and we want to make him feel at home. Besides, he may be new, but he's older than you two."

"Yes, Avery," they both intoned. Avery gave Jacob a wink and released the pair.

Avery took Jacob over to a large side table covered with trays of food. Handing a plate to Jacob, Avery took one for himself and they both helped themselves. As Avery turned to leave, Jacob hesitated. Seeing him pause, the man came back.

"Go on," he said, nodding over to the table where Nadia and the twins sat. "Don't be shy."

"Okay," Jacob said. He watched Avery go over and sit down beside Clarissa at the far end of the dining hall, then he turned and headed back to his own table. He sat down beside Nadia.

"Hi," he said.

"Hey," she replied.

She gave another quick smile, then went to eating. Not sure what to do, Jacob turned to his own plate. Suddenly, he didn't feel quite as hungry as he had before. Glancing at the other three, he realized two years had passed since he'd been around someone his own age or younger. That last day in school—the day the listeners came to take him before the council. It seemed so long ago, but he could remember the silence of his classmates, the sick look on his best friend Egan's face. He hadn't thought about Egan for a long time.

They ate for a while in silence. Even the boys were quiet, though they never took their eyes off Jacob. Nadia, on the other hand, seemed to look at everything else in the room besides him.

"So you're new, too, huh?" Jacob asked her, after finally gathering the courage to speak.

"Two months," Nadia said. "I came from Pollard. You came from Nova Campi, right?"

"Yeah," Jacob replied. "How long have you been able to see?"

"A little less than a year."

"That's all?" Jacob exclaimed.

Nadia's face reddened. "My family didn't believe me when I told them. Or they pretended they didn't. They sent me to the fixers."

Jacob remembered how his mother had threatened to send him to the fixers. He also remembered how people who went there never came back the same. They always seemed quiet, listless, as if something had died within them. Or had been killed.

"What was it like?" he asked.

She shivered. "I ran away after a few days, into the forest. Not much food in the forest. But I came to a town, finally. I made up some story about being left behind by a spaceship and a nice old couple let me live with them for a while. Then Caolas found me, came to me in my dreams. The people in town put some money together and bought me a ticket here. I told them I had family here."

"What about you two?" Jacob asked.

Eliot shrugged. "We were never Blinders."

"Our mother was, though," said Desmond.

"And our father," Eliot added.

Jacob's eyes widened as both boys' loaded forks floated up from their plates and into their mouths in perfect synchronicity before floating back down. The pair smiled at Jacob as they chewed.

"Show-offs," Nadia muttered.

A pea from Desmond's plate flew, as if flicked by an invisible finger, through the air toward the girl. Nadia waved a finger and the pea squashed in midair a foot before her face and fell to the table.

"Now who's the show-off?" Eliot teased as Desmond broke into peals of laughter.

Nadia glanced at Jacob and blushed even deeper than before.

They lingered in the dining hall long after the meal was over. In small groups or individually, different members of the community came over to Jacob and introduced themselves, told him where they'd come from, in some cases how they'd managed to escape. He met Avery's friend Marcus, joked with the twins' parents, two of the earliest members to join the group. He met June, a young woman from his own colony. Though he didn't know her—she was from Harmony's southern tier—he had a faint recollection of her disappearance, remembering how the teachers used the occasion to admonish them about the dangers of wandering alone.

Everyone was nice—he could almost feel their affection, like the warmth of the arboretum's light—but it soon became overwhelming. In the middle of conversations, he would worry about forgetting people's names, only to realize he already had. Worse, everyone in the hall was talking to one another, and while he tried to focus on those beside him, his mind kept snatching pieces of conversation around him, especially once he realized it was mostly about him. Worst of all was the sound of their voices inside his own mind. For whatever reason, he suddenly found himself picking up the projected thoughts bouncing around the room like echoes. It was a relief when Avery, perhaps sensing Jacob's growing discomfort, suggested they retire for the evening.

Back in the quarters, the four of them sat down together for a cup of hot chocolate before bed. Soon Avery and Clarissa were asking him questions about his journey, and the next thing he knew, he was telling them all about the *Odessa* crashing, about being saved by Morag and her husband, and his month on board the *Caber*. Nadia sat across from him, absorbed by the story of his travels.

He was somewhere on Reynard, making his way with Bennet to the other side of the city to book passage on a liner, when a wave of fatigue washed over him, a heaviness that settled into his eyes and made him stop, groping for the story's thread.

"Maybe it's time we turned in," Avery murmured.

Jacob glanced up to see them all watching him, their faces kind and intent.

"Sorry," Jacob said. "I forgot what I was saying."

He rose from the warm cushions of the couch and rubbed his eyes.

"You've had a long day," Clarissa said. "We've kept you up far too late."

Nadia bounced up and gave a quick good night. Before Jacob could even reply, she'd disappeared into her room. Jacob glanced over at Avery and Clarissa.

"Don't mind her," Clarissa said. "She's more excited than anyone that you're here. Someone her own age, someone else who's new. Poor thing's been through a lot. Still trying to adjust to the idea of being a Seer."

"I know what that's like."

"And don't mind the twins," Avery added. "They can be a handful, especially for newcomers. They were never blind, never had to live under Truesight. They don't know what it's like. But they have good hearts."

The couple left Jacob alone in his new room. A pair of bedside lamps in Jacob's room came to life as he entered. He sat down on the bed and glanced over at his bag, his few possessions still packed away. He would take care of them tomorrow.

He was in the process of pulling off his boots when there was a knock on the door.

"Come in," he said.

The door slid open and Clarissa took a few tentative steps into the room. Her face was drawn with a look of pain. Jacob stood up in alarm.

"I'm sorry, Jacob," she said, holding out her hands. "I know you're tired, but I couldn't wait until morning. I've been waiting for five years now. I need to know."

Jacob could hear the quaver in her voice.

"You need to know about her," he said. "About your daughter."

A wave of anguish crossed her face. Jacob could see her eyes glimmer in the low light.

"Avery said you mentioned her name earlier when you were talking to Caolas."

"I did."

She hesitated. "She was your mother's apprentice. I made sure she would be. I imagine you must have spent some time with her."

Jacob smiled. "More than you could know."

223

Clarissa smiled back, though her eyes still continued to well.

"Tell me everything," she whispered.

And so Jacob told her. About the days they spent together in Harmony, her supposed death and funeral, about following her to Melville, about the eyes Mixel had given to her and how she ultimately rejected them, about the painful return to Harmony and learning the truth about her father, about the many months of healing that followed, and the strength she'd given him, the sacrifice she'd made for him at the end. He told her everything, watching Clarissa's face turn from joy to horror then to joy again, back and forth, only to settle at the end on a kind of sadness he'd never seen before and wasn't sure he ever wanted to see again. All he knew was that if his mother could ever be told his own story, her face would look the same.

What struck him even more was how good it felt to tell her, and how the act of telling made him somehow miss Delaney both more and less at the same time. By the time he was finished, he no longer felt tired. Rather, he felt strangely refreshed standing before this woman who looked so much like his distant friend. And in spite of the sadness on Clarissa's face—or maybe because of it—he knew he'd done justice to the story.

"Thank you," the woman said at last.

"You don't need to worry," he said. "She's in good hands."

Clarissa nodded. "Leaving her was the hardest thing I've ever done. And even though I know I had to, I still suffer every day. I always will."

She closed her eyes, pushing out the tears that had gathered until they trickled down her face.

"If I hadn't confided in Martin, I might have been able to stay, as awful as it would have been. As it was, he didn't give me any choice. In the end, we agreed that it was better for me to leave. But I never felt good about leaving her with him."

"Did you know he could see?"

She nodded. "Just before the end, it came out. I begged him to leave with me, for all three of us to go, but he refused. He chose power instead. That or he was too terrified to do anything else."

Jacob tried to imagine the high councilor living among the group of men, women, and children who had welcomed Jacob so warmly, who laughed and joked together between the tables in the hall.

"I've spent all these years wondering if the change would happen to her, too. Then Caolas could have found her. We could have been together again. It was a foolish dream, but it kept me going, helped me live with the guilt of leaving her. Now any chance of that is gone."

"Delaney chose her own path," Jacob said.

Clarissa took a deep breath and nodded.

"At least you're here now. I'd like to think that I have some connection with her through you."

She gave him a quick embrace, then turned to leave.

"Wait," Jacob said.

He walked over to the dresser and reached into his pack. A moment later, he withdrew his hand and held out the small piece of silver in offering.

"Here," he said. "You should have this."

Trembling, she reached out and took Delaney's sounder from Jacob's hand, rubbing it between her fingers. She tapped its surface and the familiar note rang out, so bright and clear that Jacob could almost feel Delaney's presence in the room.

Clarissa tapped the sounder, muting the tone, as fresh tears sprang back into her eyes. She gave him another hug, tighter this time, and whispered her thanks before leaving.

Jacob undressed and crawled into bed. It was a comfortable mattress, even better than the one on board the *Justine*. And all was quiet—no more hum of ship engines, just silence beneath the layers of rock, ice, and snow.

*I made it,* Jacob thought, a thrill passing through his body. *I'm home.* All of a sudden, it didn't seem real, as if it were too good to be true. After all the long months of dreaming, to think he was finally here.

The lights dimmed, went dark. Jacob closed his eyes.

He'd just begun drifting off to sleep when he heard the music.

Sitting up in bed with a start, he cocked his head just as the lights—sensing his movement—glowed back to life.

The sound was gone. There was no one in the room. He suddenly realized he couldn't even recall what he had heard. Music of some sort—voices, bells, a ringing in the distance, like wind-blown chimes, reminding him of the sound he'd heard each time he'd broken through to otherspace.

It was probably just Clarissa in the next room, listening to the sound of her lost daughter one last time before sleep.

*Sleep,* he thought, lying back down. *Good idea.*

A wave of exhaustion washed over him, so heavy that he only half-heard the faint chorus at the edge of consciousness, an airy song that sent him into a sleep deeper than he could ever remember.

226

# CHAPTER NINETEEN

Morning was quiet among the others. Though he realized he could no longer call them that—he was now one of them.

"What *do* we call ourselves?" he asked a woman—Elise—at breakfast.

"Seers," she said, looking up from her coffee with a smile. "We are Seers."

Jacob nodded. The answer was so simple, so obvious. Perhaps too much so.

"Isn't everyone a Seer?" he asked. "I mean, everyone who isn't a Blinder?"

"On one level, yes. And in this sense we are like the trillions of others out there who have always had sight. But we are also different, special, and on this level, the word also applies. In ancient times, a seer was someone who was special, who could see the world in a different way, who even had extraordinary powers like we do. In fact, Teiresias was a famous one."

"You mean like the planet?"

She laughed. "The name is the same, yes. In the stories, Teiresias could see the future, even though he was blind."

"Is that why you're all here?"

"You have to ask Caolas. He's the one who brought us here."

She smiled once more, then turned back to her breakfast.

The laughing, the boisterous activity of the night before, had been replaced with a hush that Jacob found unsettling at first. Most of the people wandered singly or in pairs through the paths of the arboretum, engaged in whispered talk or quiet meditation, or, like Elise, sat in the dining hall lingering over the morning meal. In some ways, it was familiar. Back in Harmony, there were rules, though not strictly enforced, limiting when and where conversation could occur. In a blind world, one needed quiet space to navigate, free from the clutter, the pollution, of too much noise. Besides, one never knew who might be nearby listening. Jacob wondered at first if the group's self-imposed silence was a leftover habit from their former lives. But as the morning hour went on, he began to feel the sense of peace the quiet brought, so different from the strained, tense silence he'd often felt in Harmony.

*Follow me,* Avery said, joining him in the arboretum.

As they headed down the path, it suddenly occurred to him—maybe people were talking to each other. Maybe he just couldn't hear them.

They passed from the arboretum into the sanctuary, where Jacob was surprised to see at least a dozen people seated on the floor. They sat in no particular pattern or order, but all were quiet.

"What's this?" Jacob whispered.

*We gather every morning. Not everyone, just those who wish to. Or need to,* Avery said.

A man in the far corner—Avery's friend Marcus—stood up and approached them.

*Good morning,* the man spoke in Jacob's mind.

"Hi, Marcus," Jacob said. He wanted to project the

228

thought instead, but he suddenly felt self-conscious trying.

Marcus smiled. *I'm glad to see you here, Jacob. We all are.*

"Thanks," Jacob murmured.

"I'm off to the control room," Marcus whispered.

"I'll be there shortly," Avery replied.

As Marcus left, others began to rise and leave as well, offering smiles or quiet greetings on their way out. Soon the room was empty but for one figure.

"Come on over, Jacob," Caolas said from where he sat in the center of the room.

Jacob glanced over at Avery, who smiled and parted with a nod. He walked over to Caolas and sat down on the floor— a strange sort of rubber mat that felt hard underfoot but seemed to warm and soften the moment he settled down— tucking his legs beneath him as Caolas did.

"So what do you think of our Avery?" Caolas asked after several minutes of quiet.

Jacob paused, somewhat taken aback by the directness of the question.

"He seems strong," he said at last. "But I'm confused. From the way he talked, it sounded like you were the leader. But everyone acts like he is."

Caolas laughed. "Neither of us is the leader, at least not in any formal way. However, though we are a group of individuals come together by choice, we're still a group nonetheless, and all groups have leaders of a kind whether they're chosen or not." He paused for a moment. "But I think you're right. Avery is the one the others look to. Partly it's because he was a founding member of our band of Seers, but more so because he *is* strong. I'm too much the philosopher. Avery's a doer. I just wish the poor fellow weren't so serious, didn't worry so much. No matter how relaxed he may seem, Avery worries about everything, takes everything on himself."

Listening to this man speak of worry—this man who laughed and grinned so much, who seemed so relaxed about everything—Jacob couldn't help but smile himself.

"I don't need to be able to read your mind to know what you're thinking," Caolas said, chuckling.

"I'm sorry," Jacob said, his smile fading. "It's just that you don't seem worried about anything."

"I'm human, Jacob. Of course I worry," Caolas said. "But I try to as little as possible. There's no sense in it. But I used to all the time, worse than Avery."

"So what happened?"

"I died."

Jacob started. He thought of Maker's Drift, of the crash, of Morag's words back in the cottage when she'd asked him if he felt dead.

"I was twenty-four," Caolas continued. "I'd grown up in Robertson back on Earth. I'd specialized in administration and was sent to Pollard to serve on the colony's council. I had a wife—a skilled scent maker—and a baby girl. Then my sight came in, an agonizing three-month affair. I'd never felt at ease in my position, in politics, and it only got worse after I saw Truesight for what it really was. Then the nightmares started. In desperation, I left."

Jacob watched quietly as Caolas's face, for the first time, grew serious.

"Pollard is a cold world, brutal, like Teiresias's night side. I plunged into the snow and just started walking. I didn't know where. I didn't care. I didn't care if I died. I even wished I would. A research crew found me, just at the edge of the colony's territory. I must have just expired, for my body was still warm enough to show up on their thermal scans. They gathered me up, and their doctor managed to resuscitate me. I came back, but I was different."

He reached up to briefly touch his eyes. "Your trial came in fever, in fire. Mine was a trial of ice. But after that, I truly saw. I saw that I never had to worry, because everything was going to be okay. Everything was okay just as it was. You can cry about the world, Jacob, or you can laugh. It's better to laugh."

He put his hands out, resting them on his knees, and settled into stillness.

"I almost died once," Jacob whispered. "But I'm still afraid."

"Maybe you'll have another chance," Caolas replied with a slightly bemused look on his face.

Studying Caolas's gaze, Jacob realized there was something about those eyes that troubled him, that reminded him of Folgrin—their uniformity, lacking the separation of white, iris, pupil.

"Speak your thoughts, Jacob," Caolas said.

Jacob blushed. "What happened to your eyes, Caolas?"

Caolas reached up and touched the edge of one eye.

"I gained my sight in Pollard. Then I died. When I came back, it was gone."

"So you're blind?" Jacob whispered. It seemed incredible—the man most responsible for bringing all the Seers together, unable to see.

Caolas smiled. "No. My eyes no longer see, but I acquired another kind of sight, one that lets me view the world around me and beyond. It's difficult to explain. I suppose you could say I'm able to sense my surroundings with every part of my body, and my brain somehow turns it into sight."

"Like one big eye."

"Yes, like one big eye," Caolas replied with a laugh. "It's a strange world I live in—dark but not dark, full of shadows and forms, some of which come from beyond. From great distances and, on the rarest occasions, other moments in time."

He paused, turning his gaze down to the ground. "I miss my sight sometimes. But my gifts have more than compensated for the loss. After all, I wouldn't have been able to find any of my friends. I wouldn't have been able to find you."

They sat quietly for several minutes. This time, Jacob broke the silence.

"You said I'd start my training today."

Caolas stirred at his words. He looked up and smiled.

"So I did," he replied. "Whenever you're ready."

"Well, I'm ready now."

"Good," Caolas said.

Jacob waited in confused silence as the man turned his gaze back to the floor.

"So," Jacob began again, "what are you going to teach me?"

"Whatever you want to learn," Caolas said. "I suppose that's your first lesson, Jacob. You're in charge of your own learning, in charge of your own destiny. This place, this family is about freedom and responsibility. The two go hand in hand. You're free to choose whatever path you wish, but you're responsible for it at the same time."

"So if I wanted to leave . . . ?"

"Then you leave. Everyone here—those old enough to

make that kind of choice—understand that they can leave at any time. A few have. We only ask that those who part ways from us keep our existence secret."

"But how do you know they won't betray you? People lie. People do all kinds of horrible things to each other. Doesn't it put you all in danger?"

"Yes. But that's a risk we're willing to take. We think freedom is worth the price. We trust, knowing that trust could be broken. If it couldn't, then it wouldn't have any value. And that's what makes us different from the Foundation, from the communities we escaped from. There is no choice or responsibility there. In Harmony, people are children, all."

Jacob nodded. It felt good to talk this way. It was the kind of conversation he used to have with Xander all those evenings by the fire. He suddenly missed the soldier more than he had since leaving Nova Campi.

"So what would you like to learn today?"

Jacob hesitated. "There's only one thing that I really want, and that's to understand who I am, what's happened to me, and why. I just want to know what all this is about. For what purpose?"

"An excellent place to start, for sure," Caolas said with a smile. "I don't know if I can give you the answer, the big answer, in terms of reasons or purposes. What's the meaning of a star? What's the purpose of a blade of grass or a grain of sand? They just are. And so it is with us. But I can give you some guesses, and some facts, and perhaps you can come to an understanding that will satisfy, if only for a while.

"Nearly all the children of the Foundation, every person from every one of the colonies, were engineered to be born without sight. There are a few exceptions. You learned in school, I'm sure, of the Oedipi, who join as seeing adults and sacrifice their vision. Still, most us were made to be blind, as were our parents, grandparents, and so on. Problem is, the brain is a complicated thing. And sometimes, Jacob, nature plays funny tricks when we meddle with her."

"The ghostbox called our sight a mutation," Jacob said, recalling the words he'd heard those long months ago. "An abomination."

"Abomination? The only abomination is the one that's been practiced on us by the Foundation for the last several hundred years. But our seeing, and the emergence of other abilities, does appear to be a mutation stemming from that manipulation. Still, it's rare. Think of thousands, tens of thousands, of lives that have come and gone in each of the colonies, and look at us—a mere handful."

"But I still don't understand why," Jacob said.

Caolas shrugged. "Chance. Statistics. Environment. Conspiracy. We don't know. Does it really matter? We're here, and we've been given a gift that has made us more than what we might have been."

"You make it sound so wonderful," Jacob murmured.

"You don't think it is?"

"Not all of it. Seeing, yes. All this other stuff, I don't know."

"Understandable. You haven't had a chance to absorb it yet, learn how to control it. And of course, none of it has come without a price—for all its faults, Truesight certainly offers a warm little cocoon to wrap oneself in. We all experienced the suffering pangs of loneliness, alienation, and, in some cases, persecution. But nothing worth having comes without cost."

"Okay, so you can't tell me exactly why this happens. I can

234

accept that. But what about the other part? I have dreams—
they come true, parts at least. Sometimes they come to me
when I'm still awake. I've even had visions of the future. I've
seen things happening in other places when I'm somewhere
else. I've even been other places when I'm somewhere else."

"That's excellent," Caolas gushed. "Wonderful."

"But there's no sense to any of it. It comes and goes, as if
it's got a mind of its own. And then there are the feelings—
those prickly sensations, like my nerves are on fire."

Caolas laughed and raised a hand.

"Yes, I know all about it. We've all been there, and you'll
be comforted to know that everything you've just described is
perfectly normal. We call them growing pains, early stages
where the brain is still rearranging itself, sorting it all out."

"So how long is this going to last?"

"It depends. For some, a matter of months. In some cases,
years."

"Years?" Jacob cried. It seemed so long. Though in fact,
he realized with a start, it had been over two years since he
first began to see. "Then what?"

"Well, that also depends. We all seem to share a few basic
abilities." Caolas paused, his eyes darkening for a moment.

*For example, we can all speak without words, communi-
cate through thought alone.*

Jacob started as the voice shifted. "So you can read
minds."

"Not exactly. We only send our thoughts and hear the
thoughts others send us in return. However, we can often
sense each other's moods or opinions. It's like reading a person's body language, only on a deeper level. There are a few
who can read others' minds, however imperfectly. But as a

235

matter of course, they don't. It's impolite."

"What else can you do?"

Caolas shrugged. "We all seem to possess a certain sensitivity. It's hard to explain. Some call it a sixth sense, others intuition. Those prickly feelings you get—that's your brain telling you something is amiss. Again, there are levels of sensitivity—some have it to such a high degree, it's as if they can see a few seconds into the future. Quite amazing, really."

"So what about all the other stuff? The dreams, visions, all those things I saw?"

"This is where it gets interesting. Some of the Seers have only these basic abilities in varying degrees, but many of us have developed other powers far beyond them. There seems to be a point at which one particular ability develops, deeping to the exclusion and gradual disappearance of the others. Some have gained the ability to see incredible distances, far beyond normal human sight. Others can see in the dark, or detect extremes of heat and cold. Other powers are stranger—the ability to see events unfold from another time or place."

"You mean like my dreams?"

"Yes. Though, as you likely know by now, the future is a tricky thing. What we see is often only one possible outcome. And of course the very act of seeing the future changes it, so that it most likely will never be."

"So it really isn't the future then."

Caolas raised an eyebrow. "I suppose you're right," he said.

Jacob paused. "Last night," he said, "at supper. I saw the twins' forks lift, as if on their own, and then Nadia . . ." He hesitated, uncertain how to describe what he'd witnessed.

Caolas laughed. "Yes, your eyes weren't playing tricks on you. Most of us, Jacob, developed our powers at an older age. And for the most part, they all have seemed to revolve around seeing. But the last few I've found—including yourself—have been younger. And their powers seem to have gone beyond some advanced form of seeing. Though quite young, the twins show emerging powers of telekinesis, the power to move objects with only their mind. As for Nadia—she seems to have developed an ability to project a wall of force. Again, I can't explain these changes or why they've started to occur now. Maybe they have before, but have never had an opportunity to develop. Maybe our kind is heading in a new direction, another stage. I assure you," he added with a wink, "we're keeping a close eye on it."

Calling Nadia's image to mind, Jacob could feel the blood rush into his cheeks. He glanced over at Caolas, who, as always, stared straight ahead with his opaque eyes.

"Caolas," Jacob whispered. "What about me? What is my power?"

Caolas lifted his head.

*We'll find out soon enough.*

The sanctuary door whisked open. Jacob turned to see the twins enter, stumbling over each other and laughing as they bounced down onto the mat. Nadia followed at a distance, frowning at the antics of her younger companions. Seeing Jacob, a brief glimmer of a smile crossed her face before being replaced by the look of dignified aloofness she'd borne last night.

"Good morning, children!" Caolas called out.

"Good morning," they replied in unison. The twins rolled over to Jacob and came to a stop, still giggling. Nadia dropped

237

to the mat beside Jacob.

"Some quiet time first, boys," Caolas murmured. "Draw your thoughts together. Then to work—your practice balls are in my office as usual."

The twins rolled to opposite corners of the room and sat quietly, their eyes still open, though looking at nothing in particular.

"What about me?" Nadia asked.

"Ah, yes. I have a special task for you today, my dear. Jacob needs to learn how to mindspeak, as you did not long ago. Since you just went through the process, I thought perhaps you could teach him."

"Me?" she exclaimed, reddening as she glanced over at Jacob.

"Yes. Don't fret, Nadia. You'll find Jacob to be a quick study. He really already knows how. It's just a matter of getting his mind to accept it."

He stood up and headed toward one of the side doors.

"But where are you going?" she cried.

Caolas paused at the doorway. "I'm going to take a nap," he said. "Have fun."

He chuckled once, then disappeared through the door.

"Don't worry," Jacob said. "You don't have to if you don't want to."

Nadia paused, a look of confusion crossing her face. "No, of course I will. Like Caolas said, it's really easy."

*Can you hear me?* she asked.

Jacob nodded. "I can hear people, I just don't know how to answer back. I mean, I did it once or twice, but I wasn't really trying."

Nadia smiled. "That's the best way to do it. If you try to

force it too much, it won't work. Just sort of relax and don't think about it. Now say something to me."

"Like what?"

"Anything. Something stupid."

Jacob closed his eyes. *I like it here,* he thought.

Nadia cocked her head. "What was that?" she said, laughing. "I only caught the first part. You're trying too hard. Try to imagine that your mouth isn't actually on your face, but inside my head, then say what you have to say, but instead of moving your lips, just imagine that you are. That's what worked for me."

*Okay, if you say so.*

She broke into a grin.

*That's perfect,* she said. *Try again.*

*I've never felt snow.* It was first thing that popped into his head. *Stupid,* he thought.

*It's not stupid,* she replied, though Jacob hadn't meant to project that last thought. *I'd never felt it either until I arrived here. Don't worry, you will. Soon.*

Jacob felt a brief wave of dizziness, a heaviness in his head. Perhaps he was overdoing it. Glancing over at the boys, he realized he'd forgotten all about them. They sat at opposite ends of the room, bouncing a series of colored balls back and forth between each other across the sanctuary floor. It wasn't particularly astounding until Jacob realized their hands were folded in their laps. Not once did either make contact with the balls. It was as if the half dozen orbs moved of their own will.

*They used to draw a crowd,* Nadia said. *Everyone's used to it now.*

"Caolas told me about your ability too," he said, switching to his real voice.

"Yeah, everyone's all excited. I just think it's weird. Touch me."

"What?" Jacob cried, startled by the sudden command.

"Raise your hand and touch me," she said again, laughing. "Go ahead."

Jacob raised his hand and reached toward her. His hand suddenly froze a few inches from her face, stopped by an invisible wall. He pressed his palm against it and pushed. It didn't budge. Nadia lifted her own hand and matched it to his. She blinked and the wall disappeared so that he could suddenly feel the warmth of her skin against his own.

"Wow," he said as they both pulled their hands back quickly. "That's incredible. Is it hard to do?"

"Not something like that," she said, smiling shyly. "It was at first. I don't know, sometimes it's hard. Sometimes it really hurts. But I've been working on it."

*What do you do?* she asked.

Jacob blushed. *I don't know yet.*

*That's okay,* she said. *We'll figure it out.*

"I mean," she murmured, "Caolas will figure it out."

# CHAPTER TWENTY

The next few days passed quickly. Or slowly. Jacob couldn't be sure. Being underground at times reminded him of being in space—confined, dependent upon the corridor lights to give any sense of day or night. The Seers stuck to a fairly regular schedule, which helped. Still, between the omnipresent light of the arboretum's miniature sun and the knowledge that, beyond the glittering cave walls of the abandoned mine, the world above him was cast in perpetual darkness, Jacob always felt a mild sense of confusion over time's passing. At least in space, he had the stars. After spending several months in space, Jacob hadn't thought he would miss the view, but every time he closed his eyes at night, it was all he saw until drifting off to sleep.

That and the music. He kept catching glimmers of sound—a single chord of aching beauty—during brief moments of quiet, when sitting in the sanctuary with the others in the morning, or when walking down the corridor toward his quarters. Most of all, it came at night in the moments before sleep when the stars were in his eyes.

He spent part of the time with Avery and Clarissa, helping them as they worked in the arboretum, pruning and weeding. Other times he helped in the kitchen, washing dishes or preparing meals. He enjoyed the labor—it was nice to feel useful again, and the modest chores reminded him of life back on Nova Campi, helping Xander and Delaney with the routines of daily life. He also enjoyed the company. By now he knew just about everyone in the community, though the task was complicated by the arrival of new people. Every day, a small handful showed up so that there were now nearly fifty members sharing quarters in the renovated mining tunnels.

"Where are these other people coming from?" Jacob asked Avery one evening on the way back from the dining hall. "They're not new like me. Everyone knows them."

Avery paused. "They're returning from their jobs. Most of us take time away from the group to live and work in the outside world. Often it's to learn a particular skill or trade—remember, most of us were pretty limited in terms of what we could do when we left the Foundation. But for some, it's for more personal reasons—to spend time alone, to think and grow, or just for something different, a sense of adventure you might say."

"Oh," Jacob replied. It made sense. But why were they all coming back at once?

Much of the daytime hours were spent training in the sanctuary with Caolas, though Jacob wasn't really sure why it was called that, since they mostly just sat around talking while Nadia and the twins practiced their powers.

The day after Nadia taught him to mindspeak, Jacob sat on a couch in Caolas's quarters—the little room adjacent to the sanctuary—and spent most of the morning telling Caolas his story.

"What do you want me to tell you?" Jacob asked when prompted.

"Everything," Caolas said. "From the first moments in Harmony when you knew something was happening to you to the moment you arrived here."

So Jacob told him everything. The journey into sight, the exodus from Harmony, the search for Delaney, and his life with Xander. The onset of his powers, the fears that drove him to seek passage off Nova Campi. And then his travels through space—the crash of the *Odessa*, his brief stay with Morag and Chester, the strange episodes in otherspace, learning to read the stars, his time with Bennet. Caolas listened intently, his eyes closed for the most part, opening them from time to time to ask Jacob a clarifying question. He showed little emotion during the telling, but Jacob could tell he was absorbing every word.

It felt strange to tell the tale. He'd told the first part many times, but now, connecting it to everything else that had happened since leaving his homeworld, and telling it to someone who had gone through almost the same experience, the story seemed to take on a life of its own. He kept thinking about it as he talked, trying to find the meaning, the pattern in the whole.

When Jacob finished, Caolas opened his eyes and nodded a few times.

"Well?" Jacob asked.

"Well, what?"

"Well, what do you think?"

"A remarkable tale, to be sure," Caolas said. "The pattern is familiar, like others I've heard before, but unique nonetheless. It's your story and could never be another's. The fact that it is both, like all stories of its kind, is what makes it beautiful."

"But is there any meaning to it?"

*There you go again. Always searching for meaning.*

Jacob cast his gaze down. *I'm sorry. I just want to understand.*

Caolas laughed. *Of course you do. Don't be sorry. It would be wrong not to wonder such things. Just don't try too hard to find the purposes in your life. Or stake everything on finding them.*

*It's like the voice,* Jacob thought.

"How so?" Caolas said out loud.

"When Nadia was teaching me to mindspeak, she said the best way to do it was not to try too hard."

"Wise words," Caolas said. "But in answer to your original question—yes, I think there's a great deal of meaning in your story. Several meanings, in fact. And something important."

"Well, what is it?" Jacob asked, trying to control the excitement in his voice.

"I can't speak of it today," Caolas said. "It must be thought on."

The next day, to Jacob's disappointment, Caolas acted as if Jacob had never told him a thing. Instead, all he wanted was for Jacob to sit and listen.

"Listen to what?" Jacob asked. Nadia, Eliot, and Desmond had left after a brief session, and he and Caolas were now alone.

"To the silence. And then to whatever you happen to hear behind it. There's always something lurking beneath the quiet."

So they listened. Time passed. Minutes, hours. Still Jacob listened.

"So, what did you hear?" Caolas asked finally.

Jacob opened his eyes, though he couldn't recall having closed them.

"Music," he said at last.

"Music?" Caolas said, cocking his head in interest. "Describe it to me."

"It's not a song, really. More like just a single note, or a number of notes together in a chord. Like a dozen sounders all at once, only forming the most beautiful tone you've ever heard. Ever since I got here I've been hearing it—the smallest sound before bed, or when I'm walking down a hallway. But when I try to listen to it, really listen, it disappears."

"Musica universalis," Caolas said with a smile.

"What's that?"

"Music of the spheres. In ancient times, human beings believed that Earth was the center of the universe, encased by a series of concentric spheres of crystal, heavenly, perfect, within which moved the planets and the stars. And from these spheres came music—a series of ringing harmonics as their celestial substance reverberated through space."

"That's really what I'm hearing?"

Caolas gave a brief frown. "Of course not. It's a silly idea, after all. But a beautiful one. Your description just reminded me of it, that's all. Have you ever heard it anywhere else before?"

Jacob paused, then stirred with the realization. It hadn't occurred to him the other day, but suddenly he knew.

"Yes," he said. "Once, in a dream not long before I left Nova Campi. But it's also the same sound I heard each time I broke through to otherspace. I'm sure of it."

"That's right. I remember you mentioning that yesterday. Very odd."

"Why? Isn't that a normal sound?"

"I've never heard it before while breaking through. I don't know anyone who has."

"Oh," Jacob murmured. *Music of the spheres.* He glanced up at the faux night sky above, where myriad shards of crystal shone amid the arched vault of the ceiling, reflecting off the floor lights below.

"This was a good day," Caolas remarked. "Tomorrow, we'll go deeper."

The next morning—Jacob's fifth day with the Seers—began with another session of listening. This time Nadia and the boys joined them, as did Avery, Clarissa, and several other adults.

"I've asked the others to join us for this morning's meditation, so you can learn what it's like to share silence with others. Many minds are better than one."

*And listen carefully,* Caolas's voice sounded in his head. *You've learned to mindspeak, now we work on the sensitivity, the sixth sense I spoke of. These people have something to show you.*

Jacob glanced around quickly at the group, but there was no indication anyone else had heard the instruction.

Jacob closed his eyes and a steady quiet settled over the room. The ringing chord sounded faintly in the distance, but Jacob pushed it away. For a while, he caught echoes of voices, half-thoughts slipping out of the settling minds around him like bubbles rising to the surface of a lake. Then he could feel it—a sense of warmth, the goodwill of the Seers around him, both in the room and without. He'd felt moments of peace in his life—at the Gatherings as a child, or while listening to his mother play piano after he'd gone to bed, those many days he'd spent with Xander and Delaney basking in the sun on the beach or watching the fire burn amid the night shadows of the trees. But none of those moments matched this feeling, satisfied this longing he now realized had always been within him, a hollow space waiting to be filled.

*It is filled,* he thought. *I am filled.*

But then the sensation left him. Or rather, he left it, delved deeper where something else lurked in the darkness, something that should have surprised him but didn't.

He snapped open his eyes. The room was empty but for Caolas sitting before him.

"The session was over. I sent them away."

"I didn't notice," Jacob replied. "I was still listening."

*You felt it?* Caolas asked.

*Yes.*

*Describe it.*

"Fear," Jacob said. "They're afraid. Everyone is."

"That's right. Afraid of the dark. They all sense it moving in. Just like you did back on Nova Campi. Just like you have all along."

"But they're happy too. I felt that as well."

"Yes, it's even stronger than the fear. But that will change."

"Why? What are we all so afraid of?"

"It's quite simple, really. Primeval, in fact. We spoke of it before, when I came to you on board the ship on your way here. We're being hunted."

"The Foundation," Jacob said. He shivered, remembering how long ago the ghostbox had spoken of him as an abomination. One to be terminated.

247

"Yes," Caolas said with a grim smile. "They know of us. They fear what we've become. They see us as a threat to their control. A threat to Truesight."

*They want to destroy us.*

*You understand,* Caolas's voice sounded in his mind.

"Has it always been this way?" Jacob asked.

"No. For a long time the Foundation didn't even know we existed. One by one I found the others, brought us together, and together we formed a community, a family, traveling from one world to the next, quietly gathering those like yourself to us without notice from the outside world."

"As if no one could see you? Doesn't sound much different than life in Harmony."

"In some ways it isn't. But in Harmony we were pretending, living a lie about who we really were, about something that our entire society depended upon. You understand the difference?"

"Yes," Jacob said, nodding. "How did the Foundation find you?"

"We believe it was one of our own. There was a man, Simon Volker, from the Pollard colony who joined us a few years ago. Things went well at first, but it quickly became apparent that he was unstable. We tried to work with him, help him, but he resisted. He became paranoid, delusional. He claimed to be our messiah, the one who would lead us all to the promised world, insisted that he would be the source of our salvation."

"So what happened to him?"

Caolas frowned. Jacob could see the pain on his face. "He started to become violent, make threats. And so we banished him. We suspect he returned to the Foundation, though we don't know for sure." He sighed. "It was unfortunate for everyone. Some cannot handle the world of sight or the powers that come with it."

Jacob shuddered. Hearing the story brought back memories of Delaney's father. He couldn't help but wonder—had the same thing happened to him? The anger, the manipulation, the desire to maintain control—were they all symptoms of the partial sight? A genetic twist gone awry? Or were they symptoms of the Foundation, of Truesight, of its denial of human nature with all its frailty?

Then another, far more frightening thought occurred to him. What about himself? Could he ever become like Volker, like the high councilor? It didn't seem possible, but he had yet to learn what his true power—if he actually had one—really was. Maybe it didn't take much. Maybe it would drive him mad too. After all, Volker and Delaney's father must have been like him once—young, confused, uncertain of what fate held in store.

If Caolas sensed his sudden dread, he gave no indication.

"It wasn't long after that that the fear began, appearing in our dreams, our premonitions. We were on Albion at the time. After that, we came here to Teiresias. We've been here ever since, waiting, feeling the fear grow. These last few months, it's gotten worse. There's a chance we may need to leave this place soon."

"Avery hinted at it the first day I was here, but I didn't believe him," Jacob murmured. Staring out with his clouded eyes, Caolas gave a bitter smile. For a few moments they sat in silence. Jacob thought more about the fear, felt it again. As he did so, it changed, melded into a new form that wasn't really new, but one that had been hiding underneath all along, ever since he'd first set out.

"Caolas," he whispered.

*What is it?*

*What if it's me? What if I'm the cause of all this fear?*

He paused. He could feel his heart start pounding and closed his eyes, hoping Caolas couldn't hear it.

"Explain."

"What if I've brought them to you?"

Caolas nodded. "It's certainly possible. In fact, it's quite likely."

Jacob's stomach fell. He suddenly felt sick. "Do the others think so?"

"Some, yes. We could all feel the shadow grow as you drew closer."

"Then why did you let me come? Why did you tell me to?" he cried. But before Caolas could reply, Jacob jumped to his feet.

"I've got to leave," he said. "I can't stay here any longer." He took a few paces, then hesitated. He wanted to run, but the reality of where he was, the inability to head out on his own now struck him. Even on the warm grasslands of Nova Campi, less than a hundred miles from Melville, he'd struggled. What would he do here, in the vast darkness and cold? He suddenly remembered Caolas's story. He doubted there would be anyone close enough to save him.

Caolas laughed. It was a kind not cruel laugh, but it made Jacob stop and turn. "For heaven's sake, sit down, boy," he said, and patted the ground before him. Jacob resumed his seat.

"It's not as simple as you think. In fact, this whole issue is clouded in emotion and fear, premonitions that none of us completely understand. We knew there was danger in your coming, yes, but it goes beyond that."

"How?" Jacob demanded.

"It's hard to explain," Caolas replied. "At least right now. But if we have to leave, we'll leave. And we'll be taking you with us, rest assured." He hesitated, then shook his head. "It's quite disappointing. I brought us to this world. I was sure this was supposed to be the place."

His voice drifted off. For the first time Jacob could remember, his eyes closed and remained shut. Jacob was about to ask him what he meant, then stopped himself. In spite of Avery's earlier joke about Caolas's age, the man suddenly did seem old, tired. He remembered when Folgrin was struck unconscious in the attack on the *Odessa*. Just as Folgrin had been transformed by closed eyelids, so too was Caolas, both men made less powerful, more human.

For several minutes, the two sat in silence. Then Jacob heard the door open behind him. He turned and looked.

The twins bounded in, followed by Nadia, who came and sat down near Jacob. The two gave each other a quick smile before Eliot and Desmond jumped in between them. For a moment, they all waited in silence. Then Caolas stirred.

# CHAPTER TWENTY-ONE

Caolas opened his eyes and smiled.

"Thank you for answering my call, children," he said. Jacob looked over at Nadia in surprise. She gave a mild shrug in return. "You've all been working hard this week—seems like a good time for some fresh air. Wouldn't you agree?"

The boys whooped in unison, then leaped to their feet and were out the door before Jacob could even wonder what was going on. Nadia laughed and popped up as well. She held a hand out to Jacob and helped him to his feet.

"Come on," she said, and darted for the arboretum. Jacob followed.

They crossed the arboretum and headed for the opposite door. Jacob hadn't passed through it since the day he arrived.

The great door slid aside, revealing the bright, white corridor lined with lockers. Already, Desmond and Eliot had their lockers open and were halfway into their snowsuits.

Jacob found the locker where Avery had helped him store his thermal gear. Watching Nadia slip into her clothes, he followed her lead, starting with the pants, then the boots, jacket, hat, and gloves, until all that could be seen were their features peeking out from within the circle of their hoods.

"Let's go, I'm dying!" Desmond called out. Jacob

understood—already he could feel himself starting to sweat beneath the insulated layers.

"Okay, okay," Nadia muttered, pushing by them to open the hangar door.

They stepped out from the brilliance of the transition corridor into the darkness of the hangar. Jacob gasped as the cold, dry air entered his lungs, then paused, waiting for his eyes to adjust so that the floaters could become more than just dark shadows amid the red and green lights glowing from scattered service panels.

"Eliot, get out of there!" Nadia barked.

"Aw, come on. Let's go for a ride."

Eliot and Desmond were in the front seat of the white floater, its lights blinking on and off as they played with the switches.

The floater suddenly rose from its bed, hovered a foot or two off the ground, and wobbled back and forth. For a moment, Jacob thought they'd managed to start it, but the floater's engine was silent.

"Knock it off!" Nadia shouted again. She took a few steps toward the floater before it finally rocked gently back down to the ground. A moment later the boys emerged from the cockpit. In spite of their bundled appearance, he could see the fatigue on their grinning faces.

"Are you okay?" he asked.

"Sure," Desmond gasped, "it's just heavy."

They followed Nadia toward the hangar doors, then paused before a smaller door off to the side.

"Don't want to let the warm air out opening the big doors," she said, and smiled.

"This is the warm air?" Jacob cried.

253

Nadia only laughed, then turned the bolt on the side door and swung it open. The twins were out before either Jacob or Nadia could move, disappearing with a fading call. Jacob stepped toward the doorway. Already he could feel a new wave of cold sink in around him that made him gasp all over again, and he shivered within his suit. But before he could step through the doorway, Nadia put out an arm and stopped him.

"Better turn your suit on. Makes the night a whole lot more comfortable."

She reached up and pressed a button on the collar of his jacket. An immediate warmth circulated the length of his body, driving out the chill.

*Thanks,* he said.

*Don't mention it.*

She smiled and handed him a flat board, its edges curled up on all sides like a long, narrow platter.

"What's this?" he asked.

*You'll see,* she replied, grabbing another for herself.

Closing the door behind them, she led Jacob into Teiresias's night.

The first thing he noticed was the moon. He had noticed a moon on his journey here, but it had been small and distant. He wondered if this one—a fat, cratered crescent—was the same satellite or a different, closer one. Either way, it didn't seem to diminish the brightness of the stars much. Their presence brought an immediate sense of relief. All the anxiety and fear that had followed him from the temple seemed to slip away the moment the alien constellations came into sight. In space the stars were always moving, always shifting, coalescing and dissolving in endless patterns. But here, on the ground, just like on Maker's Drift, they suddenly became settled again. No matter that the pattern itself was different here on this world than on the others he'd been to. They provided the same sense of solace.

And while the moon didn't seem to dampen the stars' light, it cast its brightness across the land so that the snow seemed to blaze against the black sky. Jacob scrambled to follow Nadia across the packed snow, marveling at how the surface glittered under the moonlight, like the tiny crystal shards embedded in the tunnel walls beneath them.

"What moon is that?" he asked, trying to catch his breath as they trudged over the snow.

She cast a glance up.

"Luna," she replied. "It looks just like Earth's moon. That's how it got its name, I guess. At least that's what Avery told me. Although its orbit is a bit different, he said. It swings around us funny so that it's closer or farther at different times."

They took a sharp right and clambered up the slope of the hill that covered the secret refuge. Though the warmth of the suit helped ward off discomfort, Jacob could feel the cold stinging against his cheeks, burning his lungs, could see his breath cascade into quick clouds.

"Look out!"

"Coming through!"

Jacob looked up to see the twins flying toward them down the slope, hovering inches above the surface. He jumped out of the way just in time to avoid being barreled over. Nadia, however, reached out and pushed Desmond's leg, sending him rapidly spinning into Eliot, breaking both of their concentration so that they went tumbling into the snow, skidding—and laughing with screams of delight—along its packed surface down to the bottom.

*That'll show them,* she said, though Jacob could hear her laugh as well.

They reached the top of the hill and lay down on their sleds, side by side, pointing down toward another side of the hill that was less steep but longer.

*Ready?* she said.

*Whenever you are.*

She pushed off, and he followed suit. It didn't take long to get up to speed, and soon they were both hurtling across the surface, the cold wind numbing their faces, setting their eyes to tearing so that Jacob could barely see the terrain before him. All he could do was hold on and ride the bumps to the bottom.

Before long, the slope began to even out, but still they coasted until finally the sleds came to a gentle stop, the squeaking snow beneath them suddenly silent.

For a few minutes they just lay there in the silence, still feeling the rush of the hill.

"That . . ." Jacob said, pausing to turn over onto his back in the sled, "that was fun."

*It feels good to have fun,* he thought. It had been so long. He'd come so far, had endured so much. And though he'd tasted adventure and learned more than he'd ever thought he would, none of it had been fun, none of it had been as simple as this.

"It does feel good to have fun," Nadia said. Jacob wondered if she'd heard his thought, or if it was just her own.

"So many stars," he said, looking up at the glittering constellations.

"It's a beautiful night. It's always a beautiful night here," she quipped. He could hear the edge in her voice.

"You miss the daylight," he said.

"I miss the trees," she said. "The sun, the grass, the animals. To go outside without this suit. I miss all that stuff."

"I've found myself missing the grasslands on Nova Campi," he admitted. "But the snow's not bad. You can't slide on grass."

"True," she whispered. She hesitated. *Do you ever miss being a Blinder? Being back in your colony?*

"No. I'm not sure I ever have. Not really, anyway." *Do you?*

*I miss my family, my friends,* her voice sounded in his mind. *I miss my parents.*

*I know,* he replied. *I still do too. But that's not the same thing.*

"Maybe," she said. There was a long pause.

*Sometimes I wish I could go back,* he heard her say, her mindspeak so distant it was as if she were whispering. *Back to being a Blinder, back before the changes, before I could do these strange things, when things were normal.*

He turned to look over at her, remembering how Bennet had said almost the same thing on board the *Caber*. He could see the same sort of sadness in her eyes now as they reflected the moonlight.

"It's okay," he said. "I had a hard time understanding what was happening. I still do. But I don't know if the normal life was ever really good, or if it was even normal. And as much as I miss my parents and the friends I left on Nova Campi after I escaped, I just feel lucky I've got the chance to be with people who understand what I am, to be where I belong."

257

"Me too," she said at last.

She turned and looked into his eyes.

*Jacob, don't tell anyone what I thought. Please.*

*I won't,* he promised.

She nodded her thanks, then turned her face back toward the sky.

"I wonder which one's mine," she wondered out loud. "Which star did I come from?"

Scanning the night, he felt a strange wave come over him, a shiver that had nothing to do with the frigid air biting at his nose. And before he knew it, the words just tumbled out.

"That one," he said, pointing toward a tiny light near the horizon.

For a moment they just stared at each other. Then Nadia sat up, a puzzled look on her face.

"How do you know?" she asked.

He sat up as well, shaking his head. "I'm not sure," he said at last.

She stared hard at him for a moment before a grin appeared on her face. She burst out laughing.

"Good one," she gasped between laughs.

Before he could protest, something struck him in the face. The next thing he knew, he was gasping as well, brushing icy crystals of snow from his face. He glanced over at Nadia in time to see her look of dismay disappear beneath a burst of snow.

"You little brats!" she screamed, wiping her face and jumping to her feet.

Jacob whirled to see Eliot and Desmond kneeling twenty yards away, laughing hysterically, as they formed a line of snowballs, each of which flew through the air toward him and

Nadia as soon as it was packed.

*Stand back,* she said, and jumped in front of him. She held out her hand and the salvo of snowballs disappeared before them one after another in a puff of white.

It didn't seem to daunt the twins, who packed faster and faster, sending the frozen chunks of snow flying so quickly they became blurs in the moonlight, turning into magnificent bursts as they struck Nadia's shield.

Jacob could only stand back helplessly, watch and listen to their laughter, and try to push away the twinge of envy as they directed their powers at one another. There was only one thing to distract him. He glanced back up into the sky toward the star he'd called out earlier on the horizon. A dim point of light, nearly lost among the dozens of other brighter stars around it, it seemed suddenly distinct, a star like no other.

# CHAPTER TWENTY-TWO

Two days later, Avery caught up to Jacob on his way from breakfast.

"Hey, kid," the man said, throwing an arm around Jacob's shoulder.

Jacob glanced up at him. "Hi, Avery."

Avery gave him a worried look. "Hope Caolas isn't working you too hard."

"No, Caolas has been fine," Jacob replied.

He mustered a smile. It wasn't easy. All morning he'd been feeling low, wading against the ebbing tide of memory. In fact, ever since his conversation with Nadia, hearing her momentary expressions of doubt, of regret, of homesickness, he'd begun thinking about Xander and Delaney, wondering what they doing, if they were safe. But it wasn't just them. He found himself remembering Dobson—always with a pang of sadness—as well as Morag and Chester. Most of all, he found himself thinking about Bennet, missing the man's company. Was the captain still on the other side of the world, waiting for luck to shift his way? Or had he already gone back out into space to find it?

"I'm okay," he added. "I was just remembering my friends, some of the people I left behind."

Avery nodded. "Everyone goes through it. It's like, you go through so much just to get here that you don't think much about what you've left behind. But once the dust settles, it all catches up."

Jacob gave him a raw smile and nodded.

"Don't worry," Avery said. "It'll pass. Clarissa and I are looking out for you. Just be sure to ask for help if you need it."

"You don't think you can give me a power, do you?" Jacob said. Every day it was getting harder to watch Nadia and the twins go through their exercises, to hear about the other Seers and all the different things they could do.

Avery laughed. "Maybe," he said, suddenly growing serious. "That's what today is about."

Jacob realized they'd reached the entrance to the sanctuary. He expected Avery to part company from here, but today, after opening the door for Jacob, the man followed him inside.

Right away, Jacob noticed things were different. Nadia, Desmond, and Eliot were nowhere to be seen. Caolas was there, but instead of sitting on the floor in his usual spot, off to the side near the door to his quarters, he was seated on a chair in the middle of the room. Two other chairs waited, all three pointing toward the center. A circle enclosed the group of chairs, and the floor lights had been dimmed to the point where the crystals in the ceiling barely glimmered.

*Come have a seat, Jacob,* Caolas instructed.

Jacob walked to the center of the room, taking the seat Caolas offered. Avery took the third chair within the circle. Jacob resisted the urge to ask what was happening. The looks on both men's faces that something important was about to happen sent a fear-tinged thrill down his spine.

"So you've been with us for a week now, Jacob," the white-haired man said. "Are you comfortable?"

"Yes," Jacob said. "I'm grateful to be here." He tried to push away the morning's melancholy, wanting none of it to sound in his voice. For in spite of the nostalgia and anxiety stirring within him, those feelings paled against the warmth he found each night talking with Avery and Clarissa, each day he spent working with Caolas, Nadia, and the twins, each meal he shared with all the Seers.

"We're grateful you're here as well," Caolas replied, setting Jacob at ease with a smile. "Avery tells me Clarissa senses some frustration in you. An eagerness."

Jacob looked over at Avery, who gazed back intently.

"Yes," he said, nodding. "I want to know what my power is. Or if I even have one. You said before that some don't. I've been wondering ever since."

"What if you didn't?" Avery asked. "How would that make you feel?"

Jacob hesitated. He didn't want to lie, knew there was no point in it, but it was too difficult to say the truth.

"I could live with it," he said at last. "At least I would know."

Caolas chuckled. "A fair answer. What does your gut tell you, Jacob?"

Again, Jacob hesitated before answering. He couldn't help but feel as if he were being somehow tested.

"There is a power in me," he said at last. "But it still feels separate, like it's waiting for me to find it and make it mine."

"I believe you're right, though you put it more insightfully than I could've," Caolas said. "I listened carefully to your story the other day. There was much to hear, Jacob. Many clues. I think I know what you're capable of. I can only hope I'm right."

"So what is it?" Jacob cried, looking back and forth between the two men. Avery glanced over at Caolas, a tense look on his face.

"I need to be sure before I tell you," Caolas said, frowning. "You're going to need to show me. Show both of us. That's why I've asked Avery to join us. He has a power too. He can see into another's dreams, journey with the dreamer."

"I had an experience like that once," Jacob said, picturing the bright-eyed old woman in the cottage.

"Yes. Morag. I remember you telling me. It is a great gift. One I feel fortunate to share."

Avery laughed. "Only, you can do it from across the universe."

Caolas smiled. "Not very well, unfortunately—a fact to which Jacob can attest."

"So what do I have to do?" Jacob asked. "Tell me and I'll do it."

Caolas shook his head. "Just follow us in. That's the easy part. After that it's up to you." He hesitated. "You need to understand, Jacob, that normally we wouldn't do this until you'd been with us for quite some time. Your mind has only just begun its training."

"Then why now?" Jacob asked. He could feel his heart start to pound.

Caolas lowered his head. "Things are moving quickly. We spoke of it the other day. Time has suddenly become of the essence." He looked back up. "Avery thinks you're up to the challenge, though. And I, too, think you're strong enough. But the final decision is yours. You need to realize, though—you will be changed by this."

There was a moment of quiet. Jacob felt a wave of fear rise up from within. He took a deep breath and rode it, let it come and go.

"I want to know," Jacob said at last. "I feel like I've been preparing for this moment my whole life."

"In a way, you have been," Avery said.

"You want to know, and so you shall," Caolas said. "Only one thing, Jacob," he added. *This is going to hurt.*

Jacob glanced at both of them and swallowed before nodding his assent.

"Good," Caolas said. "Now close your eyes and follow me."

Jacob opened his eyes to the gray flower, the yellow grass, and leafless trees of Maker's Drift.

For a moment he just regarded the flower. It looked like the same one, only its petals were pulled in, its head no more than a pointed silver bud.

*I'm back*, he thought. *Did I ever leave? Was everything after just a dream?*

He realized he wasn't sure. Nothing appeared to have changed in the two months he'd been away—the world dormant, everything dead-looking, like the border region on Teiresias where day slipped into night. Then again, maybe it was always like this. Maybe the plants, the trees only looked dead and were just as alive as the green and purple grasses of Nova Campi. Who could account for the life of an alien world?

Then two things made him realize he wasn't back, that everything that had happened since was more than just a dream, that this was a dream.

First, he couldn't move. He felt tied to the earth as he often did at the start of his visions—sluggish, heavy, as if his bones were made of lead.

And then there was the presence behind. Two presences, and he knew both Caolas and Avery were with him. Though it comforted him a little, it made him anxious as well. He knew he had to show them something, had to figure it out. But what was it?

*Trust the vision. It will show you,* a voice sounded in his head, though he wasn't sure if it was Caolas's or his own.

It was dusk in the meadow. At least that's how it seemed. Or perhaps it was the storm clouds. Glancing up from the corner of his eye, he could see them, dark in the sky. And there was that smell in the air—the smell of moisture, the smell of rain.

Sure enough, a drop fell on his face, large and cold, splattering into little droplets that trickled down his cheek. Another followed it. Then another. Then the sky opened up. A rumble of thunder sounded in the distance. He could feel himself getting soaked, could feel the ground soaking in the rain. He watched the flower bend as the drops darkened the bud.

He was nervous for a moment. The thought of drowning ran through his head, the rain was so thick. But then he realized that there was nothing to fear. In fact, he felt as if he were coming back to the world, awakening after a long sleep. He could feel the rain dissolve the bonds tying him to the ground, wash away his grogginess even as the sky continued to darken.

The same held for the flower. He sat up, his eyes widening in amazement as the bud began to open up and blossom, come to life before him. Only now, the blood-red center eye was gone, replaced by a single point of light that brightened as the petals drew back, growing brighter and brighter by the second until he had to turn away.

The flower's light, like a piece of star fallen from the sky, illuminated the clearing, shining up into the dusk and rain so that the drops seemed to catch the light and sparkle, sending out a thousand prisms.

Jacob reached down and plucked the flowered star before rising to his feet. His hand trembled, a thrill went up his arm, passing from the blossom into his body and through him, wrapping him in electric warmth. He didn't bother to look behind him to his companions. He knew they could feel it just as well.

He lowered the flower, holding it before him so that it cast its light into the woods. Through the rain he could see an opening, the trunks of trees curving on both sides to form the entrance to a tunnel through the woods.

He passed quickly into the trees, shining the blossom before him as he went. Though it was darker in the forest, the rain was less severe, and he made good time. Soon he could see that the trees were thinning. The tunnel was coming to an end.

He came out into another clearing. The smell of wood smoke hung heavy in the air. Through the foggy rain he could see a cottage, its windows glowing invitingly. Jacob smiled. He knew that cottage.

As he started making his way across the yard, a noise caught his ear. He stopped to listen. It was music, the same chorus of ghostly voices that had been haunting him for the last week. Only there were no crystals on this world, nothing glittering but the drops falling around his light. Still, the music hovered in the air above him. And though the rain still fell from the sky, it made no noise, its patter replaced by the chord.

Reaching the door, Jacob paused to place the flower carefully in his coat pocket. He could feel its warmth against his body, and though his jacket dampened the light, he could still see its glow against his chest. He wiped the rain from his forehead and opened the door.

The music he'd heard outside was transformed as he stepped over the threshold. The notes remained the same, but their tone changed. No longer the ethereal chorus always floating at the edge of reach, it became earthly, with a rich, raw hum.

It was Chester's smallpipes. Jacob entered the cottage, rounding the corner to find the old man seated by the fire, his eyes closed as he pumped the bellows, filling the bag, setting the drones to song while his fingers worked the chanter, rocking slightly as he played, his upper body a combination of different movements made one.

Morag sat beside him, knitting what looked like a black blanket or cape, decorated with a sprinkle of stars. With a glance, he recognized the pattern: the same starry sky he'd seen his last night on Maker's Drift as he waited for Bennet to be healed.

Chester never roused from his playing, but Morag beamed when she saw him.

"I knew I'd see you in my dreams once more," she said.

"But this is my dream, Morag," Jacob replied.

"It's all the same, really," she murmured. "Either way, it's good to see you're safe."

"But I'm not, Morag," he cried. "I'm not safe at all. I

need to find a way out."

She nodded. "Very well," she said, rising from her chair. "I made you this. It ought to help."

Morag came over and spread the blanket out around him so that it draped over his shoulders and hung down.

"There you go, dear," she said, wrapping the blanket around him so that the stars folded in new patterns. "Poor thing. You're soaking wet."

"Thank you," he said. He was about to ask her how it was supposed to help when a flash of light caught his eye. He turned toward the fireplace. Its flames were gone. Like the vision he'd had the last time he was in the cottage, a sphere of light hovered in its place, growing steadily larger, coloring the cabin—the lanterns and candles now extinguished—with its bluish white glow.

*There it is again,* he thought. He looked over at Morag with grim satisfaction. Already, he could feel its pull.

"Time to finish what you started," Morag murmured, her voice now barely audible above the pipes.

Jacob nodded. A chill emanated from the brilliant orb, a shock of cold that radiated out just as its force pulled him in. He could see his breath cloud in its light, could feel his hair, wet with rain, begin to harden and freeze. He wrapped the wool blanket more tightly around him and walked toward the sphere.

Before, he'd felt heavy, had had trouble stepping across the cottage floor. But he felt no heaviness now, buoyed by the humming drones. The last few steps, he wasn't even sure if his feet touched the floor as he reached a hand out to the frosty light.

At contact, the light exploded, engulfing him, drawing

him into a blank world. He could feel himself growing stronger in its light and smiled, for by now he knew exactly where he was.

It felt good to be back in otherspace. He'd traveled it in his waking life and traveled it in his dreams, each time with increasing comfort. But this time, Jacob no longer felt its otherworldly touch, no longer felt its distortions. He no longer felt anything. He looked down and saw that his star cloak had faded, his clothes had disappeared, leaving him naked as he hurtled through the brilliant emptiness.

It was then the burning started, so slight at first that he wondered if he felt it at all. Then it grew, spread across his entire body at once, until every cell along the surface of his skin was on fire. He could feel himself accelerating and closed his eyes, wishing it would stop, wishing he could slow down, for the speed only made the burning worse. The music had followed him, no longer the pipes but a ringing chord, piercing so that he could barely hear his own screams.

He had burned before, in a fever dream back on Nova Campi, trapped in the ghostbox bunker as fire swept through Harmony. But this was far worse. He was a comet, a falling star, burning away. Glancing down, he could see himself on fire, could see his flesh blackening and splitting, turning to ash and blowing away until there was nothing left but bone, until he was nothing more than a skeleton, like the one he'd found tangled in the grass so long ago during his exodus across the plains. Then even that was gone. There was nothing left. He had become just a part of the fabric of otherspace.

The music stopped, the burning stopped. The light was gone. All was dark. And Jacob was floating.

For a long time he floated in the silence, resisted opening

his eyes. More than anything, he just wanted to savor the absence of pain. But it still hung with him, palpable through its very absence. Somehow he knew the memory of that pain would be with him forever, like a secret scar deep inside that marked him with its power, a precious pearl, a treasure.

Jacob finally opened his eyes. He was in space. Not in a ship, gazing through a window, not astride any beast or burning vessel as he had done in earlier visions. He was alone, surrounded by countless stars. No, not alone—he could still feel the presence of his watchers. But they were faint now, distant.

The stars, near and far, all different sizes and colors, glittered as they never had before, each one distinct, unique. He had the sudden feeling that he knew them, knew all of them. All those days he'd spent studying charts on board the *Caber* came back to him, and as he gazed about him, the names of stars appeared against the darkness of space, flashing for a second beside each star then fading, a steady pattern of glowing letters twinkling like the stars themselves.

Then, when the names had come and gone, a new revelation appeared. A flash of light caught his eye. Jacob turned to watch as the flare leaped forward, tracing a line of light as it streaked across space, a burning path that traveled through the dark before suddenly ending in a distant spot. A second flash appeared, tracing a new line that intersected the other, snaking in a different direction, shorter than the first.

One after another the lines appeared, beginning and ending with flashes of light, until the entirety of space was interlaced with glowing paths, a woven net that crossed between and around the stars. And, like the stars, he suddenly realized he knew them all, could pick them apart at will, for they were his, they were as much a part of him as the web of veins

270

within his body, the neural pathways within his brain.

A flash suddenly appeared right before him, blinding him for a moment. Before he knew it, he found himself being pulled into its light, just as the line itself sped away to an unknown destination.

Then he was absorbed, speeding along with the blur of light, moving faster and faster through otherspace once more. There was no burning this time, though a wave of pain rose up from within, a memory of what he'd just escaped. He soon forgot it, all his thoughts now turned toward where he was going as a point of darkness ahead punctuated the light, growing larger and larger. He was reaching the end. . . .

He felt cold. He opened his eyes to find he was lying in the snow. Gasping, he forced himself to his feet and looked around.

He was back on Teiresias. Turning to look behind, Jacob saw no sign of Caolas or Avery. He couldn't even feel their presence. He was alone.

Wrapped in Morag's star blanket, he stood at the edge of a cliff overlooking a broad expanse of drifted snow and ice as the frozen wind howled around him. Night's Head rose in the distance, the mountain dominating the horizon. The web of lines still burned in the dark sky of space above him, making the surface glow, but as Jacob watched, the lines began to fade, one after another, until there was nothing left but the stars.

A warmth against his chest made him look down. Pulling the blanket aside, he saw the glow of the flower beneath his jacket. He reached in and took it out, squinting against the brightness. It warmed his face, drove away the cold. But even as it did so, he could see the silver petals begin to wither and

curl back, watched the leaves along the stem blacken and dis-
integrate into scattered ash. Even the stalk fell apart in his
hand, so that all that was left was the brilliant point of light
that had formed its center, hovering before him.

Jacob gasped as the tiny star floated away from him. He
watched as it drifted out over the cliff, weaving across the
expanse, now gathering speed and light, growing in size as it
headed toward the mountain.

Then it disappeared. The wind suddenly died. In the
silence Jacob wondered if the star had reached the mountain
when a blinding flash burst on the horizon where Night's
Head had been, a wave of heat and light that rippled across
the land, hurtling toward him. He knew he had to run, but
there was nowhere to go, no way to escape the oncoming
blast. All he could do was close his eyes and turn away.

# CHAPTER TWENTY-THREE

*Jacob? Jacob, can you hear me?* the voice whispered softly in his mind.

*I can hear you, Delaney,* he replied.

*Oh,* she replied. Jacob could hear the pain in her voice.

He opened his eyes to see Delaney's face looking down on him, her eyes moist, her smile tight with concern.

*Your eyes,* he said. His head felt heavy, confused. He shut his lids and when he opened them again, she was gone. It was Clarissa looking down on him, Clarissa's eyes that were wet with the threat of tears.

He propped himself up on one elbow and looked around. He was on Caolas's bed in the small chamber beside the sanctuary that served as the man's quarters. Caolas was there, sitting beside Clarissa, as was Avery, watching from the corner with anxious eyes.

"It's good to see you awake," Avery said, getting up from his chair and coming over. "You've been out for a while. We were starting to get worried."

"How do you feel?" Caolas asked. Jacob could hear the excitement in his voice.

"Okay," he replied, sitting up. He rubbed his eyes. They felt sore. "I have a little bit of a headache."

"Do you remember?" Avery asked.

Jacob paused, thinking over what had transpired—the flower, the burning, the stars, the pathways of light in space, the final explosion. It was all there.

"I remember," he said, wincing at the memory of pain.

"Remarkable," Caolas said, shaking his head. "Better than I could have hoped."

"Then it worked?" Jacob whispered.

Caolas nodded with a smile.

"Your power has manifested, though the process had started long before today. When you told me of your travels, I was fairly sure of it, but this morning's journey confirmed it."

"Confirmed what?" Jacob cried. He had expected to awaken with a clear sense of what he was, who he had become, but all he had was a headache.

"Come, Jacob," Caolas said, holding up a hand. "Surely you must know. You can see things no one else can see. You can go places none of us can go."

"Do you mean otherspace?" Jacob asked. His heart began to beat.

Caolas nodded. "No one enters a wormhole without at least some trace of trepidation. For many it's terrifying. Otherspace is like a little death to most of us, a moment of nothingness from which we all fear we can never return, yet we always do. But for that period of time, everything stops."

"Except for me," Jacob whispered.

"Yes. You seem to have an affinity for it. And not just for the world between the wormholes, but for the stars as well, for all of space. You can see it like no other person can. Your mobility in otherspace, the way you learned to read the charts so quickly, read the stars and pick a path from any point in space, the innate ability to comprehend what only an experienced navigator can, and only then with the aid of a computer—all those things you experienced from the first time you entered otherspace were expressions of your emerging power."

"You mean I've had this all along?"

"Of course," Caolas replied. "We all carry our potentialities within us. It's just a matter of whether our life's journey will be enough to evoke them. Both our choices and the things that happen to us without our choosing make us who we are, regardless of what our powers may be."

"Oh," Jacob murmured. It made sense what Caolas was saying, and as his headache dissipated, as the heaviness began to fade, the meaning of his vision became clearer, so that he could begin to see it as Caolas saw it and understand how he was different. But what puzzled him was that being different, knowing his difference, didn't seem to have altered anything. For some reason, he had expected his change would have made the outside world a different place.

"You seem disappointed," Avery said.

Jacob blushed. He felt as if he'd somehow been called out.

"No," he replied. "I wanted to know, and now I do. It's good."

The other three all gave one another a sharp look. Jacob felt his stomach drop. Had he offended them?

When they turned back to him, their expressions were intent but not severe.

"It's more than just good, Jacob," Caolas murmured. "There's something else you need to know." He paused for a moment. Jacob could sense him assembling his thoughts, gathering his words for maximum effect.

"Years ago, I had a vision, Jacob. A powerful vision, of the kind you had today. I saw a world, a hidden planet waiting just for us where we could start over, build a home for ourselves without the fear that it could all be torn from us at a moment's notice. I saw a place where we all belonged and could call our own.

"All we needed was for someone to show us the way. From the moment I saw that world, I knew there would be a person who would one day come to lead us there. Only, for a long time it didn't happen. Simon Volker—the one I told you of earlier—thought he was that person, insisted it was him. For a brief time, I thought so as well. It felt right. But his madness proved me wrong."

He paused, closing his eyes for a moment before continuing.

"And so I had to wait, wait for the time when the true finder would come. I spent many hours meditating, Jacob. Many hours searching. My searching showed me a world half in darkness, half in light, half alive, half dead. It was this planet, Teiresias."

"So this is the world?" Jacob asked. It didn't make sense. They'd spoken only days ago about the fact that the Foundation was moving in on them, that they would soon have to flee.

"No. But Teiresias was more than just a place to hide. My meditations told me that this was where we should go, where we would find the answer, find the person who would show us the way. And so we came. And it worked. We found the finder."

Caolas folded his hands in his lap and smiled. Jacob glanced nervously at Clarissa and Avery, who simply watched him in eager silence. Suddenly, it all clicked. He understood the meaning of their stares.

"Me?" he cried. "You think I'm the one?"

Caolas chuckled. "Yes," he murmured. "Yes, I do, Jacob."

Jacob rose from the bed. "Just because I know the stars and can walk around in otherspace?"

"It's more than that, Jacob. You know more than just the stars, you know the paths between the stars, where things begin and end. All of space—you can see it!"

Jacob remembered what Dobson had told him about how valuable wormholes were, how few had been discovered, forcing ships to depend on breakers to bridge the vast distances between worlds.

"But I don't know where this world you're talking of is. I don't know how to get you there."

"I think you do, though you may not know it yet. But somewhere, buried in your brain, is the secret, waiting to come out. Perhaps it already has. Maybe it's there in plain sight, waiting for you to find it."

"How long have you suspected?"

Caolas paused. "From the time I first felt your presence, from those first scratchy moments we met in your fevered dream, I felt there was something different about you. I tried to be skeptical at first—I'd been fooled before—but there was no denying what my intuition was telling me. It only grew stronger the closer you came."

"That's why you let me come," Jacob murmured. "In spite of the danger. In spite of the chance that I'd be followed here by the Foundation."

"No," Caolas said. "We called you to us because you are one of us. Nothing would ever change that. Still, what you say has a certain truth. You bring hope, Jacob, something greater than whatever fear might have followed on your heels."

Jacob hesitated, looking over at Clarissa and Avery. He could see it on their faces, everything Caolas had just described.

"Does everybody know?" he whispered.

"A few sense it," Avery said, "but no one except us knows for certain."

"Knows for certain, huh?" Jacob murmured.

"We don't have to tell anybody right now," Clarissa offered.

"But they'll have to be told at some point," Caolas said. "They need to know."

"Right," Jacob whispered.

"Don't worry, Jacob," Avery said. "Everything will be okay. You'll see."

Jacob shivered. Remembering the final image of his dream, the closing rush of light, he wondered if he already had.

"Coming to dinner?"

Jacob glanced up from his bed to see Avery and Clarissa standing in the doorway.

"I'm not very hungry," he whispered. He hadn't eaten since breakfast, but his stomach was too tied up in knots to want anything in it. He'd spent the last hour lying in bed, trying to make sense of what he'd seen and, more importantly, what he'd been told.

Jacob could see the worried glances the couple gave each other.

"You go ahead with Nadia," Clarissa whispered.

Avery nodded and left. Clarissa came over and sat down beside Jacob. She didn't say anything at first, but instead drew him to her, wrapped him in a warm embrace. He took a deep breath to hold back the tears gathering in his eyes. It had been so long since he'd been held. As good as it felt, it suddenly reminded him of his mother, a pang that made the rawness more raw.

"You've had a tough day, Jacob," she murmured. "Avery told me what you went through on your journey. It'll take a while to heal from this. But you will."

"It wasn't supposed to be like this," he said. "I was supposed to come here and find you and then just . . ."

"Just what, Jacob?"

"Just *live*. Just be where I was supposed to be. That's it."

"Sounds nice," she joked, releasing him. "Sounds easy."

Wiping his eyes, he laughed as he sat up. "That's right, easy. Without all this other stuff. This savior stuff."

"Savior, huh? You make it sound so important."

"It sounded important to me. Too important."

"Jacob, we all have a part to play in life. We all contribute to this community. This is just your contribution. Don't think of it as any more than that."

"Sounds like what they used to tell us back in Harmony."

She sighed. "It is, sort of. Only there, there was no choice."

"I didn't choose this," he snapped.

Clarissa nodded. "No, you didn't. But you will choose when and how, or even if, you use your powers. And you made the choice to join us here. You make the choice to stay. But that doesn't mean there aren't any responsibilities, that there isn't a price to pay."

"But Clarissa," Jacob whispered, looking into her eyes, "what if I can't do it? What if it's not true? Caolas even admitted he was wrong once before. What if he is again?"

She put an arm around his shoulder. "Then he is. No one

will think less of you. No one will think you're any less special than you already are."

They were both silent for a moment.

"I just thought for sure that this was it. This was where I was supposed to be."

"But you *are* where you're supposed to be," she offered. "You're with us. It doesn't matter where we go, as long as we're all together."

"Then why bother with this mystery world?" he snapped. "Why not just find another place to hide?"

"A life of hiding is no way to live," she said. "Besides, what's wrong with having something to hope for? What's wrong with giving people hope?"

"Nothing, unless you can't deliver. Besides," he added, "I don't believe in a perfect world, anyway. Harmony was supposed to be a perfect world."

"If—*when*—we find our new home, it won't be perfect, Jacob. And it definitely won't be easy. We'll have to start all over, build everything from scratch. But we'll be safe and, most of all, it'll be ours and no one else's."

He suddenly found himself remembering the birthday wish he'd made on board the *Caber*, that he would one day find his place. Maybe this was the true answer to his wish. *The place to be*, he thought.

Jacob stood up from his bed.

"I need some fresh air," he said. "I think I'll go for a walk."

"I understand," she said, joining him. "I'll fix you a plate and bring it back here. You can eat when you return."

"Thanks," he said. "For everything."

She gave him another quick hug, then went to join the rest for dinner.

Jacob waited until she was gone, then left their quarters and headed down the worn passageway to the arboretum, relieved to encounter no one. A few minutes later he was under the bright lights of the transition room before his locker. He took his time getting into his thermal suit, then headed into the hangar, pausing, as always, to catch his breath in the frozen darkness. He was about to open the small side door to the outside when a voice in his mind stopped his hand.

*Wait!*

He turned to see Nadia standing in her regular clothes beside the white floater, her arms wrapped tight around herself, shaking.

*Clarissa said you were going out. I thought you might like some company.*

He hesitated. *Sure,* he said at last. *Why not.*

"I'll be right there," she called out. She ran back inside, emerging a few minutes later in her winter clothes.

As they headed through the side door, Nadia grabbed a sled.

"Want one?" she asked.

"No thanks," he replied.

*Suit yourself,* she said.

They headed up the hill in silence, following the same path they'd walked the other day. The wind had scrubbed away most of their boot prints, though a dim outline of their steps still lingered in the snow.

Reaching the top, they stopped to catch their breath.

"Today was a hard day, wasn't it?" she asked.

He nodded.

"I remember when I went in with Caolas and Avery," she said, pushing snow into a pile with her boot. "It wasn't too long before you came."

"What did you see?"

She smashed her boot down, flattening the pile before scraping it back into place.

*Beautiful things,* she said. *And horrible things. It hurt.*

*It does,* he replied.

She positioned her sled, then plopped down into it.

"Come on," she said.

"No thanks," he replied. "You go."

"Come on," she repeated. "There's plenty of room on the back. You'll feel better."

He hesitated before sitting behind her on the sled, bringing his legs around under her own.

"Hang on tight," she whispered, taking his arms and placing them around her waist. He tightened his grip, hoping it might stop the trembling he could feel working into his limbs.

And then they were off, flying down the hill. He could hear her laughter, punctuated by a scream with every bump they hit. A few times, they almost lost their balance, but each time she put her hands out and steadied them back into position. Jacob just closed his eyes and held on, feeling the warmth and softness of her beneath his arms. The sensation of speeding through the darkness sent a thrill through his body as it had so many times as a child, racing with Egan and the others down the grassy slope along the northern edge of Harmony. This was as far away from that as he could ever hope to be, but for a brief moment, the feeling was the same.

They finally slowed, laughing between gasps for air in the cold. He let go of her and rolled backward onto the snow, still laughing.

"Not bad," she said.

"You're right," he replied. "I do feel better."

He stared up at the stars. They looked different than they had the last time he'd gazed up at them, the way people seemed different after discovering some secret about them. Then he remembered that it was him who was different, not the stars. It was his secret that had been discovered. The stars were what they always were.

He started to sit up when something about the sky caught his gaze. He froze, feeling a shiver creep up his back in spite of his suit's warmth.

There was a difference in the darkness above him. He knew the stars. He could name the ones that had been named by the charts, knew the rest that hadn't been named, knew his position in relation to them all. And it was this knowledge that made him realize something was wrong.

There were too many.

He rubbed his eyes again. No. The strange lights were too pale, too indistinct to be stars. One by one they appeared across the sky. Several were quite large, blurry drops of luminosity, like the smallest of distant moons.

Slowly they began to fade away, though with a little concentration he realized he could bring them back, make them reappear.

Wormholes. He was seeing wormholes.

The knowledge sprang up, unbidden, from deep inside, from the memory of this morning's pain and beauty, and for a second he could almost see the blazing trails shooting away from each opening, twisting off to faraway points in space. It was merely an echo of the vision, but it didn't matter—deep down he knew where each one came out, could sense what path it took.

He scrambled to his feet and searched the sky in all directions, pausing over each wormhole that appeared, hoping one would emerge, stand separate from the others. Caolas had believed that Teiresias was where they—where he—would find the way to the hidden planet. It just had to be somewhere in the endless night above him.

But he saw nothing. Nothing in those lights between the stars that gave him any sense of what he should be finding.

*What are you looking for?*

He glanced down to see Nadia now standing beside him, gazing up into the sky.

*Hope.*

*What about it?*

"Do you have hope?"

"I do. I wouldn't be here if I didn't. I never would have left."

"That's right," he said. "That's true."

She smiled. "Ready to go again?" she asked, picking up the sled.

"Absolutely."

"Race you to the top," she cried.

She tore off up the slope, and he followed, letting the wormholes fade back into the night.

His sleep was restless from the start, his headache returning not long after he closed his eyes, a dull residue of the vision's pain. The ringing chord, its timbre appearing at the edges of his dozing, didn't help. He could almost feel the crystals in the rock around him reverberating, growing, filling the carved-out passages, crushing them all.

The discomfort carried over into his dreams. He was

stumbling through the snow, a thousand wormholes blazing overhead, holding his finder out before him, sweeping it back and forth. But it was silent. He knew why it wasn't working—he had no name to give it, nothing for it to lock on to. Once he thought he knew, but when he tried to speak it, his mouth refused to work. It was frozen shut. Looking down, he realized all of him was frozen, coated in ice. He had forgotten his suit, had wandered out into Teiresias's night with nothing more than his old smock from Harmony.

Suddenly, the finder began to beep. He turned until the signal reached its height, then pushed numbly through the drifts, his heart pounding, matching the finder's rapid pulse.

A distant figure appeared in the direction where the finder was pointing, marching steadily toward him. Jacob called out and waved his arms, and the figure waved back. But as the silhouette drew closer, began taking on its familiar black shape, Jacob pulled to a stop. He tried to run, but his legs were frozen into ice. He could only stand and shiver as Folgrin came to him, that same dark smile on his face. . . .

The lights rose as Jacob sat up in bed with a gasp. There was an uneasiness, a prickling in his spine the likes of which he hadn't felt in weeks. At first he thought it was simply the nightmare, but he suddenly heard Avery and Clarissa stirring in the next room.

He jumped out of bed and ran into the common room only seconds before the couple appeared.

"You sense it too?" Clarissa asked him.

"Yes," he cried.

Nadia emerged from her room, a look of worry on her face. "What's going on?" she murmured.

"Hush," Avery whispered. *Listen.*

285

There was a cry in the distance, faint, muffled. Jacob went to the door of their quarters and opened it, listening again. There it was—the sound of a woman's screams echoing down the corridor.

He tore off down the tunnel, the others close behind, dashing past sleepy men and women stepping out in confusion.

The woman's screams grew louder as he entered the arboretum. Squinting against the brilliant orb overhead, he rounded the path to see Elise—the woman who had spoken with him his first morning at breakfast—kneeling on the ground in her nightclothes before a fountain, her head in her hands, shrieking.

Avery pushed past him and took Elise in his arms, calling her name as she struggled, still screaming. Then she slackened, breaking into sobs as Avery rocked her.

"They're coming!" she cried. "They're almost here."

Over and over she repeated the words as people congregated in the clearing. Jacob could see the looks of worry on their faces as they whispered to one another. The fear that had been slowly gathering underneath had finally risen to the surface.

The whispering stopped. The crowd grew quiet. Jacob looked over to see Caolas standing nearby, a grim smile on his face.

"We had better get ready," he said. "It's time to leave."

# PART SIX
## Night's Head

# CHAPTER TWENTY-FOUR

The sky seemed to brighten by the second as the floater made its way across the terminator, passing from night to day. Jacob kept an eye out below, watching the surface, noting how the snow gave way to dark earth, then to the pale grass of the tundra, which soon became dotted with low-lying shrubs and trees before turning to forest. The sun's emergence on the horizon made him blink, more out of instinct than from any real brightness on its part. Though barely more than a week had passed since he'd last seen it, somehow the time seemed much longer.

He and Avery spoke little on the ride to Tendrille, allowing the floater's hum to fill the silence. There was a strange sense of peace in the cockpit, as if both of them were making a conscious effort to put aside their fear and savor the last few hours of what passed for normalcy, neither knowing how long it might last. For much of the journey, Jacob tried forgetting the sound of Elise's screams and the nightmare that had preceded them. Mostly, he tried fending off the guilt that was steadily building at the edges of his mind, the feeling that he—the person most likely responsible for both their detection and their salvation—was supposed to somehow fix this whole crisis. Jacob wondered if Avery was thinking the same thing about him in the silence.

In spite of all that, Jacob was just glad to be along. After people had retired back to their quarters, and Elise had been treated with a sedative and returned to bed, Caolas had called a quick conference in the sanctuary with Avery, Clarissa, Marcus, and a few others. To his surprise, Jacob had been included as well.

The reason why quickly became apparent.

"I realize today was exceptionally difficult," Caolas told him as the others looked on. "The pain, the powers, the burden they entail—it is all most regrettable. But this is a desperate time, Jacob, so I will ask you simply—if you have any sense of where we should go, now would be a good time to let us know."

Jacob felt the blood rush to his face. He hesitated for a moment. "I went out earlier and studied the sky," he said at last.

"And what did you see?"

"Wormholes. They were everywhere. I studied each one. The stars too," he said. He could sense the anticipation of the adults, as if they had all drawn a collective breath. "But there was nothing," he murmured.

The collective breath exhaled. Jacob could almost feel the deflation, though their faces remained placid.

"It's okay, Jacob," Marcus offered with a smile. "Don't worry about it."

"That's right," Caolas said. "You will see it someday. And when you do, you'll know it."

The others voiced their agreement. Jacob nodded his thanks before looking away.

"In that case," Avery said, "there's no time to lose. It's

going to take us most of a day to get everything together."

"Do we really have to leave now?" Jacob asked.

"Elise is one of our most sensitive Seers," Caolas said. "If she says they're coming, then they are."

"I still don't understand," Clarissa murmured. "I thought that the way would be found here. Teiresias was supposed to be the place."

"Maybe it is," Caolas replied. "We can always come back. But for now, we can't risk waiting for them to find us."

"How could they find us, though?" Jacob asked. "The Foundation wants nothing to do with any of the Seers. And they can't see themselves."

"They won't likely come, Jacob," Avery said. "But they have resources. And there are plenty out there who would be willing to do their work for a price. The Foundation will hold its nose and reach out if they feel there's a need."

"Then it's settled," Caolas said. "Avery, you must leave for the port at once and find us a ship. Anything will do at this point. The rest of us will start packing."

"Got it," Avery said. They all began to rise.

"Wait!" Jacob said. "I want to go too."

Everyone turned to look at him. Even he was surprised— the words just came out. But he had the sudden feeling that he had to make the trip, a prickling along his spine that told him it was vital. An image of Bennet sitting in a booth in the Mandrel appeared in his mind. Or maybe that was it—just wishful thinking he might see his friend again.

Caolas hesitated. "I don't know if that's wise," he said. "After everything you've been through today."

"But I know someone who might be able to help," Jacob replied. "If he's still there."

"He doesn't happen to have a ship, does he?" Marcus joked.

"No," Jacob said. "At least, I don't think so. But he can help us find someone who does."

There was a pause. They all glanced at one another for a moment before Avery put a hand on Jacob's shoulder.

"I don't mind the company."

"Very well," Caolas said, giving Jacob a smile. "Good luck."

The sun had moved high into the sky by the time the port city appeared in the distance. Though there were a few silver towers of the kind Jacob was used to, Tendrille lacked the high profile of Nova Campi's Melville. On the other hand, BiCo's colony was much more expansive, its elaborate wooden halls and buildings spreading out through the surrounding jungle in a sprawling maze. Soon they were floating over half-hidden neighborhoods toward the port, as busy as ever with the coming and going of dozens of ships.

"So you really think Bennet's still here?" Avery asked, casting a sidelong glance toward Jacob as the floater slowed and lowered onto a back street near the port.

"Maybe," Jacob said. "He was going to try to find some friend of his who had a ship, another smuggler. If he did, he might still be here. Or he might be waiting for his friend to come back. It's only been a week."

"Does his friend have a ship?" Avery asked as the floater came to a stop.

"I think so."

"That would be nice," Avery said. "But if he doesn't—or even if Bennet's gone—it's not the end of the world. I've booked passage before, though maybe not under these circumstances. I can do it again."

"Do we have enough money?"

"That's the question. We've got a little nest egg. Those of
us who spend time away working always put what we've
saved into the pot. But it'll be a squeeze. It's short notice, and
that's never cheap."

"I've got this," Jacob offered. He took the diamond earring from his pocket and showed it to Avery. He'd kept it on
him the whole time. "Bennet said it was worth a lot of
money."

"Good," Avery said. "We'll probably need it."

Jacob reached down into his bag and pulled out the stunner Xander had given him.

"Think we'll need this?" he asked, offering it to Avery.

Avery's eyes widened at the sight of the weapon.
"Hopefully not," he murmured, taking the stunner and checking the settings, "but you never know." He handed the pistol
back to Jacob. "Here, you keep it. You can be my backup," he
said with a wink.

They stepped from the cruiser out into the blazing heat
and brightness of the sun's perpetual zenith. Though Jacob
balked for a moment at the temperature shift, it did feel good
to be outside without layers of clothing, to feel real sun on his
skin.

Avery handed him a pair of sunglasses and donned his
own.

"All right," he said, "stay low and keep close. They may be
looking out for us."

"I don't think so," Jacob said. "Not yet." Though he could
sense the danger underneath, stronger than he had for a long

time, he couldn't feel the eyes on him the way he had on Nova Campi. He reached into his pocket and felt the diamond. Maybe it was working after all.

A large passenger liner had recently made orbit, and waves of passengers, fresh from the shuttles, were leaving the terminal and filling the streets, eager to visit the shops and bars. Avery and Jacob fell in with the flood of people, dropping out only when they reached the alley that ran behind the Mandrel.

"I like to go in the back way," Avery said, "especially during times like these."

"Good idea," Jacob replied. As they started down the alley, Jacob suddenly thought of Xander. *I wish he were here,* he thought. *He would like something like this.*

But as they approached the back door of the bar, a dark wave of fear rose, a sharp twinge that set his hair on end, a foreboding of the kind he'd felt before boarding the *Justine,* though far more sinister in its depth. It stopped him in his tracks.

Avery had frozen as well. He turned to Jacob.

*You felt it too, huh?* he said.

Jacob nodded, his face pale. "Should we still go in?"

"I don't know if we have much choice," Avery murmured. "Most of the spacers who are likely to even consider us are probably in there. It's the best place to start. Just keep your eyes open."

"Right," Jacob replied. He took a deep breath and followed Avery in.

They moved slowly down the hall, letting their eyes adjust from the outside glare, listening to the clamor grow. When they reached the end, Jacob poked his head around the corner and scanned the area.

The place was packed with men and women of all sizes and colors, spacers telling stories, making deals, shouting over the sound of music and the clinking of glasses. As Jacob peered over the bar and between the crowds moving across the floor, his heart suddenly gave a leap.

"I see him!" he cried.

*Quiet down.*

*He's in the same booth as before.*

*Is he alone?*

Jacob stretched for a better look.

*I think so,* he said at last. *But I can't see very well from here.*

"All right," Avery said. "Follow me."

They left the doorway and moved along the wall, traveling parallel with the far side of the bar before settling into a place in the shadows opposite from Bennet's booth. Jacob was shocked at how different the man appeared, as if all the life had been sucked out of him from a week ago. The captain sat, staring down at his drink, his face somber as he checked his watch.

*You see him?* Jacob asked.

*Yeah, I see him.*

*So let's go.* Jacob started to leave the wall, but Avery grabbed him by the shoulder and pulled him back.

"Hold on, kid. You felt that back out in the alley, didn't you? Something's not right. Just wait."

With a look toward the door, Bennet suddenly stood up. Jacob prepared to follow him, but the man didn't leave. He just waited by the table. The crowd suddenly shifted, and Bennet disappeared.

"What's he doing?" Jacob asked. He kept craning for a glimpse, but there were too many people in the way. Finally, the crowd parted for just a moment. But it was long enough.

Jacob watched in horror as Bennet reached out and shook LaPerle's hand.

"Oh no!" Jacob whispered, grabbing Avery's arm. "No, no, no."

It seemed impossible, like some strange dream, far stranger than any vision. How could that man have followed him all the way to the far end of space? Even worse, what was Bennet doing greeting him? For a moment, Jacob wondered if he was just seeing things. He closed his eyes and opened them again, but LaPerle was still there, shaking Bennet's hand, wearing that same smarmy grin.

*Who is that guy?* Avery asked.

*He works for the Mixel Corporation,* Jacob replied.

Avery gave a grim smile and shook his head. Jacob was about to explain who he was, but before he could, the crowd shifted again and another man stepped forward to shake Bennet's hand.

This time, Jacob nearly cried out loud. He hadn't imagined there would be anyone he'd rather see less than LaPerle. But that changed as soon as the man in the black suit appeared at LaPerle's side.

Avery moaned. *Oh, God, not him. I should've known.*

Jacob glanced over at Avery in shock. *You mean you know Folgrin?*

Now it was Avery's turn to be stunned. His face turned grim.

*Jacob, that's not Folgrin. That's Simon Volker. He used to be one of us.*

Jacob felt his heart begin to race. *But that's the man from the* Odessa*!* he said, fighting the urge to cry out. *He was on Nova Campi. He would have followed me all the way here if we hadn't crashed.*

"Looks like he made it after all," Avery murmured.

They watched as the three men sat down in the booth, Bennet on one side, LaPerle and Volker on the other.

A sudden thought made Jacob start. He reached over and grabbed Avery's arm.

*Avery, if he used to be one of the Seers, does that mean he can hear us? Can he know we're here?*

Avery hesitated. *I don't know. I can't sense him, though. I don't think he can hear our thoughts. But I don't know why.*

"Caolas said he went crazy," Jacob said, his eyes on Volker, suddenly afraid to mindspeak in spite of Avery's words.

"You could say that. Though I think he was half crazy from the start. Either way, he's trouble."

Jacob shivered at the thought of those days he'd spent on board the same ship with the man, all the times he'd caught him watching him with those glistening, black eyes.

"Do you think he's working for Mixel now?"

Avery shrugged. "That, or Mixel's working for him."

"How's that possible?" Jacob asked.

"It's not, unless he's with the Foundation now. It's what we've feared all along. Simon hinted that he was going back. I just can't imagine they would've taken him in."

"He had plenty to offer them. Like information about you, not to mention being someone who can see, who can do their dirty work for them," Jacob spat. "And I brought him here. It's all my fault."

"No, Jacob," Avery said. "Simon may have followed you from Nova Campi, but the Foundation already knew we were here. Caolas said you told him that the ghostbox back in Harmony said as much."

"Then why bother with me?" Jacob demanded.

Avery shrugged. "They probably hoped to use you to get to us. Easier than trying to search a whole planet."

"Yeah, they probably did," Jacob whispered, feeling suddenly sick. Watching Bennet and Volker together, talking once more like they had on the *Odessa*, seeing Bennet's betrayal play out before his eyes made his stomach turn. And then there was LaPerle.

"I just want to know what Mixel has to do with all this," he said.

"Me too. Nothing good, I'm sure. But they'll have to keep a low profile. This is a BiCo-owned planet. If their suits knew Mixel was poking around here, there'd be real trouble. In the meantime, Bennet doesn't have a clue where we are. So don't worry, Jacob. As long as we're careful, we'll be able to chart a ship and sneak our way off this world before anyone's the wiser."

The men's conversation didn't last long. At one point, it looked as if some sort of exchange was taking place as Bennet slid something across the table, but it was difficult to see with the shifting crowd. All Jacob could tell was that Bennet never smiled. Then Volker and LaPerle were standing. A moment later they were gone. Bennet stayed behind, staring at some small object in his hand before tucking it into his jacket.

"Well, I guess we better go. We'll have to come back when Bennet's gone," Avery said. "Doesn't look like your friend's going to help us. I'm sorry, Jacob. In the meantime, we'll go down to the hangars, poke around, and see what's there."

"I just don't get it," Jacob murmured, watching Bennet as he downed the rest of his drink and got up from the booth. "I thought for sure I could trust him. I had such a good feeling about him from the very start. I was so sure."

*It happens sometimes,* Avery said, putting a hand on his shoulder. *Nothing's foolproof—we all make mistakes.*

Jacob watched as Bennet headed for the door. After all those weeks they'd spent together on board the *Caber,* all those conversations, all the jokes, all the things Bennet had taught him—only to betray him in the end? Jacob could feel a wave of anger rise up.

Jacob broke away from the wall and headed toward the front door.

*What are you doing?*

*I've got to talk to him,* Jacob replied. *I need to understand this.*

"Forget it, Jacob," Avery said, catching up and putting out an arm to stop him. "Putting aside the fact that it's too dangerous, we don't have the time for this. Just let it go."

*I can't,* Jacob replied. "Besides," he said out loud, "we need to know what's going on, what he said to them. I think he gave them something. We have to find out."

Avery hesitated, before shaking his head.

"Fine," he said at last. "Just keep that stunner of yours handy. We might need it after all."

Jacob smiled, but he could feel the knots in his stomach tightening. He could still remember the first time he'd seen Xander pull the weapon from his cruiser's dashboard before their incursion into Mixel's headquarters to rescue Delaney.

The possibility that they would have to use it had sickened him. And now, here he was, carrying it himself. He could only wonder if he'd changed enough to be able to use it.

Coming out onto the sidewalk, they managed to spot Bennet just before he turned the corner. They quickly caught up and trailed him as he made his way down a brief series of streets before reaching a hotel. The Bradbury, a worn-looking wooden four-story building, had a series of staircases and balconies that ran the length of the hotel's face. Jacob and Avery watched as Bennet climbed to the third-story balcony and disappeared into one of the rooms.

"Hope you're right about this," Avery said.

"Me too."

They crossed the street and slipped up the stairs. A minute later they were at the door.

Taking a deep breath, Jacob pulled the stunner from his pocket, then reached up and knocked on the door.

Bennet opened the door and, seeing the pair, froze. Jacob watched as one wave of emotion after another—surprise, joy, worry, guilt—swept over Bennet's face in quick succession. Looking down at the stunner, he stepped back and held up his hands.

"You don't need that, kid," he said.

They moved into the room. Avery shut the door behind them.

"Don't I?" Jacob cried. He could tell the hand holding the stunner was shaking. He only hoped it wasn't shaking so much that either man noticed. "After what I just saw in the Mandrel, I have a hard time believing that."

Bennet swore. "The earring," he said, his voice rising. "Do you have it?"

Jacob hesitated.

"Do you have it?" Bennet cried, his eyes widening. He took a couple of steps toward Jacob.

"Yes!" Jacob cried, holding the stunner up higher, his hand shaking harder now. Bennet pulled up and thrust out his hand. "Give it to me," he commanded.

"Why should I? It's one of the only things protecting us right now."

"Just give it to me, dammit!" Bennet shouted.

*Do it,* Avery's voice sounded in his mind. Jacob glanced over at him in disbelief.

Avery nodded.

Jacob reached into his pocket and took out the diamond. He looked down at it for a moment, watched it sparkle in his palm before flicking it to Bennet.

Bennet snatched it out of the air and dropped it to the floor. Before Jacob could say anything, the captain stomped his boot down onto the jewel. There was a faint crunch. Jacob watched in horror as Bennet ground his foot back and forth. The captain pulled his boot back, revealing nothing but a glittering pile of dust.

"What'd you do that for?" Jacob cried. "We needed that to buy passage off this world. Not to mention the fact that it was keeping us safe."

"Sorry, Jacob. I hate to waste a good cloaker too," Bennet said, "but I had to."

"Why, so your friends can find us now?" Jacob snapped.

"No," Bennet snapped back. "So they can't."

"Homing device," Avery explained to Jacob, shaking his head as he realized the truth.

"One of its features," Bennet said, looking down at the

floor. "In case you ever need to find it."

"So that's what you were giving LaPerle and Folgrin," Jacob said. "Some sort of finder."

Bennet nodded, his face ashen.

"We'd better get out of here, Jacob," Avery said. "For all we know, they might have activated it the moment they left the Mandrel. Thank god you didn't leave it back home."

"Why'd you do it?" Jacob demanded, giving Bennet a hard stare. "I thought you were my friend."

"I am, Jacob," Bennet whispered. "It's just—it's too complicated to explain."

"Try," Jacob retorted.

*We don't have time for this,* Avery broke in.

*I need to know.*

"Folgrin came to me on Nova Campi, right after you stopped by," Bennet began. "He told me he worked for Mixel, that there was an outfit that owed them a lot of money. Said they'd stolen it and were hiding out on Teiresias, and that you'd be able to lead him to them to recover it. He offered so much money, Jacob. Enough to pay off the *Odessa*. Hell, enough to buy a whole new ship. All I had to do was get the two of you to this world as fast as possible and keep a low profile."

"So that's why you were so excited to see me back on Maker's Drift," Jacob snapped.

Bennet sighed. "I figured that even if Folgrin was dead, if I could get you to Teiresias, I could still get Mixel to pay up."

"But after all that time we spent together on board the *Caber*, the *Justine*," Jacob said, feeling his voice quake. "All those things you taught me, our talks, the birthday cake, even. It was all just a sham."

"No," Bennet cried. "You're a good kid, Jacob. Tough. You remind me of how I was at your age. I would just as soon have kept you with me, only you insisted on going."

"So even after all that," Jacob retorted, refusing to relent, "after learning the truth about the Seers and why I was really going to Teiresias and knowing that Mixel's story was all a lie—you still decided to turn us in?"

"They said they wouldn't hurt you," Bennet whispered. He hesitated. "You don't know how hard it was for me to do what I did. It took me four days just to call Mixel."

"Four whole days," Jacob sneered. "Wow. I feel so honored."

Bennet looked away.

"That would've been three days ago," Avery broke in sharply. "How'd they get here so fast?"

"They were already on their way," Bennet replied. "Those bastard pirates captured Folgrin and ransomed him back to Mixel. LaPerle met up with him on Reynard not long after we'd already left on the *Justine*. They were coming here to start the search without you. They just got here this morning."

He turned back to Jacob, a look of forlorn desperation on his face.

"Their offer—it was too much, Jacob. I'm sorry. I really am." He put his head in his hands. "I needed a ship. I just can't be without one, you know. I'm nothing without one."

Jacob shook his head, returning the stunner to his pocket. In spite of everything, he couldn't help but feel a pang of sympathy.

"You told me before that a captain without a ship was a pathetic sight," he whispered. "I guess you were right."

He turned with Avery toward the door. "Well, I hope you

get your precious ship," he called back.

"Actually, I did," Bennet said.

Jacob and Avery froze, giving each other a quick glance before turning back.

Bennet pulled a rainbow-hued card from his jacket pocket. "That was the deal. Instead of cash, they brought me a ship, a used trader. I'm now the proud owner of the *Mabel*. It's waiting in the port as we speak. I was just getting ready to leave when you showed up."

Avery walked up and grabbed him by the collar. Bennet didn't resist.

"Then how about smuggling us off this world?" he said. Avery had been standing by through most of the exchange, keeping an even temper, but Jacob could now hear the edge in his voice. "I can't think of a better way for you to make it all up to us."

"Neither can I," Bennet said, gently removing Avery's hands.

"Do they know where the rest are hidden?" Jacob demanded. There was a sudden burn along his spine. He could feel the familiar sense of dread rising to the surface.

"I used the tracker earlier," Bennet said. "Just to see if it worked. Enough to see you weren't in Tendrille, to know you were on the nightside. But there's no record of the scan in the device. And no," he added, "I didn't tell them anything."

"Still, we'd better get going," Avery said. "When they get around to trying that thing and discover it doesn't work, they're going to come for you, and that doesn't do us any good."

The burning now erupted, an electric alarm set coursing

304

through his body. "Avery," he gasped, "I'm afraid—"

He whirled to see the group of men in the doorway. There was Volker, regarding them with malice. But it was LaPerle, beside him, who spoke.

"Afraid of what, Blinder?"

# CHAPTER TWENTY-FIVE

Jacob's heart leaped into his throat as the five men stepped into the room and shut the door. Volker stared at Avery with open hatred, while LaPerle simply regarded Jacob with a smile of derision.

"Fancy meeting you here, Jacob," he sneered. "It's been so long. And with both of us so far from home."

"This is my home now," Jacob replied.

"Well, not for long," LaPerle said. "Still, you must miss Xander and dear Delaney, especially after her touching sacrifice." He shook his head. "Those beautiful eyes. What a shame."

"You better not have hurt her," Jacob cried. "Or Xander."

LaPerle snorted. "Hurt them? We're not barbarians, Jacob. Truth is, we have no need for either of them now. They're forgotten."

He turned to Bennet. "As for you, Captain, you should leave," he said. "Fly away in your ship while you still have it. After all, this doesn't look very good. If it weren't for the fact that your device worked long enough to give us these two, I'd have my men take you out into the jungle somewhere and shoot you."

"I thought you weren't barbarians," Bennet retorted.

"Inflicting pain on people when they deserve it doesn't count. In fact, I consider it quite civilized."

Bennet paled and closed his eyes.

"However," LaPerle continued, "a bargain is a bargain, so you may go. Besides, I'm sure we'll have continued use for your services in the future, especially after this little affair."

"I want Jacob," Bennet said. "Let me take him with me."

"No, Captain," Volker broke in.

"That's right," LaPerle said, smiling. "I'm afraid Jacob's already spoken for."

Bennet opened his mouth to protest.

"Leave," Volker snapped, drawing his own pistol. Jacob gasped at the sight of the hand holding the weapon—a skeletal mesh of steel and wire, encased in clear plastic, a crude replacement for the severed original.

The captain hesitated, glancing over at Jacob and Avery.

"I'm sorry, Jacob," he murmured at last. He picked his bag up from the bed and walked past them out the door.

LaPerle turned to one of the three men. "See that he makes it to the hangar," LaPerle ordered. "And make sure he takes off."

The man nodded and followed after Bennet.

LaPerle turned his attention back to Avery and Jacob.

"Let's not drag this out," he said. "Mr. Volker here has chartered a ship, a rather nice one, I might add. It's waiting for you to take us to your friends. So let's all calmly make our way to the hangar, and you can show us where we need to go."

*Just stay calm and follow my lead,* Avery said. *Whatever happens, we can't tell them anything.*

*I know,* Jacob replied. He wondered if his mindspeak sounded as nervous and sick as his real voice would. He glanced over at Volker, but the man gave no indication he'd heard them.

"So once you've gathered us all up, where are you going to take us in this nice little ship of yours, Simon?" Avery asked.

"Back to the Foundation," Volker replied.

Avery started to laugh. Jacob could see an annoyed look appear on LaPerle's face, while Volker's darkened further.

"What's so funny?" Volker snapped.

"You," Avery said. "I don't know what's worse—the fact that you went crawling back to the Foundation or that you're working with the fancy suit here. Though I will say, that's not a bad one you've got on, either."

"Rich words," Volker replied, "coming from Caolas's lapdog."

"You know they're just going to kill us," Avery said, turning to LaPerle. He looked back at Volker. "We're abominations, right, Simon?"

"That's right," Volker said with a grim smile. "But we're not going to kill you. You are children of the Foundation. We're going to fix you. Fix you and return you back where you belong."

"Fix us?" Avery exclaimed. "Is that what they did with you, Simon? Did they fix you?"

Jacob watched, fascinated, as Volker began to shake. As Folgrin, he'd always seemed to be in control, coldly commanding with a dark presence. Now, as Simon Volker, he suddenly seemed a different person, a strange, somehow broken creature. Jacob could see his composure slipping away with every word Avery spoke.

"Yes," the man spat. "I submitted myself to them and they

took me in. I was sick—just like all of you are—and they healed me."

"Well, I don't care to be healed, thank you very much," Avery retorted. "And I don't think they did a very good job with you. You're as sick as ever, Simon. I can sense the hollowness in you. Whatever powers you once had are gone. You gave them everything, and they took it all. Including your eyes, it appears."

"It's true," Volker said. "They no longer burden me." He reached up and pressed a spot along his temple. Jacob watched in horror as the black lenses of what he had thought were eyes slowly rolled up into the lids above, revealing a pair of empty sockets.

LaPerle looked away in disgust. "Ugh!" he exclaimed. "I told you not to do that around me."

Volker pressed his temple again. The lenses swiveled back down into place, glistening as brightly as ever. "Unfortunate though they are, the synthetics are a temporary necessity," he said. "But I'm willing to taint myself to fulfill the mission."

"The mission?" Avery snorted. "Oh, yeah, that's right. You're going to heal us. Still looking to play the hero, huh, Simon? You were going to save us once before, as I remember. Isn't that what your dreams said? Take us to the Promised Land?"

"You'll find it soon enough," Volker replied, his voice suddenly mournful.

"He's lying," Jacob said, turning to LaPerle. "They're not going to heal us. The ghostbox back in Harmony told me so. The Foundation has orders that all of us are to be terminated. They're afraid of us."

"Well," LaPerle sighed, "they can be a little shortsighted. Pardon the expression," he said, glancing at Volker. "Fix you, terminate you—either way, it's really none of my concern."

"What is your concern?" Jacob broke in. "Why are you even here?"

LaPerle shrugged. "Business," he said. "What else? The Foundation needed our help. We were kind enough to offer, and they were smart enough to accept."

Jacob could see Volker's face sour at LaPerle's words.

"I'm surprised," he said, turning to Volker. "They always taught us in school that the Seers were to be avoided at all costs, that they were impure."

*Good. Keep them talking,* Avery said. *Meanwhile, now's the time to start thinking of a way out of here.*

*I thought that's what you were doing.*

"They have their uses," Volker growled.

"We certainly do," said LaPerle. "A fact I'm happy to say we managed to persuade them on. I put together the presentation myself. Quite a challenge when your audience can't see. But in the end, they came around."

"You hacked into our systems, then blackmailed us, you filth," Volker spat.

"Ouch," LaPerle said, putting a hand against his chest with a grin. "Actually, Jacob, I have you to thank for it."

"Me?" Jacob cried.

"Of course. After we decided to write off the affair with Delaney—a decision that I was against, by the way—I started thinking more about you, about things you'd said those first few times we'd met, about the way you acted. Something didn't add up, so I followed a hunch. The next time our technicians went to Harmony to service the ghostbox, I had them install a tap. It didn't take long to learn all about you, about Simon's former friends, their powers, their possibilities. Fascinating stuff."

"I thought there were strict laws against interfering with the Foundation or any of its colonies," Avery interjected.

"There are," Volker hissed.

"Yes, there are," LaPerle agreed. "With huge fines, or worse. It was certainly a risk. But business is all about taking risks. And we were willing to risk that the Foundation was more interested in keeping its secrets than turning us in. And we were right."

"Don't look so glum," he added, seeing the anger on Volker's face. "A little spying, a little blackmail—everyone does it."

"That's why you're Seers," Volker muttered.

"Right," LaPerle retorted. "I'd be careful about slinging too much indignation my way. After an hour of poking through your people's dirty secrets, I felt refreshingly honest."

Feeling the tension rise in the room, Jacob began trying desperately to think of a way out. It was just him and Avery against the four of them, at least three of whom had weapons. All he had was the stunner. Avery had nothing.

*Got any ideas?* Avery asked.

*I'm thinking,* Jacob shot back. *What would Xander do?* he wondered to himself. He knew the former soldier would have come up with something by now. But Jacob needed more time.

"So why bother coming after me?" Jacob said, stalling.

"Well, we knew the ghostbox had told you about Teiresias. And Simon guessed the others had contacted you. It was just a matter of getting you here. But you were taking too long. So, we decided to give you a little push from that cozy little nest you were in."

"By threatening me. By scaring all of us with those cheap stunts."

LaPerle shrugged. "It worked."

*How good are you with that stunner?* Avery asked.

*I've never actually fired it before.*

*Great.*

"Let's go," Volker barked.

"So what is Mixel getting from all this?" Avery blurted out.

"A cut," LaPerle said. "The usual fifteen percent." Jacob could hear the pleasure in the man's voice, the same sound of smug satisfaction he'd heard back at Mixel Tower in Melville when LaPerle had bragged about profiting off Delaney.

"Fifteen percent of what?"

"Why fifteen percent of you, of course. Well, of your group, actually. The Foundation thinks you're abominations. Fine, they can take care of that however they like. But we think you're special. We think you can be valuable assets."

The stunner came back to Jacob's mind. It's the only thing he really had to work with. *Keep talking,* he told Avery.

"What are you going to do? Make us your pets?"

LaPerle laughed. "More like valuable employees. Sounds better, doesn't it? Better than anything they're going to offer you, I can promise you that," he said, nodding toward the scowling Volker. "In fact, we'd like you to be one of them, Mr. Warrick. You and Jacob, here. After Mr. Volker's story about Jacob's otherspace perambulations, we're especially intrigued."

Jacob tried surveying the two heavies behind Simon and LaPerle. Whom should he try to shoot first? Could he get both? Could he get himself to stop shaking? *Don't be afraid,* he told himself. *Xander wouldn't be afraid.*

"I can't speak for Jacob, but I don't think I'd have much to offer your fine organization," Avery shot back.

"Oh, but Mr. Volker told me all about the wonderful things you people can do. Read minds, see the future. Do you realize how valuable those skills would be to our business? And if we could figure out how you work, then duplicate it? We've spent considerable millions in the past trying—all the corporations have—but with no success. The subjects always die. Or they just go crazy."

"Enough!" Volker cried. "Enough of this!" He raised his pistol and pointed it at Avery's head. "You, shut up."

"You don't need to shoot," Avery murmured, raising his hands.

*You don't need to shoot,* Jacob thought to himself. *That's it.* His heart began to race as he slipped his hand into his pocket.

*I've got it,* he told Avery. *I think I know what to do.*

*Good,* Avery said, *because one way or another this meeting's coming to a close.*

LaPerle sighed. "Don't mind him," he told Avery. "He's just mad we're taking you. They all are. It was almost a deal breaker, in fact. The Foundation wanted simply to pay us. But we wanted you instead. Doesn't that make you feel good?"

Jacob closed his finger around the trigger and gently squeezed halfway like Xander had showed him. He took a deep breath and tried to steady his hand. He felt like there was electricity running through every nerve in his body. All it took was for him to pull too hard, make one slip, and it would be over.

"Come, Mr. Volker," LaPerle continued. "Mr. Warrick's quite right. We don't need to shoot anyone. Not yet, anyway. And not here."

"Thank you," Avery said.

Jacob wondered. Was the trigger halfway down? He couldn't tell. *It's going to have to be,* he thought, creeping his thumb up the handle until it reached the power setting. Slowly he began adjusting the dial, doing his best to keep even pressure on the trigger. *Click, click, click.* The dial's turning echoed in his ears. He winced.

"Don't thank me until this is over, Mr. Warrick," LaPerle snapped. "In fact, you probably won't want to thank me at all."

*Click.*

A high-pitched whine began emitting from the stunner. *One, two, three.* He fought back the urge to yank it from his pocket and toss it away. He needed to be patient. He needed to count the seconds. It needed to be just right.

*Get ready to drop,* Jacob warned. *Four, five, six.*

The whine grew steadily louder as it rose in pitch.

*Got it.*

*Seven, eight.*

"What's that noise?" Volker asked.

LaPerle's eyes narrowed. The guards stirred.

*Drop.*

Jacob pulled the stunner from his pocket and hurled it past Volker and LaPerle, past the guards, toward the front door. He didn't even notice their reactions. He simply dove to the ground, glancing from the corner of his eye to see Avery do the same.

The blast was even bigger than Jacob had expected, a burst of light and sound that filled the tiny space, washing over him. As quickly as it was over, Avery was pulling Jacob to his feet. He opened his eyes to a smoke-filled room, the sound of an alarm throbbing somewhere close by. The furniture was scattered, as were the men. No one seemed badly injured, through they all appeared stunned. Feeling dazed himself, Jacob watched them struggle on the ground, heard their groans.

*Let's go*, Avery said, grabbing him by the shirt and staggering toward the front door, wide open from the blast.

Wiping their eyes and coughing, they stumbled from the hotel room, ran across the long balcony, and made their way down the stairs to the street, doing their best to ignore the bewildered looks of the growing crowd.

*Good job, kid*, Avery said as they crossed the street. *You saved us.*

Pausing to glance back at the smoke pouring from the hotel room, Jacob imagined Volker and LaPerle inside, rising to their feet, brushing themselves off.

"Thanks," he said. But he couldn't help feeling that he hadn't saved anyone yet.

# CHAPTER TWENTY-SIX

Jacob never thought he'd be so happy to see the dark side of Teiresias again, but as they slipped across the terminator, the floater hugging the surface as it sped along, he breathed a sigh of relief. Soon the forest and vegetation below turned gray, dissolving into the shaded mix of rock and ice. Then it was all snow and darkness, and he couldn't help but feel safer the more distance they put behind them.

"I still can't believe Bennet betrayed us. I thought for sure I could trust him."

"It's tough," Avery agreed. "But you saw the look on his face—he knows he did the wrong thing. He wanted to make amends."

"So you're saying I should just forgive him?"

Avery shrugged. "Part of being a Seer is learning to accept other people's frailties, especially in the people we care about. It's not easy. It's something the Blinders never could do."

Jacob turned away to look out the window. He wanted to be angry, but he knew Avery was right. Strangely enough, it only made him angrier.

"So what do we do now?" he said at last.

Avery shook his head. "We don't have many options.

They'll be keeping a close eye on the port, talking to captains, offering bribes. We're not getting off this planet anytime soon."

"Can't we just keep hiding?"

"Sure we can. It's risky, though. They'll be looking for us, doing sweeps. It's only a matter of time. For all I know, they're tracking us now."

"You really think so?" Jacob cried. The safety he'd started feeling suddenly disappeared.

"Mixel's got more than just those goons that showed up with Simon and LaPerle. Their people probably watched us leave the hotel. For all we know, they let us go."

"So why are we going back?" Jacob cried. "If we're just going to lead them to the others?"

Avery frowned. "Because I don't know for sure. And we need to warn everybody. If we don't come back, then they might come looking for us, and then they'd be even more exposed. We just have to hope we got away clean."

"So where do we go after that? There must be other places we can hide."

"We've got a few holes here and there, some bare-bones places we've set up. We can split up and try to wait them out. But like I said, it's only a matter of time. You saw the look in Volker's eye—he won't stop."

"We could go to BiCo, tell them what Mixel's doing."

Avery nodded. "That would get rid of Mixel, but I'm not sure BiCo would be any better. Still, it's something to keep in mind. We'll talk to the others, see what they think."

"Caolas will know what to do," Jacob murmured.

"That's what I'm hoping."

They'd reached the great basin, a smooth expanse

stretching for miles like a frozen sea. As he had before, Jacob noted the lights of the mining operation on the far side. He tried to imagine the men and women working there, digging down deep under the surface for the beautiful crystal shards upon which so much depended, each jewel a precious key, opening the door to anywhere. How many people lived there? Perhaps they would be willing to take them in, hide them under the earth.

He was about to ask Avery about the mine when he noticed a light at one spot on the horizon, a glow that seemed to fill the sky around it.

"What's that light?" Jacob asked.

Avery squinted through the windshield. "What light?" he asked.

"There on the horizon."

"I don't see it. Probably just an aurora. They pop up along the northern sky from time to time."

"Oh," Jacob murmured.

They sped along, Avery pushing the floater full-throttle. The light continued to grow. Then, as Jacob watched, a dark spot appeared in the midst of the glow, a black wedge of the horizon rising up into the light. As they drew closer, Jacob's heart began to pound. He sat up in his seat and pressed his forehead to the window's cold glass.

*Night's Head.*

*What about it?*

Once more he was standing on the edge of the cliff from his vision, once more he watched the star-bud leave his hands, fly across the land to the vast peak calling in the distance. And he could feel it now, calling to him, could see the halo still alight over its growing peak like a signal beacon as bright as any of the wormholes he'd seen yesterday in the sky.

"We have to go there," he whispered.

"What do you mean?"

"It's the place. Where we're meant to be," Jacob said, his voice louder now. "It's the gateway!"

"I don't understand," Avery said, glancing at Jacob with concern. "It's just a mountain. Are you sure?"

"Yes!" Jacob cried. "Yes, I'm sure. I can't explain it—I just feel it. Like Caolas said I would. After I went through the last wormhole in my vision, I ended up back on Teiresias, and I saw Night's Head in the distance. The starflower flew from my hands right toward the mountain." He could feel himself shaking now. "It has to be it. Why else would I have seen that?"

"I don't know," Avery replied, shaking his head. "I wasn't with you for that part. Caolas and I—we lost you when you went into the wormhole. We thought that was just the end of your journey."

"Well, it wasn't," Jacob murmured, remembering the flash of light sweeping over him.

"Okay, Jacob," Avery said at last. *I hope you're right.*

"Me too," Jacob whispered.

Jacob could sense a ripple of excitement wash through the crowd when Caolas told them the news of their departure.

They'd all gathered in the arboretum to hear Avery's report. Jacob had watched the worried faces of Marcus, Clarissa, of all of them as Avery told of Simon's reappearance, of the Foundation's plan for them, as well as Mixel's.

Then it was his turn. He struggled to keep his voice even, to remember to keep taking breaths as he related the details of his vision and the revelation that had appeared to him on the way back from the port. Hearing himself talk, he couldn't help but think it sounded crazy. But it didn't matter what he thought, it was what he felt, what he knew underneath to be true, that mattered. It was enough for him. Would it be for the rest of them?

There was a long pause afterward as they all stood still beneath the domed arboretum's light. He closed his eyes, not wanting to look at them, afraid to see their doubt. Instead he listened. He could hear the birds singing, could hear the water splashing in the fountains, but still there were no words from anyone.

"We all have many gifts," Caolas said at last. "Some that we share, some that are ours alone. This is Jacob's gift, this knowledge. Yesterday, Avery and I accompanied Jacob on his journey, watched as his power blossomed and unfolded. If he says that we must go to Night's Head, if that's where we'll find our escape, then that's good enough for me."

The murmuring of voices brought Jacob back. He opened his eyes and looked at the faces watching him, so different from those of the crowd he'd faced on Harmony's stage so long ago. And though he did see a flickering of fear, even doubt, he saw far more love and kindness. More than anything else, he saw hope.

"Those who wish to stay here are welcome. We will leave a floater and plenty of supplies. No one need make this journey against their will. For as all of you, I'm sure, can sense— there's plenty of danger ahead."

It was true; Jacob could feel it—the darkness closing in, nearly as strong as the mountain's beckoning light. It had followed him all the way back. He could tell the others felt it too.

But in the end they all went, said their farewells to the home they'd built, the home that had kept them safe for the last three years. It didn't take long. They'd been busy while Jacob and Avery were away. All of the essentials were already packed and loaded. It was just a matter of gathering a few last things, whatever could be stored, and shutting down the power. They watched the little sun slowly fade, then bundled up and made their way to the hangar.

Soon the convoy was slipping over the snowy landscape—a small hauler and three floaters—in the direction of Night's Head. Toward the light that only Jacob could see.

"So what next, Jacob?"

Jacob leaned in toward the front seat and looked out through the windshield at the snowy mountainside. As impressive as Night's Head was at a distance, it was even more so up close. It seemed impossible that anything could be so big. Having reached the mountain, he could no longer see the glow, but he could still feel the mountain's pull, stronger than ever, as if his whole body were vibrating beneath his winter clothes.

But there was another feeling as well—the feeling of all eyes on him as everyone in the floater regarded him with expectation. Between Avery and Clarissa up front, Caolas, Elise, and another man behind him in back, not to mention Nadia beside him, he could sense their anticipation, their anxiousness. He could only imagine what those in the other craft must be wondering as they hovered in place.

"I'm not sure," he said at last. He closed his eyes, tried clearing his head. What was he supposed to do next? The feeling that this was the place, that this mountain was somehow

321

the gateway to another world, was so strong in him that it had never occurred to him what he should do once he got here. Now, looking at its steep slopes, its rocky cliffs and icy flanks, he could only stare in dismay as the night around them seemed to grow darker by the second.

He felt a warmth and looked down. Nadia had taken his hand.

"Don't worry," she said. "We'll find it." She gave his hand a squeeze and smiled.

"We'll go around," Avery offered, giving Jacob a hopeful glance.

Jacob nodded. "Okay."

"What's going on?" Marcus said, his voice coming over the speaker.

Avery glanced toward the floater off to his left. Jacob followed his gaze, noticed the pale faces at the window.

"Just tell everybody to follow me and stay calm," Avery replied.

They circled the base of the mountain. Nothing. Jacob felt nothing but a growing sense of horror and doubt. Here they all were, gathered together, in the open, vulnerable. And he'd brought them to this place.

They continued to circle Night's Head, moving in a spiral up the mountain, each swing shorter than the last as the mountain narrowed toward its peak. And still nothing.

"Wait," Jacob said, a prickle running down his back as he caught sight of the dark patch not far below the peak. Drawing closer, he realized it was a plateau, one of the few flat spots they'd encountered on the mountainside. "There."

"You mean where the slope juts out?" Avery asked.

"Yes. Bring us down there."

"But I don't see anything," Avery replied.

"Just do it," Clarissa said.

Jacob glanced behind to see Caolas watching him. The man stared with his opaque eyes, and though Jacob knew the eyes themselves no longer worked—at least not in any conventional way—he could tell they were now looking deep inside him. Caolas nodded and smiled.

They touched down a few moments later. Jacob watched through the windows as the hauler and the other two floaters settled down beside them.

One by one they left the craft, gasping at the summit air—even colder and far thinner than Teiresias's normal nightside air. Soon they were gathered, and once again they turned to Jacob and waited.

The plateau was barren but for a scattering of rocks and ice. The wind had blown the snow away, scouring it down to clear, dark rock. At his feet, Jacob could see the glinting flakes of crystal mixed into the stone. Across the way, the side of the mountain rose, a sheer cliff with a large crack running down its face, a dark separation wide enough for perhaps a single person, but that was all. No tunnel waited, no gate, no path to any world that he could see.

Jacob kneeled down and, removing a glove, placed his bare hand onto the surface. He could feel the cold run through his palm and up his arm, its burn mixing with the tingling along his spine. He could hear it now—the hum, the ghostly chord. It was everywhere around him, loud enough to hear over the growing murmur of voices behind him. He closed his eyes.

*Please*, he thought, feeling his hand grow numb, *show yourself. Please.*

"Jacob," Avery's voice called gently from behind him.

Jacob opened his eyes and stood up. He turned to see everyone watching him, the steam from their breath rising under the dim light of the moon and stars.

"What do you think?" the man asked.

Jacob hesitated.

*It's okay, Jacob,* Nadia's voice spoke in his mind. *Don't be afraid to say it.*

"I don't know," he said at last, his voice choking on itself. "I thought I would, but I don't."

He could see their faces fall at his words, but he saw no anger, no ill will. He almost wished he had.

"We'd better go, then," Marcus said. "Find someplace to hide until we can figure out what to do."

"You're right," Avery agreed.

They all turned back toward the floaters, a flurry of discussion breaking out as they began weighing their options, their voices sounding loud now after the long spell of silence.

Only Jacob stayed where he was, staring down at the gleaming stone. He felt as if he could stand in this spot forever. Maybe he should. Maybe he would.

This time, there were no words from Nadia, no silent thoughts dropped into his mind. She simply came up beside him, wrapped her arm around his, and pulled him toward the floater.

He let her pull him, felt the warmth come back into his hand as she reached down and took it.

He was about to thank her when he froze. They all did, and he knew they could feel the shock run up their backs just as he could. Several people cried out.

A moment later they heard the noise, a roar that seemed

to come from nowhere. He turned in time to see the ship appear, banking around the mountainside and over their heads.

*Too late,* he thought, though he couldn't tell if the words were his own or the echo of the thirty other voices around him, all crying out at once.

*Too late.*

# CHAPTER TWENTY-SEVEN

The ship—a slim, dark craft smaller than the *Odessa*—made a sudden turn as it passed overhead, lowering its nose as it swiveled to face them.

"Run!" Avery cried.

They all broke for the transports, but before they'd gone more than a few steps, a flash of light made them pull up. Jacob gasped as a series of bursts flew from the ship, striking each one of their vehicles in succession. As each burst struck, it sent a ball of energy cascading over the craft, a web of blue lightning that engulfed the entire shell before dissipating.

"What are they doing?" Jacob called out to Avery.

"Pulse guns," he shouted back. "They're knocking out the electronics on the floaters."

"Can you fix it?"

"It would take at least fifteen minutes to reboot the systems. And that's *if* those pulses didn't fry the circuits."

As Jacob turned to watch the ship maneuver to a landing, he realized they didn't have fifteen minutes. They didn't have five. And with all sides of the plateau dropping off in nearly vertical slopes, they had nowhere to go.

They gathered together into a group, holding one another for support, as a ramp lowered from the belly of the ship, scattering light over the stone, making the crystal grains sparkle like snowflakes under a full moon.

Jack LaPerle strolled down the ramp, followed by Simon Volker and a dozen armed men, all dressed in winter garb.

LaPerle pulled up a dozen yards away, his face screwed back in shock inside the hood of his parka.

"Dammit, it's cold!" he cried in disbelief. He looked strange in his overstuffed jacket, so out of place that Jacob would've laughed if he hadn't felt so sick. The men spread out behind him, their rifles held loose but ready, while Volker said nothing. He simply hung back with his hands thrust deep in his pockets, his hood covering his pale hair and black eyes.

"Well, here we all are," LaPerle said. He spotted Jacob, who stood at the front beside Avery and Caolas. Jacob could feel Desmond and Eliot behind him, peeking out from each side of his jacket.

"That was quite the escape you managed back at the hotel, Jacob," LaPerle said. "Very impressive. I was rather put out until I realized it was far simpler to just have you followed back than to try to get one of you to talk, a process that I'm sure would have been both messy and unpleasant. Now I get to have both of you, undamaged."

"You don't need to do this, Simon," Caolas called out, taking a step forward.

Volker recoiled at the words, drawing back farther. "I have nothing to say to you, Seer," he replied, his voice so bitter Jacob wondered if it was even the same man.

"We aren't a threat, Simon," Caolas continued, ignoring him. "We have no wish to undermine the Foundation. We just want to be left alone."

"You have rejected Truesight," Volker shouted. "That's enough."

"Just let us go," Caolas said. "Jacob, here, has found the way to our new world. Soon, we'll be gone."

Jacob winced at these last words. He glanced over at Caolas and swallowed.

"That boy has found nothing," Volker cried. "There is no other world! You know that as well as I do!"

"Nonsense!" Caolas shouted back. "It exists. You saw it, just as I did. You even believed you would take us there."

Volker shook his head. "That was the foolish dream of a Seer, a symptom of the sickness in my brain. But you are right about one thing, Caolas. You will soon be gone."

"All right, enough!" LaPerle shouted, holding up a gloved hand. "It's too cold for this. Everyone onto the ship. You can argue all you want about who's right and who's wrong later."

"Wait!" Jacob cried, stepping forward.

LaPerle shook his head and swore.

"Take me," Jacob said. "Forget the others. I'll work for Mixel. I know where the wormholes are, all of them. I can see them! Imagine what you can do with that knowledge."

*Don't do this,* Avery said.

*I have to. I got us into this. I can get us out.*

LaPerle snorted. "But I'm already taking you. Like I told you before, it's been arranged. Still, it's good to know what you're capable of. Looks like we'll be getting a good return on our investment."

"You'll get nothing unless you let the others go," Jacob shouted. "Otherwise, you'll get nothing from me. Nothing from any of us. We won't be owned by anyone."

LaPerle sighed. "We're all owned by somebody. Or something. You'll come around, trust me. Besides," he added as he turned back toward the ship, "I've already made my deal with Mr. Volker here. A bargain is a bargain."

"I'm afraid Mr. Volker has no intention of keeping his bargain with you," Caolas called out. "Isn't that right, Simon?"

LaPerle froze in his tracks and turned toward Volker.

"What is he talking about?" he snapped.

Volker pulled both hands from his pockets. A black sphere lay in one, a small control in the other. "You always understood me, Caolas," he called back.

"Oh God, no," Avery whispered beside him.

*What is that?* Jacob asked.

"A micronuke?" LaPerle cried, his voice cracking in dismay. "What are you, crazy?"

"Of course he is, Mr. LaPerle," Caolas said. "Don't tell me you didn't know."

Jacob could see the stunned panic on LaPerle's face, could see his men stirring in alarm, turning their rifles toward Volker.

Volker made a strangled noise, a laughing sort of sob that made Jacob shiver.

"The Foundation once had the right idea—terminate the Seers, destroy the abominations. But they've grown soft now. They want me to bring you back. They want to fix you, like they think they did with me. But there's no fixing any of us, Caolas. They can take away our eyes, go into our heads, it doesn't make any difference. We're still sick. We're all still abominations."

"No, Simon," Caolas said. "Only you."

"Hold on, Volker," LaPerle cried, raising his hands as he backed toward the ship. "Just hold on for a minute. You want

329

to blow yourself and all your people up, that's fine. Just let us go. We'll get on our ship and out of your way."

Volker's face twisted in contempt. "You're as rotten as anyone. We're genetic accidents, corrupted against our wills. But you're corrupt by choice." He looked down at the ground. "It doesn't matter. We're all Seers. We're all guilty."

He pressed a button on the control in his left hand. The black orb in his right began flashing a green ghostly light.

LaPerle gave a cry, turning frantically in every direction as if the way out were somewhere right in front of him, just waiting to be seen. Everyone else seemed to freeze, even the men with their rifles, transfixed by the blinking orb.

For a moment, Jacob froze as well. Then, staring at the ticking bomb, an idea popped into his head.

*Snowballs.*

"Eliot, Desmond," he hissed. "You need to get rid of that thing. Pretend it's just another snowball."

"What?" Desmond replied, confused. Then, "Oh!"

"Right!" Eliot said. Both boys closed their eyes.

Volker cried out as the micronuke flew from his hands. Everyone gasped as the orb sailed through the air, then hit the ground and began rolling across the smooth stone toward the mountain's face, blinking faster as it sped along.

"Get it!" LaPerle shouted to his men. "Throw it over the side!"

All of them scrambled after the rolling ball, nearly tripping over themselves in a desperate race.

"Uh-oh," Eliot cried, realizing their mistake.

"Sorry," Desmond whispered.

Jacob could only watch in fixed horror as the flashing sphere bounced across the plateau toward the mountainside before disappearing into the crack.

Time suddenly slowed down, so that Jacob felt as if he were seeing and hearing everything that was happening at once—Volker looking toward the sky in anguish, LaPerle pulling to a stop, bringing his hands to his face, all of the Seers crying out in fear. Only Caolas stood unmoved, his face placid, smiling, his clouded eyes radiating a sense of peace that made Jacob forget everything else. Jacob couldn't think of a better way to die than to be caught in that gaze. He was so distracted, he didn't notice Nadia pushing by him until it was too late.

This time there was no explosion like back in the hotel, only a sound so loud it was no longer sound, a light so bright it was no longer light, spreading out to encompass everything in its path. Jacob watched as one by one they disappeared— LaPerle, his men, Volker, even the ship, all swallowed up in the slightest fraction of a second as the wave closed in on him. The last thing he saw was Nadia's form, a dark silhouette, arms held out, as if to embrace the light now singing the ancient chord of his dreams.

"Jacob, wake up!"

Jacob opened his eyes to see Clarissa kneeling over him, her steaming breaths coming quick in the purple light. He sat up and looked around at the other Seers picking themselves up or helping others to rise. The floaters and the hauler waited nearby, their sides glowing faintly against that same purple light. He thought he could still hear the chord, the same collection of notes that had haunted him in his visions and amid the caverns of their former home, though perhaps it was merely an echo of the blast still ringing in his ears.

"What happened?" he asked.

"Something terrible and wonderful and strange," she said, her eyes welling.

Jacob turned and gasped.

Most of the mountaintop was gone, leaving a giant crater, of which their plateau formed a kind of lip. The interior of the crater seemed to glow with a life of its own, and as Jacob stood and walked over to the edge and looked down, he could see why, could see the millions of crystals glinting in the light, as if the interior of the mountain were one large jewel that had been blown to pieces.

But it wasn't the crater or its glowing bed that made him gasp, but the source of light instead, hovering above them all.

From where Jacob stood looking up, the wormhole appeared in the sky as a beautiful flower, like a purple rose in full bloom, a blossom like the ones his mother grew in Harmony. Of all the things he'd seen since gaining his sight, it was by far the most spectacular, and as he watched it ripple and pulse, he could feel the tears gather in his eyes.

A hand clasped his shoulder. It was Caolas.

"Do you see it?" Jacob asked.

"We all can. It's beautiful."

Jacob shook his head. "Where did it come from?"

"We're not sure. Perhaps all those crystals vaporized in the blast. But it doesn't really matter. Only one thing is important."

Jacob nodded. "Where it goes," he said.

Caolas squeezed his shoulder gently.

By now Jacob could sense others gathered around him, could sense their eagerness at the sight of the pulsating cloud. It didn't bother him, didn't distract him as he gazed up into the purple swirl, allowed the light to draw him in, pull him from himself into otherspace and race along its brilliant path to a faraway point. There it was. The feeling that had drawn him to the mountain, a certainty that warmed him to the core.

He opened his eyes, not realizing he had closed them.

"I know where it goes," he said. He pointed to a star, so tiny, so faint among the thousands of other stars it could barely be seen with the naked eye. But it didn't matter. Even with his eyes closed, he could see it in his mind—a warm, yellow star, waiting for them.

"How far?" Caolas asked.

"Beyond the Rim. It's on the charts, but well beyond the settled worlds."

"Perfect," Caolas said.

"It's just like you said," Jacob whispered.

"Yes," Caolas said, smiling sadly. "But with a price I hadn't foreseen."

Jacob paused for a moment, glancing down at the crater. Then the awful truth struck, a sudden memory of the blast that ripped all the joy from him.

*Nadia.*

He pushed past Caolas and the others and ran over to where Clarissa and Elise were kneeling, supporting the figure in their arms.

Nadia was covered in a blanket, her clothes now nothing but burned rags, her face pale and still, her eyes closed.

"Is she dead?" Jacob whispered, not wanting to hear the answer.

Clarissa looked up.

"She's not dead," she murmured. "But she's far away."

"Can you bring her back?"

She shook her head. "I don't know," she whispered. "We have to hope we can." She turned back to caress the girl's face.

*Nadia?* Jacob said, kneeling down and taking her hand. He called out again, but there was no reply.

*I'm sorry, Jacob.*

Jacob looked up to see Avery standing over him. The man reached down and held out a hand. Jacob accepted it and rose to his feet.

"She saved all of us," Jacob said, shaking his head. "Using her shield. Absorbing all that power."

"I never would have thought she'd have that much strength," Avery said.

Jacob remembered the way she'd held his hand, how she'd whispered those words of encouragement, remembered the way she'd spoken of hope.

"I would," Jacob replied.

They returned to the crater where Caolas still stood, gazing up at the wormhole.

"It's shrinking," he said, glancing at them.

Jacob gazed up at the swirling cloud in alarm. Caolas was right—the wormhole was smaller than when he'd last seen it. He could feel it drawing back into itself, the blossom closing.

"How much time do we have?" Jacob asked.

Caolas shrugged. "Not long, that's for certain. How are the transports coming?"

"I got the hauler going," Avery said. "Marcus says one of the floaters is fried, but the other two are almost there."

"Good, good," Caolas murmured. "Keep going."

"Caolas, we can't take the transports into the wormhole," Avery warned. "Floaters need gravity to work. They weren't made for travel too far above the surface. If we come out in space, we won't be going anywhere."

"It's okay," Jacob said, seeing the disappointment on Caolas's face. "I know where the wormhole goes. I can take us there anytime."

Caolas nodded. "Very well," he said at last. "But we need to get out of here soon, regardless. An explosion of that magnitude will surely have been noticed. BiCo is probably already on its way. And for all we know, there are still Mixel agents searching for us."

He turned to gaze back up at the wormhole. "Looks like Simon had a role in getting us to the other world, after all."

"A ship!"

They all turned toward the cry. Jacob ran to the edge of the precipice and looked out. A craft had appeared in the distance and was closing fast. Already Jacob could hear its engines.

"Must be BiCo," Avery said, pulling up beside Jacob.

"Maybe it's Mixel," another cried out in fear.

"We'd better get everyone on board," Caolas said.

They all moved, quickly now, driven by a fresh sense of urgency toward the hauler and the two working floaters. Avery scooped the unconscious Nadia into his arms and headed for the nearest transport, his own floater now worthless.

"No!" Jacob called. The others paused and looked back.

"We don't need to run," he said. "Not this time."

They stopped and turned back to join him along the cliff's edge. This time there was no questioning, no fear. They could tell by the certainty in his voice, or maybe they could sense it for themselves, that their time of running was coming to an end.

The ship, an angular craft slightly smaller than the *Odessa*, swept in, landing gently on the narrow bit of plateau left unoccupied. The ramp lowered to the surface of the rock. This time there were no bright lights, only dim shadows as a man trotted down the ramp.

*Bennet.*

Jacob stirred at the sight of the captain stepping out from under the ship. He remembered Bennet in the Mandrel, shaking LaPerle's and Volker's hands, remembered what the captain had told him at the hotel. He wanted to be angry at Bennet. But seeing the grin on the captain's face, seeing the man's relief as he caught sight of Jacob, Jacob suddenly remembered Avery's words on the way back.

"I've got this nice new ship with nowhere to go," Bennet called out.

"How about there?" Jacob replied, pointing toward the shrinking wormhole.

Bennet gazed up at it and smiled.


Before long they were all on board. Though it was a tight fit, they even managed to squeeze the transport and one of the floaters into the cargo hold.

"I came looking for you," Bennet told Jacob as people hurried onto the ship. "I had a rough idea of where your hideout was from the scan I'd done, so I made some low sweeps, but nothing. Then I saw the explosion."

"You're probably not the only one," Jacob said. They followed the last group up the ramp.

"Good point," Bennet said as the ramp closed behind them. "And I'd rather not stick around to answer questions."

A minute later they were in the cockpit—Bennet and

Jacob, along with Caolas and Avery. Clarissa remained with Nadia, now settled in the ship's tiny sick bay, while the remainder of the Seers rested in the main body of the ship.

"Think we can make it?" Caolas asked as the *Mabel* lifted from the surface and rotated in the direction of the wormhole, now visibly collapsing.

"No problem," the captain answered, glancing at the man beside him. "Though I'm afraid I'm going to have to ask you to switch seats with Jacob," he said.

"Why's that?" Caolas asked.

"That chair's reserved for the first mate," Bennet said, looking over at Jacob with a smile.

Jacob took the seat just as Bennet throttled up the *Mabel*, sending the ship forward with a burst of speed. Then they were gone, into the light.

# EPILOGUE

The sun was preparing to set as they gathered around the ship to say good-bye. A warm evening breeze brushed the tops of the grass, a whisper that blended with the nearby river's flow, setting up a hush so calm it seemed to quiet even the birds calling from the trees along the far bank. All three moons had now broken the horizon's edge, the first one, large and full and orange, pulling its younger yellow siblings behind it into the sky.

"Thank you, Captain," Caolas said. "For getting us here, and for the use of your ship these past few days as we got ourselves in order."

"My pleasure," Bennet said, shaking his hand. He glanced over at the collection of shelters nestled along the top of the rise, encircling the hauler. All week they'd worked on converting it into a kitchen and dining room, a place where people could gather.

"It's a nice settlement," the captain added. "But I'll be back before you know it with everything you need to make this place a real home."

"It already is," Caolas said.

"You sure you'll be okay until then?"

"We've got enough supplies for the next few months,"

Avery said, reaching out to take Bennet's hand. "And our scans show edibles all over. We'll be fine."

Bennet nodded, then turned toward Jacob.

"You ready?"

"I'm ready," Jacob said with a smile.

"Good. I'll be in the cockpit, getting the *Mabel* fired up. You can join me there." He gave the crowd a quick salute, then headed up the ramp.

Jacob turned toward the Seers. The warmth of their smiles matched that of the breeze flowing in from the plains that reminded him so much of his own homeworld. But that wasn't all—he could also see the sadness in their eyes, in spite of their efforts to hide it.

He'd held off telling them until today, still unsure himself about the decision that had been growing in him all week.

But that changed in the early hours of the morning when, waking before dawn's light, he left the shelter and wandered out into the damp grass. The moons had just set, and a million stars blazed in the sky, joined by the glow of wormholes in their midst. Seeing them, feeling their pull, he realized that he couldn't stay.

It wasn't that he didn't want to stay. He knew that he could be happy here on this new world with these people who loved and cared for him, just as he now knew he could have been happy staying on Nova Campi with Xander and Delaney. Or with Morag and Chester on Maker's Drift. But there was only one place he truly belonged.

He'd waited for the sun to rise, then went on board the *Mabel*. Bennet was in his quarters with a cup of coffee, reading one of Jacob's books.

"Sure," Bennet said, his face widening in surprise and

delight when Jacob told him he wanted to return with him to space.

"But there's a catch," Jacob said. He told the captain his plan.

"It's a deal," Bennet said, reaching out and taking his hand.

"What?" Avery cried when, shortly after, Jacob had told them of his decision.

"I'm sorry," Jacob said. "I need to go."

Caolas nodded, putting a hand on Jacob's shoulder.

"Jacob knows where he belongs," he said. "And where he's needed."

"Needed? He's needed here, with us." Avery paused, shaking his head. "I'm just surprised," he murmured. "After everything you went through to find us. And to find this world. I mean, look at it, Jacob. It's beautiful."

"It is."

"And it's safe."

*I know,* Jacob replied. They all knew. For the wormhole had disappeared behind them, leaving no trace. To the Foundation, to Mixel—to everyone—they were dead. Like Volker, like LaPerle, all of them gone, forever.

"That's why I can't stay. There are others of us out there, Avery. Other Blinders who will begin to see. Maybe some already have. And they'll need someone to find them and bring them here."

"And that person's going to be you," Avery murmured.

"That's right," Jacob said. "With Bennet's help."

Avery nodded and gave Jacob a smile. "I see," he said. "So how will you find them?"

"Caolas will be searching. He'll be able to tell me where they are."

Avery glanced over at Caolas. "Were you in on this?"

Caolas shook his head. "I found out just now, same as you. But I see the sense in it. Jacob has a special kinship with the stars. His place is among them. Either way, it doesn't really matter how you or I feel—it's his choice to make and his alone. His future, his life."

"I know," Avery said. He turned to Jacob. "I just want to make sure he knows."

Jacob smiled and nodded. *Thanks for looking out for me. Just try to stay out of trouble.*

*What fun would that be?* "Besides," he added. "It's not like you'll never see me again. I'll be coming back from time to time."

"I'm sure you will," Avery replied. "Especially now that Nadia's on the mend."

Jacob laughed as he felt his face redden. It had been two days now since Nadia had finally emerged from her coma, shaken and weak, but able to recognize everyone. Jacob sat by her side and told her everything that had happened—how she'd saved them, how they'd come to this new world. Knowing that she was going to be okay made his decision to leave easier. It also made it harder.

Now, standing before everyone at the bottom of the ramp, he suddenly found it hard to say good-bye, hard to leave, in spite of the fact that he and Bennet would be back. There was a strange sense of finality in the leave-taking. For even though he knew he would always be a part of them, he suddenly realized that things would be different upon his return. Next time, he would just be visiting.

"Everything changes," Xander had told him. "Nothing stays the same." The words had always terrified him. But

341

thinking of them now, he realized they no longer did. Not because they weren't true, but because he'd finally accepted them as true, as perhaps the most important truth of all.

"Good-bye, Jacob," Clarissa said, coming forward to embrace him. "Stay safe."

"Thanks, Clarissa. And who knows," he offered with a smile, "maybe when I return, I'll have someone else with me."

She gave him a look of wonder, then hugged him a second time, this time tighter. When she let go, there were tears in her eyes.

"I'll hope," she whispered.

One after another they came forward to wish him farewell—Nadia, Caolas, Avery, the twins, all came to say good-bye. And then he was up the gangplank and making for the cockpit, already thinking of the stars.

Fifteen minutes later they were through the atmosphere, back into the endless night of space.

"Where to?" Bennet asked.

Standing at the tip of the cockpit's nose, surrounded by glass on all sides, Jacob looked in every direction.

"That way," he said at last, pointing to a wormhole two days' journey away. From the other side it was only a few weeks' travel through deep space before they'd reach another world, one of mild plains and zephyr trees orbiting a great ringed giant, a world he'd once called home. He knew that he would now just be a visitor there, as well.

Gazing out at the clusters of stars and galaxies burning in the dark, he realized it didn't matter. No matter where he went, he would always be home.

TELL THE WORLD THIS BOOK WAS

| GOOD | BAD | SO-SO |
|---|---|---|
| | | |